THE PERFECT DAUGHTER

ALEX STONE

First published in Great Britain in 2021 by Boldwood Books Ltd. This paperback edition first published in 2023.

1

Cover Design by Head Design

Cover Photography: Shutterstock

A CIP catalogue record for this book is available from the British Library.

Paperback ISBN: 978-1-83533-938-1

Hardback ISBN 978-1-80280-308-2

Ebook ISBN 978-1-80280-306-8

Kindle ISBN 978-1-80280-307-5

Audio CD ISBN 978-1-80280-314-3

MP3 CD ISBN 978-1-80280-311-2

Digital audio download ISBN 978-1-80280-305-1

Large Print ISBN: 978-1-80280-309-9

Boldwood Books Ltd.

23 Bowerdean Street, London, SW6 3TN

www.boldwoodbooks.com

For all those who encouraged me to follow my dreams.

1

NOW

I lied.

I never used to lie. I never used to do anything my mother would disapprove of. I was a good girl. A good daughter. A perfect daughter. At least, that's what I tried to be.

But perfect doesn't really exist.

'I love him.' I paused. The word caught in my throat. 'I loved him.' It was amazing the difference putting one little 'd' on the end of a word could make. It changed everything. Our future had become the past with that one little letter. But it also made it less of a lie. I had loved him. Once.

The police officer shifted slightly in the armchair opposite. I could feel pity emanating from him. It made me uncomfortable. I wasn't used to pity.

I had mastered the art of always maintaining the appearance of being fine. Always just fine. It was a balancing act. A show I put on for the outside world regardless of how I felt inside, like the smile I painted on with pink lipstick each day. It was always the same shade, subtle and pale, nothing too bright. Never a vibrant red. That would look too fake, as though I was trying too hard. It had to look natural. Plausible.

Except today. Today it wasn't acceptable to look like I was fine. Today I was expected to be sad, heartbroken and mournful.

I twisted my hands together in my lap. I heard Mum sniff beside me. She reached out and placed her hand on top of mine with a gentle squeeze. It was a sweet gesture. Supportive. Motherly. She was letting me know she was there for me. But there were no tears in her eyes, not for Adam. Never for him.

She'd hated him. She'd made that clear from the start. There was never any pretence with her. She wasn't one to mask her feelings. She said that would be insincere. False. A lie.

Mum despised lies. To her there was nothing worse. It was unforgivable. It didn't matter what kind of lie it was. Big or small, it was irrelevant. A lie was a lie. That was all that mattered.

She had a sixth sense for them. She was like a human lie detector. She always knew. Maybe I looked guilty and my fear betrayed me. Or maybe it was just that she was too suspicious.

Mum saw deception all around her. She didn't trust anyone. Not even me. Not even when I was innocent. Perhaps she saw something in me. I took a shaky breath. What did she see in me now?

The police officer cleared his throat. I squinted at his name badge, trying to make out the letters from across Mum's living room. I was sure he'd introduced himself when he'd arrived. It had only been a few minutes ago and yet his name had evaporated from my memory already. Ironic, really. There were so many things I would like to forget and yet they stayed with me. Taunting me.

And then there were other things; things that didn't seem possible; things I had no recollection of; but things that changed everything.

'Miss Harper, I'm sorry to have to ask you this, but were there any problems in your relationship?'

I blinked. I paused for a moment, debating how to answer. 'Is any relationship without problems?'

He studied me carefully and I tried not to shuffle under his gaze. Perhaps my response had been too reasoned. Too formal.

'So there *were* problems?'

I bit my lip. 'Occasionally.' I shrugged. 'But nothing of any real consequence.' Another lie.

'How long had you known Adam?'

'We met in May.' I smiled slightly at the memory. Everything had been so different then. Our lives had been full of possibilities. New relationships were like that; full of firsts. First date. First kiss. First lie. First betrayal.

Nine months, that's all we'd had together. It didn't seem much. Nine was such a small number. But when we were together it had seemed like an eternity.

2

THEN

'Hi, Mum,' I called as I turned the key and pushed open her front door.

'Oh, you're here, then.'

My body tensed as I closed the heavy wooden door behind me. Her unspoken 'at last' hung heavily in the air.

I glanced at my watch: 6.08 p.m. I winced.

'Sorry, traffic out of Bournemouth town centre was—'

Mum grunted, cutting though my excuses. 'The traffic wouldn't be a problem if you left on time, Jessica.'

I met her penetrating blue eyes and tried not to squirm. 'I know, but the meeting overran. It was only a couple of minutes, but…'

She rolled her eyes. 'They know what time you finish. You should just tell them that you have to leave. You're letting them take advantage of you. They only pay you to be there until 5.30 p.m.'

I swallowed but said nothing. What could I say? She was right, of course. I'd never been good at leaving dead on time. It just wasn't that easy. Delays happened. Sometimes I needed to finish what I was working on, or a meeting ran long. It wasn't like I planned to be late, but then it also wasn't as though it was critical for me to leave exactly on time. Was it?

Most of my colleagues had kids to get home to. They had football practice, or dance lessons to drive them to. And yet even they stayed sometimes. Whereas me... How could I explain that I needed to be at my mother's at 6 p.m. promptly without fail?

Mum stood in the kitchen doorway, watching me. She looked so sad and alone. Guilt churned in my stomach. Those few minutes didn't seem significant to me, but they mattered to her.

'I'll be sure to leave on time tomorrow.'

She smiled and I felt my shoulders relax as I slipped off my jacket.

'When did you buy that?'

I froze at the sharpness of her tone. I frowned slightly, trying to catch up with the change in conversation.

I followed her gaze to my red top.

'You went shopping without me.'

It wasn't a question, but an accusation.

'No. I mean, yes, but...' I shook my head and let out a feeble laugh. 'It wasn't like that. I met Karen for coffee in town last weekend and had a few minutes to kill before my bus home.'

'I could have come with you.' Mum's voice was small and dejected.

My jacket weighed heavily in my hands. I'd hurt her.

'It was only a couple of minutes.' I tried to justify my neglect.

'I could have met you after you'd seen your friend. I wouldn't have got in the way. We could have gone for lunch and made a day of it.' Mum lowered her gaze and stared at the floor. 'Unless you didn't want me there...'

'No, of course I did. That would have been nice. Lovely, even.

In fact, we should do that.' I was babbling. I knew it, but I couldn't seem to stop myself.

It was the expression on her face that did it; pinched and pained. The hurt showed in the hunch of her shoulders that made her seem smaller and more vulnerable. The realisation that I'd made her feel unwelcome and unwanted tore at my heart.

'This Saturday?' Mum stared at me, her eyes wide and hopeful, watching me intently for any sign of hesitation.

I smiled. 'Yes, absolutely.' The agreement slipped easily from my lips as my mind raced. I was meant to be meeting the girls from work for lunch on Saturday. I would have to cancel now. I'd just tell them something had come up. They wouldn't question it.

'You're a good daughter.'

I smiled, feeling a warm glow wash over me. I was redeemed. My earlier thoughtlessness had been forgiven.

'I don't know what I'd do without you.'

My smile wavered. She was pleased with me. I was still loved. And yet there was an implication behind her words; a desperation. Beneath her appreciation I could hear her unspoken words.

You can never leave.

I rubbed my arms as I shivered. The early evening chill must have followed me inside.

Mum nodded, a sharp, short nod of approval, and then disappeared into the kitchen. I stared after her, feeling strangely unsettled. It wasn't as though I'd really wanted to go out with the office crowd anyway. Had I?

I shrugged as I hung my coat on a peg. Of course not. A mother and daughter day was far more 'me'.

Mum was already sitting at the table when I walked into the kitchen. I glanced out of the window behind her and smiled slightly. The sight of the ocean always comforted me. It was one of the things I loved about this old house.

I frowned and turned away. Perhaps more accurately, it was the only thing I loved.

'I bought some minced beef. I thought we could have spaghetti bolognese tonight,' Mum said.

I smiled and stifled a groan. So much for my plan of popping yesterday's leftover homemade chicken casserole into the microwave and giving me a night off cooking.

'Sure, why not?' I said with another shrug.

I pulled a frying pan from the drawer beneath the hob and rummaged through the fridge for the packet of minced beef. I tipped it into the pan to cook and took a deep breath. Neither my evening nor my weekend were going to work out quite as I'd planned, but at least I still had Friday night to look forward to. I felt a smile tug at the corner of my lips. Just one more day and then—

'You're very smiley this evening.'

I heard the suspicion in Mum's voice.

'I got asked out on a date.' I set a pan of water to boil, feeling like a teenager, full of excitement and pride when a cute boy in my class had spoken to me.

Mum stared at me, her lips parted. 'A date?'

She questioned it as though she didn't understand the words.

'By who?'

I laughed nervously, playing for time as I opened a tin of tomatoes and emptied them into a pan with a sprinkling of herbs. I knew my response would elicit a reaction. I doubted it would be a good one. There simply wasn't a right answer to that question. Whoever the guy was, Mum would find an issue with him.

I took a deep breath. 'The plumber.'

Mum shook her head. 'I'm sorry, I thought you said the plumber.'

I swallowed. 'I did.'

Her expression darkened. I shouldn't have told her. She didn't need to know every detail of my life. And yet, somehow, she always did. She knew how to draw information out of me, even things I'd promised myself I wouldn't say.

She didn't even have to try hard to get me to talk now. It was so ingrained in me. Her need to know had become my need to tell her. She didn't believe in secrets. That's what she always said.

We don't have secrets, Jessica. Not between us.

It was too late now, though. I'd already opened the door, inviting her judgement in.

'He came to repair the leak under my kitchen sink, and we just got chatting.' I clamped my mouth shut. Why did I always feel the need to justify myself to her?

Mum's eyes narrowed. 'Why would he be interested in you?'

I froze. Some part of my brain was telling me I should feel slighted and insulted by her question. But mostly all I felt was numb.

My mind raced for an answer, but I felt like I was swimming against the current, where my ability to think was drowned out by one terrifying realisation. Mum was right. Mum was always right. What would Adam see in me?

'Well, it's not as though you'll have anything in common,' Mum continued, giving weight to her question.

'We have lots in common.' I grabbed hold of the lifeline she had inadvertently thrown me, and felt a tiny glimmer of satisfaction. 'We talked about music, books and—'

'A shared appreciation of music is hardly enough for the foundations of a lasting relationship.'

I shook my head, refusing to let her dismiss the connection I'd felt to Adam. 'It doesn't need to be. It's just a date. We'll get to know one another better then.'

She stared at me, her left eyebrow arched upwards.

'It's just a date,' I repeated. But I could hear the wobble in my voice.

'You know you don't attract the right sort of men. You're too gullible. It always ends badly.'

My earlier happy glow had been doused by reality. Mum was right again. I was a magnet for disastrous relationships. The guys always seemed okay at the start. Nice, normal guys and then... I stirred the tomatoes with more force than necessary.

Maybe it wasn't their fault. Maybe it was me. Could something about me drive them to it? Did I change them?

I flinched as the tomatoes spat at me, burning my hand.

'So when is this *date*?'

'Friday night.' I glanced at the clock hung over the kitchen door. Just over forty-eight hours to go. The tick-tick of the seconds passing filled the silence. The countdown had begun.

I swallowed. There was still time. I could call him and cancel. He'd probably be grateful.

'I suppose you won't be home for your dinner on Friday, then?'

Home.

It had been years since I had lived here, but somehow this was still classed as home. Mum was in denial that I had ever left, but then perhaps I hadn't really. At least not properly. I seemed to spend more time here than I did in my own apartment.

I added the spaghetti to the pan of boiling water. What if I didn't cancel? It would be nice to have a meal cooked for me for a change. It wasn't as though anything was likely to come of it, but it would be an evening out.

'Well, will you?' Mum asked.

I gave the tomato sauce another stir. 'No.' I smiled at the certainty in my voice. 'I won't be here on Friday.'

3

NOW

'They were very happy together,' Mum said. 'They had a very close relationship.' She glanced sideways at me and I knew what was coming. 'If anything, it was too close.'

The police office arched his eyebrow. 'How so?'

I gazed out of the window, watching the mist settle over Old Harry Rocks in the distance. A squawk caught my attention as seagulls circled over the waves crashing beneath them. Is this how it felt to them? To look down on the world below them, observing, but not participating?

'They were inseparable. Jessica always did whatever he wanted, went wherever he wanted. Of course, she was too preoccupied with him to bother about spending time with her own mother.'

'That's not true.' Indignance surged through me as my attention jolted back to focus on Mum. I'd still spent time with her. Not as much as I used to, but things were different. I'd had a boyfriend. I'd had... a life.

I slumped back against Mum's sofa, as I realised just how

much I had lost. Not just Adam, but our life together. A life with someone by my side. A life where I wasn't alone.

Mum rolled her eyes at me and patted my hand. 'You were obsessed with him, dear.' She turned back to the police officer. 'She was totally devoted to him. I don't know how she'll survive without him.'

The police officer's gaze burned into me. He was weighing me up; judging me against Mum's description. Did I seem like the broken-hearted girlfriend who couldn't survive without the love of her life?

I squirmed in my seat. Possibly not.

I was sad. Of course I was sad. At one point I'd begun to think we might have a future together. But I learnt a long time ago that people always let me down. Adam was no exception. He'd just been a little harder to let go of.

We'd had so much potential at first. I'd truly thought that he was different, he was special.

I was wrong.

Was it fair to blame him for it, though? Maybe if we'd met sooner, before my life had become jaded by lies and betrayal, things might have been different for us. Maybe I would have been different.

I let out a long sigh and tugged at a loose thread on my blue sweater. Maybe it didn't matter. Maybe I was destined to become who I was and changing the past wouldn't have prevented it. Perhaps the darkness was always there, surrounding me, waiting...

4

THEN

I glanced around the crowded bar, my eyes desperately searching the unfamiliar faces. Would I recognise him? Would he recognise me? Or, for that matter, would he even spot me at this table, tucked away up the corner?

I leaned forward, hoping to find another table, a more visible one. But there weren't any. It was standing room only now, and that was assuming you didn't mind being on close terms with your neighbours.

I shrank back in my seat. It was better here.

Laughter erupted from a group near the bar. They cheered as they clinked their glasses, sending beer and wine slopping on the floor. They certainly didn't seem to mind. Or perhaps they didn't even notice. They were just happy to be done with work for the week, and relaxing amongst friends with drinks in their hands. What else mattered?

I turned my glass of orange juice round on the wooden table before me, and tried to ignore the sticky beer-stained rings that surrounded it. It seemed both my orange juice and I were out of place here.

Another cheer broke through the din, raising the volume another notch. Friday night had been a bad idea for a first date. We'd never hear one another in here. I stared at the empty chair opposite me. Not that it mattered. He probably wouldn't even come. I was just taking up a table unnecessarily.

I checked my watch for the sixth time. It was still early. Too early. I sighed. My desperate need to not be late had resulted in me being absurdly early. I rolled my eyes and sank a little lower in my seat. I should at least wait until 7 p.m., just on the off chance that he actually turned up on time; I couldn't have him thinking I'd stood him up.

'Jess?'

I practically leapt out of my chair, and stared at him as I half stood, half stooped, vaguely aware that I was supposed to reply, but my brain was preoccupied. He was here. He'd actually come.

'Sorry, I hope I haven't kept you waiting long.'

I shook my head as I attempted to gracefully sink back into my chair. 'No.' I forced the word out. 'Not at all.'

His gaze dropped to my half-drunk orange juice and he raised his eyebrows.

I attempted a casual shrug. 'Well, maybe just a couple of minutes.'

The corner of his mouth twitched and I laughed.

'Okay, fine. So, I may have been ridiculously early.' I held my hands up in defeat. 'I just hate being late.'

Adam nodded. 'Punctuality is definitely an admirable quality, except...'

I drew back slightly and swallowed, waiting for the criticism. 'Except?'

'Except, it kind of makes it hard for a guy to make a good impression by being early, when his date has beaten him to it and bought her own drink.'

I laughed again, as a little bit of tension ebbed away. 'What can I say? I'm an independent woman.'

The lightness withered from my smile as I spoke. Was I independent, or was I just alone?

'Fair enough.' Adam nodded. 'But would this independent woman like some company?'

I bit my lip and gestured to the vacant chair, not trusting myself to speak.

He slipped his coat off and swung it over the back of the chair. 'I'll just get a drink first. Can I get you anything?'

I shook my head and lifted my glass with a nervous laugh. 'I already seem to have one, thanks.'

Adam rolled his eyes and laughed before heading off towards the bar. I watched him manoeuvre through the crowd with ease. I envied that. He didn't get stuck trying to squeeze through tiny gaps between people who were oblivious to his presence. An 'excuse me', a nod and a smile were all it took and the crowd seemed to expand a little to absorb him. They granted him passage as though he belonged there.

Adam re-emerged with a lager in hand in half the time it had taken me to get served, despite the fact that the pub was even busier now. Not that I was jealous, of course.

'So, Jess, what do you do?' Adam asked as he sat down.

'I work in law.'

'Wow.' Adam's eyes widened as he leaned back in his chair studying me. 'I'm impressed.'

I shook my head. 'It's probably less impressive than you think. I'm a contracts assistant.'

He frowned as confusion weighed on his brow.

'I spend all day submerged in reading the fine print of business contracts, rather than going head-to-head in a courtroom.'

'Ah, I see.' Adam shrugged. 'Still impressive, though. It just sounds a little more behind the scenes, that's all.'

I smiled. I liked that way of putting it. Usually, people's eyes glazed over when I said the words 'contract law'. My career instantaneously lost its intrigue and both it and I suddenly became boring and dull.

'It's a lot of red tape, really, but…' I cringed. Why was I making it sound worse?

'It's important, though.'

I blinked and nodded slowly. 'Yes, it is.' I sat up a little straighter. 'One missed clause or badly placed word and it could open the firm up to a huge amount of risk.'

Adam leaned forwards on the sticky table, his dark brown eyes fixed on mine. 'It sounds a lot of responsibility.'

'It is, but I kind of like it.' I shook my head. 'Not the work itself exactly – to be honest, that is incredibly boring. But I like the satisfaction of knowing it's important, that what I'm doing makes a difference to the company I work for. I'm protecting their interests. It makes me feel like what I do matters.'

I clamped my mouth closed, holding back the words that threatened to escape.

It makes me feel like I matter.

I swallowed and forced a smile back onto my lips.

'I'm not sure I could do your job, stuck sitting at a desk all day would drive me crazy. It's so…' Adam frowned. 'Confining.'

'Really?' I raised an eyebrow. 'I'd never thought of it that way.' I studied my glass of orange juice as I pivoted it on the table between us. There was something comforting about the routine of going to the office five days a week. I knew what I was expected to do. How I was expected to behave. What I was expected to be. There was a certainty to it that gave me purpose.

I tipped my head to the side. Or perhaps the routine just stopped me from having to decide anything for myself.

I glanced up at Adam. 'Your job seems so unpredictable to me. I don't know how you plan anything when you have to slot travelling and emergency call-outs into your day.'

'I like it that way. Always different. Never the same.'

I shuddered. The mere idea was terrifying to me. Adam's eyebrows raised and I winced. He'd seen my reaction, he probably thought I was being dismissive and rude about his career.

I clasped my hands together on my lap. I needed to say something positive. Something to detract from my thoughtless dismissal. 'It must be interesting, though, meeting new people every day, seeing a glimpse into their homes, their lives.' It was feeble, but at least it was sincere. I'd always been curious about other people, the way they lived, who they were.

Adam smiled. 'It can be, but most of the time I end up twisted into tight spaces and trying not to judge them on the cleanliness of their bathrooms.'

'Ah.' I wrinkled my nose. 'So not exactly the highlight of your day, then.'

Adam shook his head. 'I wouldn't say that.' He winked at me. 'Sometimes you can end up meeting a fascinating person whilst fixing her kitchen sink.'

I laughed. 'I hardly think I class as fascinating.'

Adam tipped his head to the left as he studied me. 'I don't know, I get the feeling there are hidden depths to you behind that serious façade.'

Heat crept into my cheeks. 'And I get the feeling that I might not be the only customer you've asked out on a date.' I cringed as I spoke. I hadn't intended to announce my fear to him, but Mum was right, why would he be interested in me? He must meet so many interesting people; interesting women, why would

I stand out from them? I wasn't beautiful or sexy, I wasn't even that interesting or funny. I was quiet and nondescript. My most distinguishing attribute was my ability to blend in. I was like a chameleon that could hide in plain sight. Except I never actually intended to hide. It wasn't my aim, at least, not consciously. I wasn't even sure how I achieved it. Somehow I was just invisible.

Yet, Adam had noticed me.

'You're the first,' Adam said, as he raised his hand in a mock scout salute.

My eyes narrowed and I studied him dubiously.

'Seriously,' he added. 'Most of the time people try to ignore that I'm there. They might offer me a cup of tea, sometimes without prompting, but that's it. I'm just there to do a job. I'm an inconvenience, a disruption to their routine. I try to keep out of the way and get the job done as quickly as possible so I can get on to the next.' He paused and his eyes met mine. 'Until I met you.'

I shook my head and let out a nervous laugh.

'You're lovely.'

I waited for him to continue, but he just smiled.

There were no caveats, no clarifications, no suggested improvements. Just lovely.

I shuffled awkwardly, willing him to keep talking and move the conversation on, but his comment just hung there between us. I cleared my throat. 'But do you like being a plumber?'

The corner of Adam's mouth twitched, at my avoidance of his comment. He shrugged. 'It's like any job, I guess. It has its good days and bad days. But, yeah, for the most part, it's okay. I like the jobs that are a little different, though; not the same mundane repairs where you barely even need to think.'

I tipped my head to the right and studied him. 'You like a challenge.'

Adam chuckled. 'I guess I do. It makes life more interesting that way.'

I nodded slowly, and resisted the urge to tell him to be cautious. I knew better than most that interesting challenges weren't always as they seemed. Then again, perhaps he was exactly the kind of guy I needed. The kind of guy who wouldn't run when things got a little complicated.

I sipped my orange juice. Maybe Mum was wrong. Maybe this time I'd found exactly the right sort of man. Now all I had to do was convince him that I was the right sort of girl for him.

5

NOW

'How...?' My voice cracked and I took a breath. 'How did it happen?' It wasn't a question I wanted to ask, but the policeman would expect it, wouldn't he?

'His van went off the road at Anvil Point.'

I flinched at that name. It jarred against me. It was a place I knew well. A place of beauty and serenity. Or, at least, it had been.

'But you haven't found his...' I swallowed. 'His body. You only presume he's dead. There's a chance...' My words trailed out. A chance for what? For him? For us? My shoulders sagged. We'd never really had a chance. Not before, and certainly not now.

'The cliff there is...' The police officer shifted in the armchair again and cleared his throat. 'The damage to the van was extensive. It's unlikely anyone could have survived a crash like that.'

'But you didn't find him,' I urged. I was clinging on, even now. Despite everything, some part of me still couldn't let him go. Not completely. Not yet. But then that had been the problem, hadn't it? I never had been able to let him go, even when I should have.

'We're searching, but when the tide changes it's likely that, well...'

Silence filled the room.

'That he'll wash ashore.'

I cringed at Mum's bluntness and closed my eyes, trying to hold back my tears. But the darkness was consumed by images of Adam's lifeless body, battered and bruised, as it was tossed carelessly by the brutal sea. He'd deserved better. Better than that. Better than me.

'Do you know why Adam was at Anvil Point?'

I blinked my eyes open, dragging myself back to the present. 'He'd been doing bathroom renovations for the holiday cottages there.'

The police officer nodded and scribbled in his notebook.

'So it's not unusual for him to be there early on a Saturday morning?'

I shook my head. 'It was a big project, but he'd been keen not to let it take him away from his regular clients. He'd worked out there most weekends for a while.'

At least he used to.

I bit back the words that had sprung into my head.

A memory niggled in the recesses of my mind. Last weekend Adam had celebrated the completion of a successful job. He'd been so happy to have his weekends back to himself.

'I thought he surfed at the weekends?'

Mum's question startled me. She'd never seemed to pay any attention to Adam's interests or routines.

'He did. He hated missing it. The last few weeks had been torture for him. Being away from the sea had driven him crazy. It was the thing he loved most.'

More than he'd ever loved me.

I swallowed. 'He tried to teach me once. But...' I shrugged and tried to brush away the memory. 'It wasn't really my thing.'

The officer tipped his head to the right, curiosity etched in his features. He wanted to ask more, I could tell. He wanted to know about Adam, about us. What kind of man had Adam been? What kind of relationship had we had? Our stories were our life, our history, our undoing.

We'd worked for a while. We'd fitted together like pieces of a puzzle. But it wasn't enough.

I wasn't enough.

I'd tried to be. I knew I had. But like my attempts at surfing, I'd failed.

'Did Adam have a problem with alcohol?'

The curtness of the question grated on me and I frowned. Adam would hate to hear himself discussed like this. His life dissected. His habits analysed. I shook my head. 'He liked a lager, but not to excess.'

'Lager?'

I swallowed. There was something about the way the police officer repeated that word. Something dubious and unsettling.

'We found an empty bottle of whisky in his van.'

Whisky.

The word jarred against me. It was unnatural and wrong. I started to open my mouth to speak, but clamped it closed. Maybe that wasn't something the police officer needed to know. It would raise too many questions. He'd want to know why Adam would drink something he didn't like.

Adam wasn't the kind of man to do anything he didn't like. Not without a reason. Everything he did had a purpose, an intended outcome, something to gain.

What did he have to gain from drinking something he hated, whilst driving clifftop roads where he had no reason to be?

Nothing.

But, like me, he had everything to lose.

6

THEN

My stomach churned as I stepped off the bus at Bournemouth square. It was only May and already the town centre was chaotic with weekend visitors meandering aimlessly. I glanced at the pub, just visible above the heads of the crowd before me. It wasn't that far. My fingers wrapped around the strap of my handbag, which hung from my shoulder, and I lowered my gaze to the pavement ahead of me. I ploughed forward, sidestepping feet that veered towards me. I could do this.

I pulled open the door to the pub and stepped inside. It was still busy, but somehow it seemed a little less daunting today. I lingered in the doorway, contemplating where to sit, when a movement caught my eye. Adam was waving to me from the corner table where we'd met yesterday.

I headed towards him, slipping off my jacket as I walked, suddenly feeling flustered and warm.

'You look amazing,' Adam told me as his gaze travelled from my eyes to my toes and back again.

I laughed, and shuffled from one foot to the other. 'Thank

you,' I mumbled as heat rose to my cheeks. I wasn't someone who heard good things about myself very often.

He frowned. 'Why do you laugh? It's true.'

I shrugged. I was more accustomed to criticism than compliments. I didn't know how to take them. Worse still, I didn't even believe them. I was always sceptical. They were just words to say because he felt he ought to, because custom dictated it, not because he meant them.

'Thank you,' I repeated. What else could I say?

'There's nothing to thank me for. I'm just telling you the truth.'

'You're early,' I said, changing the subject.

'Even earlier than you, you mean.' He tapped his watch with a laugh. 'Something tells me neither of us will ever be late in this relationship.' A pink glow crept into his cheeks. 'I mean... Not that this is...'

I bit my lip and tried not to smile too broadly.

This relationship.

Is that how he thought of it? Of us?

We were only on our second date and he was already thinking in terms of a relationship. It had been a slip of the tongue. He hadn't meant it, of course. It was too soon for that. But the fact he'd said it implied a possibility. A future.

'Plus, I was here early enough to get us our table, before it got too busy,' Adam continued.

Our table.

I smiled again as I slid into the chair opposite him. We had something that was 'ours'. I liked that.

'I got an orange juice for you, I hope that's okay?'

'Perfect, thank you.' I nodded at the second glass of orange juice on the table. 'No lager today?'

Adam shook his head. 'Maybe later.' He shrugged. 'To be

honest, I don't drink that much, and I never touch the hard stuff. I'm such a lightweight.'

I lifted my glass. 'Looks like you're in good company here.'

He laughed, raised his glass and clinked it against mine. 'I couldn't agree more.'

* * *

We wandered down the stairs from the Odeon and out into the mild evening air.

We paused by the entrance. I waited for his goodbye. Would he hug me? Kiss me? Or maybe just walk away with a casual wave and a cheery goodnight like yesterday?

'It's still fairly early. Maybe we could go for a walk on the pier?' Adam asked.

I smiled. 'That would be nice.'

Nice? Was that all? I tried not to laugh as my heart pounded with excitement. Could he hear it? Could he hear the relief in my voice? The hope?

We wandered down the path beside the gardens in silence. The tourists still lingered, but somehow their presence didn't bother me as much now. The crowds separated as we approached as though Adam somehow repelled them from our path.

I searched for something to say. Something interesting. Something funny.

My mind was blank.

'What are you doing on Monday evening?' Adam asked.

I hesitated. Did he want to see me again? I could tell him I didn't have any plans. I didn't have to have any. I could cancel them. For him.

'I'm having dinner with my mum.' The truth slipped out. I couldn't cancel on her again. Not so soon.

'And Tuesday night?'

The same.

I kept my mouth shut. He didn't need to know we ate together every night. He didn't need to know I had no other plans. 'Nothing I can't cancel.'

Adam grinned. 'I'm glad.'

He reached for my hand, his fingers entwined around mine.

'Are your parents not together?'

Every muscle in my body tensed.

'It's just you only said you were having dinner with your mum, not your parents.'

'Oh.' I let out a long deep breath. 'Right, yes, it's just Mum and me. It has been for a long time.'

'And your dad?'

'Left.'

Adam blinked at the abruptness of my tone. 'I'm sorry.'

My stomach stirred. I didn't want Adam's pity. I didn't deserve it. I shrugged as I tried to free myself from the weight that had descended upon me. 'Like I said, it was a long time ago.'

'But you're close to your mum?'

His question startled me. Not because of the answer, but because it went without saying. It was just a fact. The way it was for everyone. Wasn't it?

'Aren't you close to yours?'

'Yeah, of course. But...' He shrugged. 'It's just different, I guess.'

I turned to face him. 'How?'

His shoulders lifted as he took a deep breath. 'My parents haven't always approved of my choices.'

'Oh.' My heart ached for him. There was something so unbearably sad for a child to be a disappointment to their parents.

Like I was to Dad.

I shivered, despite the warmth of the evening. I didn't want to think about Dad. Not now. Not ever. He'd moved on and so had I. Or at least I was trying to.

But this wasn't about us. This was about Adam.

'I don't blame them,' Adam continued. 'I haven't always made the best decisions,' he added quickly, as though he didn't want me to think badly of them. 'I tried to, I did. But sometimes, well, I guess, sometimes knowing something is wrong makes it much more tempting.'

I frowned, as I tried to follow his logic. 'How can wrong be tempting?' It didn't make sense. If something was wrong, then you didn't do it. There was no question about it. No appeal. No desire. Not even a choice. Just an obligation. An instinctive obedience.

'It's hard to explain.' Adam shrugged. 'Not that it matters now. It's in the past.' He smiled and winked at me. 'The future is far more interesting.'

He leaned towards me slowly, as though giving me time to pull away. But I didn't. I couldn't. My feet were rooted to the spot. Waiting.

His lips touched mine, soft and warm. A thousand thoughts rushed through my head, but I couldn't grasp any of them. I didn't want to. All I wanted was this. All I wanted was him.

* * *

'I've been trying to call you for hours.'

I pulled the phone away from my ear, softening the volume. Mum spoke as though she hadn't seen me in days. The fact that I'd spent the morning with her, traipsing around store after store, searching for something she approved of, seemed to have been forgotten already.

My credit card had survived the trip unscathed. The only

thing I'd bought was our lunch in a café before we'd given up. Our shopping sprees were always economical. Somehow we never found anything that suited me.

'Sorry, Mum. I had my phone off in the cinema and forgot to turn it back on.'

'The *cinema*?'

I cringed. She hadn't needed to know where I'd been. Now I'd opened myself up for the questioning that would inevitably follow.

'Who did you go to the cinema with?'

I rolled my eyes; and so it had begun.

I hesitated. I could lie. I could tell her I'd gone alone. The problem was it wouldn't be believable. Not to her.

'With Adam.'

There was a lingering pause and I wondered if she'd heard.

'The plumber?'

I took a deep breath. 'Yes.'

'You saw him again? *Already?*'

I could hear the contempt in her tone.

I shook my head. It was just motherly concern, that was all.

'That was too soon,' she continued, seemingly not needing to wait for my confirmation. 'He'll know you're desperate.'

He'll know.

That was how she saw me. Desperate. She said it like it was a fact. That was what I was. Who I was.

'We went to see a movie together. That hardly classes as desperate, Mum.'

I swallowed. Did it?

Mum scoffed. I hated that sound. It was full of condescension and disapproval. Her way of telling me I was wrong. I was being a fool. Again.

'So, I suppose it's serious, then?'

This relationship.

Adam's words whirled around my head and I felt a funny little charge of electricity pass through me.

I hope so.

I caught myself smiling and tried to compose my emotions. It was too soon to be thinking like that, but still... The idea was appealing. There was something about him, something that made me want our dates to never end. He was different. He didn't have flaws. Not like the others.

'I'd better buy a hat then, had I?'

There was laughter in Mum's voice. It wasn't a real question. It was a taunt. She didn't believe she'd need a hat, because she didn't believe there'd be a wedding. Any wedding. Not for me. The mere idea of it was laughable.

I wanted to yell at her. I wanted to tell her how much her sarcasm hurt. But mostly I wanted to ask why she found it so funny.

I was a joke to my own mother. Not even she believed I could find someone who could love me.

7

NOW

The police officer rose to his feet. 'We'll be in touch when we have more news.'

When they've found Adam's body.

My brain silently translated the meaning of his words and I nodded. I wondered how he'd learned to be so tactful. Was it his training, or experience? How many times had he delivered news like this?

'Will you be staying h—'

'Yes,' Mum replied for me. 'She'll be staying here, at home, where I can look after her.'

There was that word again. *Home.*

I had a home.

My home.

One I'd shared with Adam.

It had still been mine. He'd still kept his rented apartment. At least for now. But we had plans... We'd *had* plans.

The police officer smiled slightly. 'Well, we know where to find you, then.'

I nodded.

He'd already known where to find me. He'd come here to deliver his news. He'd tracked me down so easily. But then where else would I have been?

He'd gone to my apartment first, of course. He said my neighbour had redirected him here. Everyone knew where I'd be. I was predictable. Reliable.

'But if you think of anything in the meantime,' he pulled a business card from his pocket and handed it to me. 'Just give me a call.'

'Your room is all made up and ready for you,' Mum said as she walked back into the living room after seeing the police officer out.

My room was always ready for me. Waiting. Just like Mum. Both were hoping for my eventual return.

'Maybe you should lie down for a little while, and I'll get us some lunch ready.'

I nodded again; it seemed to be the only thing I could do. It didn't require speech or even thought. Just an instinctive movement of my head. A sign of my agreement. I always agreed.

I stood up and headed towards the stairs. I wasn't tired. I wasn't hungry. I didn't want to lie down. I didn't want to eat. I only wanted one thing. Adam. But then that was the one thing I could never have.

I lay on my bed, staring at the ceiling. I could hear Mum moving around downstairs. The banging and clattering grew louder with each passing minute. Maybe this is why she usually left the cooking to me.

'Jess?'

I ignored her. She could manage without me just this once.

'Jess!' Her voice was louder, more urgent.

I sat up and swung my legs over the side of the bed. 'I'm coming.'

I walked onto the landing and peered down the stairs.

She looked harassed. Her hair, which was usually perfectly positioned, was wild and dishevelled. 'Have you seen my notebook?'

I blinked. 'Huh?'

'My notebook,' she repeated, dragging the words out as though I was a child who didn't understand plain English.

I shook my head. 'Isn't it in your bag?'

She sighed. 'Would I be asking you where it is if it was in my bag?'

I stared at her, her words tumbling off me without impact. I didn't even flinch at her tone. That struck me as odd. Usually her words bothered me, but today... I frowned, probing my feelings, trying to pin down what it was I felt.

Nothing.

That was it; I felt nothing. Just empty and numb.

'Jess, focus. I need you to help me find it.'

'A notebook?' I'd lost everything and she was worried about a lost notebook?

'It's important.'

'So was Adam.' I turned on my heel and marched back to my room. For the first time in my life, I slammed the door behind me. It felt good. It felt rebellious. It was tiny and insignificant and yet... I smiled slightly as I realised Adam would be proud of me.

8

THEN

'That's some house,' Adam said as I pulled my car up on the driveway of the imposing whitewashed six-bedroom house before us.

I nodded but didn't speak. He was right, it was quite spectacular.

'You grew up here?'

'We moved here when I was about six. Mum inherited it from her parents. They died in a hit and run.' I took a deep breath. 'It was a drunk driver. The police caught him. He went to prison. But...'

'It couldn't bring them back.'

I shook my head.

'I'm sorry. That's so sad.'

I mustered a half shrug. 'It was a long time ago.'

'But you still miss them.'

I nodded.

'I can hear it in your voice.' He squeezed my hand. 'There's a touch of wistfulness to your tone. They were important to you.'

I nodded slowly. 'Yes, they were and...'

'And?'

I shook my head. 'It doesn't matter.'

Adam leaned towards me. 'Yes, it does.'

I took a deep breath and looked back at the house. 'It's just, things changed after they'd gone.'

The house that had once been somewhere exciting to visit for the occasional weekend or school holiday had become home. Our lives were upended and slotted into somewhere none of us had really fitted, no matter how hard we tried.

Anyone who saw the house, or knew of its location, was envious of us and the new life we had acquired. But appearances could be deceptive. Reality was always subjective.

I shook my head again, trying to cast off the wave of sadness that threatened to engulf me. 'Come on, we can't sit out here all afternoon.'

I opened my door and clambered out. I took another deep breath and straightened my long blue skirt.

'Are you all right?' Adam asked as we fell into step and started walking towards the house.

I tried to smile, but it felt too forced to look natural. 'Just a little nervous.'

He chuckled. 'Shouldn't I be the one who's nervous here? I'm the one who's about to be grilled by your mother.'

I cringed.

'Wait.' Adam stopped dead, as uncertainty flashed in his eyes. 'I was only joking. She's not actually that bad, right?'

I gazed at him helplessly. I wanted to deny it. To reassure him that it was just an informal quiet afternoon with my mum, who was excited to meet the guy that had made her daughter so happy over the last few weeks. But I couldn't. It wasn't. He was auditioning for her, and my mother was a harsh critic. Few ever made the cut.

'I should have turned her invitation down. You should have told me this was a bad idea and that you didn't want to meet her.'

'But I do.'

I squinted at him. 'You do?' I couldn't keep the surprise out of my voice. 'Why?'

Adam stepped forward and his gaze met mine. 'Because she's important to you. She's part of your life. I want to know everything about you. Even your mother.'

'But it's too soon. I should have told her that.'

Adam rested his hands on my shoulders. 'So, why didn't you?'

'Because...' I swallowed. How could I answer that? I wasn't sure there even was a reason, just a compulsion. 'She wanted to meet you,' I finished lamely. That was all that had mattered. She'd wanted it.

Adam nodded. 'Then we'd best not disappoint her.'

He reached for my hand, our fingers intertwined like pieces of a puzzle slotting perfectly in place. It felt natural. Right.

We started walking again and I felt stronger. I was worrying unnecessarily. Adam had got this. His calm thoughtfulness would win Mum over. How could it not? He was everything a mother could want for her daughter. Everything I wanted for myself.

The front door swung open as we approached and I automatically pulled my hand from Adam's. I felt like a child caught doing something I shouldn't. Something wrong.

I saw Adam's startled expression, before he quickly replaced his smile and reached out his hand to my mum. 'Mrs Harper, it's great to meet you.'

Mum studied him, her lips pinched into a straight line that added years to her age. She left his hand outstretched in front of her for a few seconds too long, before finally gripping it with her own. 'Yes, well, you'd better come in.'

She released his hand, turned on her heel and disappeared inside.

I didn't dare look at Adam. What must he be thinking? It was hardly a warm welcome. I half expected him to turn around and head back down the drive. I wouldn't have blamed him. Perhaps I should even encourage him. I could go with him.

It was stupid to have brought him here. I wasn't ready to share him yet. Our time together was precious and new. It was ours. Just ours.

'After you.'

I looked up and realised Adam was holding the door for me to go first.

I smiled and stepped inside. I should have known he wasn't the type to run from anything. Not even my mother.

* * *

'Wow! I thought the house was impressive, but this view...' Adam's voice trailed off as he stared out of the kitchen window.

The long stretch of freshly cut lawn led to a rocky cliff edge, and beyond it was a vast expanse of blue. The sky met the sea somewhere on the distant horizon. It was perfect.

'Come on, you need to see it properly.' I swung the patio door open. I grabbed Adam's hand and led him outside. 'I love it out here,' I told him as I hurried him along the winding path to the end of the garden.

I pointed to the right. 'Over there you can see Old Harry Rocks near Swanage.' I signalled to the left. 'And over that way you can see the Isle of Wight.'

'Wow!' Adam repeated as we reached the edge. He glanced left and right again before leaning forward, peering down the steep cliff face to the promenade and beach below. 'This is incredible.'

I watched the waves crashing on the shore. 'Dad and I used to stay out here for ages, just watching the waves.'

Adam turned his head to look at me. 'You've never talked about your dad before, other than when you told me he left when you were a kid.'

'I don't talk about him.' I shrugged. 'Mum didn't allow it.'

'Allow it?'

'Like it.' I laughed. 'I mean, she didn't like it. It was...' I searched for the right words.

'Too painful,' Adam finished for me.

I nodded, but somehow it didn't feel right. Had it been too painful for her? She'd never really seemed sad that Dad wasn't around. She didn't seem to miss him. It was more that she was angry.

I rolled my eyes. Of course she was angry. He'd abandoned her and left her to raise a kid all alone.

Except, it hadn't really felt like she was mad at him, but more like she was mad at me.

I closed my eyes and willed the tears away. I was wrong. I had to be wrong. Mum loved me. She'd always loved me. It was just her and me. Together.

'Jess?'

I opened my eyes and my gaze met Adam's. I cringed as I realised he'd been watching me.

'Are you okay?'

I pasted my smile back in place and saw his shoulders relax.

It wasn't just Mum and me any more. I had Adam now, too.

'So what do you think?' I asked, nodding back at the view before us.

'It's quite something,' Adam said with a laugh. 'I'm kind of envious of you growing up here. It must have been amazing.'

I swallowed. 'Yeah, I guess.'

'Can you get down to the beach from here?' Adam asked as he brushed an overgrown bush aside with his foot.

'I wouldn't recommend it.' I leaned forwards slightly. 'The cliff side is unstable.'

Adam pouted and edged a little further forward. 'That's a shame. You'd have your own private beach access if you could clamber down here.'

'You should mind your footing up here,' Mum said as she walked up beside me. She nodded towards the edge. 'One mistake and...' Her gaze travelled to the promenade below the rocky clifftop and then back to Adam.

I bit my lip as I studied her. There was something about her expression that I couldn't place as she stared at Adam.

It was just concern, of course it was. That's why she was warning him about the cliff.

'Mum's right,' I said, turning back to Adam. 'Dad and I used to joke that we'd try it one day but...' I swallowed and glanced at Mum.

Her expression had hardened.

I'd mentioned Dad.

We don't talk about him.

'We should go back inside,' I said, as I turned my back on the beach and the past.

* * *

'It's very...' Adam paused as I handed him a delicate flowered china cup and saucer. 'Traditional.'

I bit my lip and tried not to let the tea spill. Mum would be so cross if it splashed on the beige carpet. It was spotless. A little threadbare in places. But spotless. It, like the rest of the house, had been cleaned to perfection. Mum had always been very particular about this house.

I sat on the three-seater sofa beside Adam and sighed as my mind drifted.

'Mum, can Susan come round after school tomorrow?'

Mum's hand froze; her fork suspended in front of her lips as her gaze darted around the kitchen. 'The house isn't really tidy enough for visitors.'

'It's perfect. It's always perfect.'

'Well, yes. I suppose it's not too bad, but...'

'We won't make a mess, I promise. I'll get her to take her shoes off and we'll stay in my room. No one would even know she's here.'

'But I would know.'

My gaze drifted to the photo of the two of us that hung over the fireplace. Just Mum and me. Her arm wrapped around my waist. A smile on her face.

It was the only addition she'd made to the décor since we'd moved in. She'd insisted on having the photo taken a few months after Dad had left. It was as though she was trying to prove to the world that she and I were fine alone. We'd lost everyone who'd mattered to us; first her parents and then Dad, but we still had each other.

'What happened with your dad?' Adam asked. I glanced at him and realised he was staring at the photo.

I shrugged. 'Sometimes things don't work out.'

'Does he still live in Bournemouth?'

'I don't know.' I shifted on the lumpy sofa. 'I never heard from him after he left.'

Adam gaped at me, his eyes wide. 'But you seemed so close.'

'We were.' I shrugged again, trying to brush off the past as though it no longer bothered me. 'Or, at least, I thought we were.'

A movement caught my eye and I saw Mum in the kitchen picking up a chocolate cake.

'I guess things aren't always as they seem,' Adam said softly.

My head jolted back and I stared at him, wondering what he'd meant. But he was still studying the photo.

I shuffled forward on the sofa and leaned towards the coffee table. I reached out to move a notebook that lay beside the tea tray to make space for the cake.

I frowned as I picked it up. There was something familiar about it. The navy blue hard cover. The worn corners. It wasn't just any notebook. It was *the* notebook. The one Mum had had for years. At least it appeared to be the same one. She'd scribbled in it frantically when Dad left. For days she had been inseparable from it. And then suddenly it was gone.

For a while.

It was like a phase that re-emerged periodically. She'd write in it obsessively for a while and then it would disappear for months, sometimes even for years.

But it always came back.

Curiosity niggled at me, urging me to turn back the cover and take a quick peek inside. My fingers twitched as I ran them along the edge of the pages. It would be so easy, Mum wouldn't even know...

I let out a deep breath. But I would know.

The notebook wasn't mine. I had no business poking my nose into Mum's personal affairs.

Not that that ever stopped her.

I froze, stunned by the hostility of that thought. There was a truth to it, but it was different. She was my mum. That came with certain rights, certain responsibilities. She looked out for me; protected me. That was all.

I frowned. Wasn't it?

'That looks amazing, Mrs Harper.'

I jumped and quickly set the notebook down on the sofa beside me.

'Mum always makes the best cakes,' I told Adam proudly.

'That's because I use your grandmother's recipe. Sometimes it's better to stick with tradition.'

Mum's gaze locked on Adam as she spoke and I cringed. She'd heard his comment. His slight on her house; her way of life. He hadn't meant it that way. To him it was probably just an observation. But to Mum every comment meant something. Not just the words that were spoken, but what was left unsaid. She prided herself on being able to read people.

It was an impressive skill to possess. If it worked.

Somehow it never had on me. If it had then wouldn't she know how much I loved her? How much I cared?

How much I needed her to love me back?

I blinked, startled by that stray thought. It was random. It was wrong. She loved me. She always had. In her own way.

She just didn't know how to show it, that's all.

She loved me.

She'd stayed.

Mum cut the cake, slid a slice on to a plate and handed it to Adam. She did the same with a second piece and turned to pass it to me. I lifted my hand to take it from her but she froze.

'Mum?' I squinted at her. Was it my imagination or did her hand tremble as she held the plate? 'Are you okay?'

She laughed. A contorted chuckle that lasted for just a moment. 'Sorry,' she said as she shoved the plate into my hand. 'I was miles away.'

I nodded slowly.

She dropped the cake knife down on the coffee table with a thud.

'Aren't you having any cake?'

'Yes, yes, just got to tidy up a bit first.' She slid past me, scooped up the notebook from the sofa, hurried to the dark oak desk by the window and shoved the notebook into a drawer.

I turned back to Adam and realised he was also watching Mum. He turned to me and arched his eyebrow. I shrugged, but there was a heaviness in my stomach. One afternoon in Mum's house and he's already started to notice her strange habits.

Mum returned and cut a piece of cake for herself, before sitting in the armchair opposite.

Adam shuffled forwards on the sofa. 'Are they your grandparents?' he asked, nodding at a photo on the sideboard.

'Yes, that photo was taken at the hotel they always used to go to in Majorca.'

Mum tutted. 'It was Menorca.'

I squinted at the photo. 'Really? I thought it was Majorca.'

'You know your memory isn't reliable.'

Adam's eyes widened as he turned to me. 'I haven't noticed your memory being bad.'

Mum laughed. 'Not bad, just selective.'

I froze. I felt like a cornered animal, caught between my instinct to fight and an overwhelming fear telling me to run.

Adam turned back to my mum. 'You make it sound like Jess can choose what she remembers and what she forgets.'

'Not choose exactly.' Mum stared at me. She was taunting me. Reminding me who was in charge. She knew my weaknesses; my secrets.

I swallowed. I should intervene. I should make her stop. And yet, I couldn't.

'Jessica just has a way of forgetting the bad things.'

I held my breath waiting for her to continue, but Mum shrugged, as though signifying the end of her revelations. She'd made her point. She didn't need to elaborate. The power balance had been restored in her favour.

Adam patted my knee. 'Sounds like a useful skill.'

Mum nodded. 'It can be, sometimes.' She leaned back on the sofa and took a sip of her tea. 'Luckily, Jessica has me to help remind her.'

* * *

'It was lovely to meet you, Mrs Harper. Thank you for inviting me to your beautiful home.'

I stared at Adam, trying to read his expression, but his smile appeared as genuine as his words. Except, how could they be? How could anything about the last three hours be described as lovely?

Beside me Mum nodded, and she and I watched as he headed towards the door. I started to follow, but Mum caught my arm. She leaned in close to me.

'Are you going to marry him?'

Her voice was barely a whisper and for a moment I thought I must have misheard her. But then I saw her expression, doubt and questioning fuelling her piercing glare.

I stared at her, conscious that my jaw had dropped open. 'I've only known him for a few weeks.'

She snorted. 'That doesn't seem to matter. You can't bear to be apart from him. If you're not with him, you're messaging him.'

I heard the contempt in her voice. She thought I was getting too involved too fast. Maybe she was right. Maybe I had got caught up in the excitement, the newness, the attention, the company.

There was a voice in the back of my head telling me to be careful and go slowly. But I was tired of listening to that voice. For once I didn't want to be cautious and sensible. I wanted to be adventurous and carefree.

But there was another reason too; I was afraid to lose him. I still couldn't believe he was actually dating me; that we were a couple. What if I didn't reply to his messages at midnight when he wanted to chat and I just wanted to go to sleep? What if I didn't agree to go to the Mexican restaurant he loved, even though spicy food gave me stomach ache? Maybe he'd realise I wasn't fun enough, interesting enough, or adventurous enough. Quite simply he'd realise that I wasn't good enough.

It was the conclusion everyone came to eventually. At some point my usefulness expired. I was always temporary.

'It's not always good, you know?'

I stared at her, unable to find the words to express my shock. She actually wanted to dissuade me from the idea of love, of marriage, of being happy. I knew life wasn't perfect. I'd lived through enough heartache to know that. But love and marriage was every little girl's dream. It was my dream. It's what she'd wanted for herself. And yet, not for me...

There were no motherly reassurances. No comforting, 'don't worry, you'll find the right guy', or 'it'll all work out'. She wanted to shatter the dream. My dream.

It was like telling a child that Father Christmas didn't exist.

Except I already knew.

9

NOW

I lay on my bed and stared at the phone in my hands. Adam's smiling face stared back at me. I missed that smile. I missed him. But then I'd missed him for a while, not just today.

He'd been slipping away from me. I'd known it. I just hadn't known how to stop it. But I'd still wanted him.

What you want doesn't matter.

I cringed and rolled over. Those words had taunted me my whole life. There was an inescapable truth to them now, just as there had been the first time I'd heard them.

'When's Daddy coming home?' I asked as Mummy and I sat at the kitchen table. He was usually home from work before dinner. We always ate together.

Mummy wasn't eating either. She hadn't even made herself anything to eat. She just scribbled in a notebook as though she couldn't get the words onto the page fast enough. I peered at the notebook. It looked new. She'd only written on a couple of pages so far, but it would be full soon if she carried on writing at that speed.

'He isn't.' Mummy's voice was strange and hollow.

I swallowed the half-chewed mouthful of scrambled egg and toast. I stared at her with wide eyes, as an uneasy queasiness lodged itself heavily in my stomach. 'What do you mean?'

'He's never coming back.' She carried on writing.

'Never?' My voice was barely a whisper.

Mummy shook her head. 'Never.' She smiled. But it looked wrong. Her lips were thin and taut and her eyes were narrow and dull. 'It's just you and me now.'

I blinked. She said it like that was a good thing, a treat, like the weekend we'd spent together at the old house, just the two of us, when Daddy had to go away for work. Mummy and I had built a fortress under the kitchen table. We'd played in it all weekend. But that was different. It was special. It was just a weekend. Not even the whole weekend. Daddy had come home in time to tuck me into bed on Sunday night.

But never was longer than a weekend. Never was too long.

'Come on, eat your dinner before it gets cold.'

I glared at the pale yellow egg and pushed my plate away. 'I don't want dinner. I want Daddy.'

I heard Mum's sharp intake of breath and knew she was cross. 'What you want doesn't matter.' She leaned forwards and pushed the plate back in front of me. 'Now, eat.'

There was a sharpness to her voice and a coldness to her eyes as she glared at me, almost as though she was daring me to defy her. I shuddered and slumped in my chair.

'Now!'

I flinched and grabbed my knife and fork, my hands trembled slightly as I cut the toast.

I dropped the phone on my bed. Mum was right. It hadn't mattered. I hadn't mattered. Not enough to make Dad stay. Not enough to make him come back. He hadn't even called.

I hadn't mattered enough to Adam either. I wanted him to love me, to be with me. Just me. I wanted him to want me the way I wanted him.

'Jess?' The bedroom door opened slowly and Mum peered in. 'I've been calling you. Dinner's ready.'

I turned away and stared at the ceiling. 'I'm not hungry.'

'You have to keep your strength up, honey.'

'What for?' It was pointless. Adam was gone. I was back here again. Back to the life I'd had before I'd met him. A life alone. 'I don't have anyone.'

The mattress dipped as she sat beside me. 'You have me.'

I stared at her. There was indignance in her tone. She thought that should be enough. That she was enough.

But it wasn't.

Was it wrong for me to want more from life than this? Than just her? An all-consuming job that I hated and evenings spent alone with my mother. She was important, of course. I loved her. I wanted her. I needed her. But I needed something more as well.

It was like time had stopped. Most kids grew up and moved away. The bond between parent and child still existed but it changed, it flexed to allow for growth. But not for us. Mum and I were different. Our lives were still enmeshed like they had been when I was a kid, only our roles had reversed. Not fully. Not consistently. I flipped back and forth like a pendulum that was constantly changing speeds. One moment I was taking care of her, the next she was influencing my decisions like I was still a child. It was messy and chaotic. It no longer worked. Perhaps it never really had.

10

THEN

'Nervous?' Adam asked as he parked the van in the multi-storey car park.

I tried to laugh, but it came out as a strangled cackle.

'I'll take that as a yes.'

I swatted his arm with my hand. 'I just want to make a good impression.'

He leaned over the handbrake and kissed my cheek. 'You always make a good impression.'

I rolled my eyes, but inside my stomach flip-flopped.

I slid my hand round the back of his neck and pulled him back towards me. Our lips met and my nerves dissipated as thoughts of anything but him evaporated from my mind.

Slowly he pulled back and smiled, a big lazy grin, as his eyes locked with mine.

He tickled my ribs. 'Come on, stop trying to distract me, you're just trying to postpone the inevitable.'

We clambered out of the van and met behind it. His hand reached for mine immediately.

'What if they don't like me?'

'Well,' Adam took a deep breath and shook his head slowly. 'Then we'll have to break up.'

I gasped. 'I can't believe you just said that.'

'I mean, it would be hard. I've known them for years.'

I frowned. 'Wait, you mean break up with them?'

Adam looked surprised. 'Of course. You didn't think you were going to get away from me that easily, did you?'

His bottom lip quivered and he couldn't keep up the act any longer. We both laughed as we walked towards the stairs.

I cast sideways glances at Adam as we walked. I still couldn't believe we were together.

How had I been so lucky to find him? I'd just called a plumber. It had been chance that it was his number I dialled. But because of that call he'd walked into my apartment and into my life. It was so simple. And yet so unexpected.

Now all I had to do was not screw it up.

* * *

'What are you drinking, Jess?' Steve asked after Adam had finished making introductions.

I shuffled into the booth and glanced at the unfamiliar faces staring back at me. Josh and his girlfriend, Kate, were already seated, with drinks in their hands.

'A white wine, please,' I said, turning back to Steve as he stood beside Adam.

Adam's left eyebrow arched upwards, but he didn't comment. 'I'll give you a hand, mate,' he said, slapping Steve on the back and they headed to the bar.

I watched the back of his head retreating, and cursed his good manners. Why did he always have to be so helpful? Why couldn't he have left Steve to it and stayed with me?

Coward.

The accusation dug into my core. I was being pathetic. I didn't need Adam to hold my hand every second. I was perfectly capable of making conversation with his friends on my own.

Wasn't I?

'So, how do you guys know Adam?' I smiled at Kate and Josh. I could do this.

'Adam, Steve and I went to school together,' Josh replied, with a shrug.

'Wow, Adam said you'd been friends for years, but I hadn't realised it was that long.' We were in our early thirties now, surely it was unusual to have maintained school friendships for that long?

'Don't you keep in touch with any of your school friends?' Kate asked.

Friends.

The 's' on the end of the word struck a nerve. I'd only had one friend after we moved to Bournemouth.

An image of Susan flashed into my mind. We'd been insepa-rable throughout our childhood. She was the one constant in my life. She'd learnt not to ask questions. She didn't get mad that I wouldn't talk to her. She didn't pry. She just stayed.

Until she left.

I shook my head. 'No, we lost touch in college.'

Kate tipped her head to the right. 'In college? You didn't go to the same college, then?'

'Yes, we did, but we had different subjects.' I shrugged. 'Ran in different circles. You know how it is?'

Kate nodded, but she couldn't know. Not really. No one could.

Only Susan.

What was she doing now? I shook that thought away. It was better not to wonder; not to think. It brought back too many memories; too much pain.

Just tell me the truth, Jess.

I flinched at Susan's voice in my head. I hadn't thought about her in years. I hadn't allowed myself to.

'Are you okay?' Kate leaned forwards across the table, her brow creased in concern.

I forced my smile back in place. 'I'm fine.'

Kate glanced at Josh, neither of them looked convinced.

'I was just wondering where she—' I licked my lips. 'Where they are now.'

'Maybe you should look them up?' Josh suggested. 'It could be fun to catch up.'

Fun.

I nodded, but the idea of facing Susan again sent a shudder through my body. It certainly wouldn't be fun.

'Josh is right,' Kate said. 'Wouldn't it be amazing to see how their lives have changed in the last twelve years? You would have so much to talk about.'

'We really would.' I laughed, praying that my fear wasn't audible. As much as I missed my old friend, I couldn't track her down. I couldn't risk bringing her back into my life. Not now.

I caught sight of Adam approaching with drinks in his hands.

I had too much to lose.

* * *

'They like you.'

'Really?' I beamed at Adam as we walked hand in hand towards the beach. It was our tradition now, every time we came to town we always took a detour to the beach.

'Couldn't you tell?'

I laughed and nodded. It had gone well, I was sure of it, but... I nibbled my lip. Was that enough?

I studied Adam's profile as we walked. He knew them better than I did. He could read them. He'd know.

My shoulders lifted as I took a deep breath. It was silly to be so bothered about their opinion of me. They were Adam's friends, not mine. If they hadn't liked me, so what?

But it didn't lessen my relief. Having them on side was an advantage. A big one. Whether I wanted to admit it or not, I needed their approval.

'Must be nice having such longstanding friendships. You must know one another really well after all these years.'

'Yeah, those guys know all my secrets.' Adam laughed, but for a second I could have sworn I saw him wince.

'You have secrets?' I groaned inwardly. It was a stupid question. Everyone had secrets. Even me.

We reached the railing and leaned over the beach.

'I did.' His nose twitched as he kept his gaze fixed ahead of him. 'But it was a long time ago.'

My mouth opened. Instinctive curiosity formed questions that threatened to tumble from my tongue.

I clamped my jaw shut.

Curiosity worked both ways. It's how it was in a relationship. Whatever questions I asked, I would be giving him a free pass to ask them back of me.

Just because he had secrets, it didn't make them equal to mine.

'Do your parents like your friends?'

Adam blinked. Confusion passed across his face. Was it my sudden change in topic, the fact I'd missed an opportunity to learn more about him, or the seeming randomness of my question?

'My parents?' He hesitated, as though trying to figure out what it mattered if his parents liked his friends or not. 'Yeah, they like them, I guess.' He chuckled. 'Though they probably like them better now than when we were kids.'

'How come?'

'Seriously?' Adam raised his eyebrows. 'Three teenage boys can be a little bit much for any parent to handle.'

'You were troublemakers?'

'No, not exactly.' Adam winked. 'But we weren't angels either.'

I laughed and gave him a playful shove.

'What about you? What were you and your friends like?'

'We were...' I swallowed.

Adam rolled his eyes. 'Let me guess, angelic.'

I gripped the railing. 'Something like that.'

Adam placed his hand over mine. 'It must have been tough, growing up without your dad around.'

'Mum and I managed. We still had each other.' I watched the waves break on the shore. 'But sometimes I wonder...'

'What?'

I hesitated. I pushed myself away from the railing, suddenly feeling the need to keep moving. I hadn't intended to say anything. I should just shake it off and say it didn't matter. But the unvoiced thought niggled at me. It wanted to be heard. I wanted to be heard. We fell into step as we walked along the promenade. 'After Dad left, Mum said it was just the two of us and that was enough. But, I don't know if she ever believed it. To me it always felt as though she'd cut herself off, even from me. It happened after she lost her parents. A wall went up around her. She was isolated in her grief.'

We reached a bench and we sat, staring out to sea. 'I couldn't reach her. Neither could Dad. He tried. I know he did. I guess it just wasn't enough.' I shrugged. 'After he left she was different. Still distant, but...'

I bit my lip. It felt wrong to talk about Mum like this. She'd be so mad if she could hear me. Mad and hurt.

'No one needs to know about Daddy, do you understand?' Mummy said as I put my school uniform on.

I caught sight of my reflection in the mirror. My eyes were all puffy and red. I'd cried myself to sleep last night. I'd buried my head beneath my pillow so Mummy wouldn't hear. She wouldn't like it.

'We don't talk about him, Jess. We don't talk about him leaving yesterday. We just don't talk at all.'

'Why not?' I stared at her, my mind racing as I tried to make sense of her instruction. Why couldn't I tell anyone? Why couldn't I tell Susan? At least she wouldn't mind if I cried. She'd give me a hug and tell me it would be okay. It's what we always did when one of us fell and grazed a knee. It's what grown-ups did. It's what Mummy used to do.

Mummy's face softened and she reached for my hand. Her touch was warm on my skin. My hand seemed so tiny cocooned in hers. It felt safe. It felt special.

I couldn't remember the last time she'd held my hand. She used to. I knew that. She always used to hold my hand. She always used to give me hugs.

And then she didn't.

'Because they'll ask us why, Jess.' Mummy leaned closer to me. 'They'll ask us why he left. They'll ask what you did wrong.'

My throat felt tight. 'Did I do something wrong?' My words were barely a whisper.

Mummy stroked my cheek. 'You didn't mean to, I know that.'

I stared at her, my eyes wide as tears dripped on my toes. 'What did I do?'

'You were just...' Mummy sniffed and wiped her own tears with her other hand. 'You were just you.'

I tried to choke back the sobs, but I couldn't. My body shook as her words circled my mind.

It was my fault that Daddy had left.

But worse than that, it was my fault that Mummy was hurting. I'd made her cry. She never cried. Not even at Granny and Grandad's funeral. But now tears streamed down her face.

I'd let her down.

I'd made her sad.

Somehow I'd caused this. I'd done something wrong. Or maybe I was wrong. I was just me. That wasn't enough.

'Somethings are best forgotten and just moved on from. Do you understand?'

I nodded. 'I'll be better, Mummy,' I whispered between sobs. 'I promise.'

She squeezed my hand tightly. 'I know you will, Jess. I know.'

'But what, Jess?'

I shook my head as I fought back the tears that threatened to fall.

'You said your mum was different after your dad left. Distant but...'

'Clingy.'

I laughed at Adam's bewildered expression. I couldn't blame him for his confusion. How could someone be both distant and clingy at the same time? The two were so contradictory. It was impossible. And yet it was real.

'It felt like she kept me at arm's length. We never hugged or really even talked; at least not about our feelings. It was as though our emotions didn't exist. They weren't allowed.'

I twisted my hands together in my lap. 'But we were still close. Inseparable, really. She looked so sad and lonely every morning as I left for school, my heart ached to stay home with her. It was like she needed me to be around. Not really for any purpose, just to be there. She still does.'

'But you have your own life. You can't be with her all the time.'

'I know, and I'm not. But I still feel guilty for not being there. I owe her, Adam.'

'You owe her?'

I laughed again and started to stand up, as though trying to put distance between me and my confession. 'You wouldn't understand.'

Adam caught my arm and pulled me back to the bench. 'Try me.'

I stared at his warm hand still resting on my arm. Could I tell him? It was tempting. How would it feel to open up; to confide in someone? To finally share my secrets?

'We've been through a lot together.' My reply was a cop out. Cagy and uninformative.

Adam studied me, patiently waiting for me to elaborate.

'She's always been there for me. When everyone else leaves, she stays.'

'Everyone?'

My body tensed at my slip. 'My dad.'

'And?'

I shook my head. 'It doesn't matter. Not now. It's all in the past.' I smiled and traced my fingertips along his jawline. 'I'm more interested in the future.'

Adam leaned towards me. 'Our future,' he whispered before his lips met mine.

* * *

I clambered into bed and flicked off the light switch, plunging myself into darkness. It had been a good day. A great day.

Adam had been happy. That was all that mattered. I hadn't embarrassed him in front of his friends. I hadn't let him down, or scared him away. All in all, it had been a huge success.

I pounded my pillow, trying to get comfortable. If it was such a great day, why did I feel so unsettled and restless?

I should feel so happy and pleased with myself. I should just be able to close my eyes and lose myself in wonderful memories as I drifted off to sleep.

I stared at the ceiling through the darkness. I wasn't even the slightest bit sleepy. My mind was racing. One thought repeated in a loop.

Susan.

Seeing Adam with all his old school friends had triggered an old game of 'what if' in my head. What if Susan hadn't fallen out with me? What if we had gone away to university together as planned? What if we'd made new friends there? What if I'd studied different subjects? If I'd had a different career? If I'd had a different life?

Everything had changed because our friendship had crumbled. She'd been my lifeline to the real world, and without her that link had severed. I'd still gone to university, but I'd stayed in Bournemouth. I'd lived at home.

With Mum.

University didn't change anything. It was just a continuation of what my life had always been. The only difference was that I caught the bus to a different destination. One where I was very much alone.

I fumbled for my phone on the bedside cabinet and squinted as the screen lit up. I opened Facebook and typed in her name. Susan's profile was at the top of the list. We weren't friends, not in real life, nor on Facebook, but I'd visited her page so often that she stayed in my phone's memory, just as she did in my own.

I told myself it was just curiosity. But I knew it was more than that. I was living vicariously through her. The parties, the holidays, the boyfriends, and eventually, the husband. Hers was the life I might have had.

If I hadn't destroyed it all.

11

NOW

'Jess! What are you doing here?' Karen rushed towards me, her chair spinning behind her desk from the speed at which she'd left it.

I froze in the aisle of the open-plan office feeling exposed. It was Tuesday. I'd only taken one day off. That wasn't too much, was it?

'I work here.' My voice was wobbly and uncertain. They still wanted me here, didn't they? I still belonged somewhere.

'But it's too soon.' She flung her arms around me, engulfing me in a hug that I couldn't escape from.

I glanced at the faces that peered at me from behind their computer screens. Everyone was watching me silently. Judging. Wondering.

Stacey hurried up beside her. 'Karen's right, you need to give yourself time.'

Karen stepped back and I studied her. Concern oozed from her. It was almost tangible.

I turned to Stacey. 'What will time change?'

Stacey flinched at the sharpness of my tone and glanced at

Karen. Guilt kicked me in my gut. I hadn't meant to be harsh. But I knew that the idea that time could heal all wounds was laughable. It didn't heal anything. Not for me. It never had.

Stacey touched my arm. 'Has there been any news?'

I knew what she meant. It was the same question that I asked myself every time my phone rang, or the doorbell chimed.

Have they found Adam's body?

I shook my head.

Her hand fell away. 'I'm sorry.'

'That must make it so much harder,' Karen added.

I tipped my head to the right. 'Why?'

Karen blinked. 'If they found him, if you knew for sure...'

'Then what? I could move on?'

She twisted her lips together. 'It would help, wouldn't it, at least you wouldn't constantly be waiting; wondering...'

'What's to wonder about? Adam is gone.'

They exchanged a look that I couldn't fully distinguish. It lay somewhere between stunned and afraid.

Were they afraid for me, or perhaps of me? I rammed my hands into my coat pockets, feeling chilly.

Perhaps Karen was right. It was too soon for me to be here. Not for me, but for them.

They didn't understand that I was okay. I was coping. It seemed impossible to them that I could continue without Adam, without knowing where he was, without knowing exactly what had happened.

They didn't know that it was possible to carry on. That questions were pointless when the answers were more damaging than the unknown.

'Come on, I'll walk you to your car.' Karen linked her arm with mine.

'But I can't just leave.'

'It's fine. Management won't care.'

My body tensed.

'I mean, they'll understand,' Karen corrected quickly. 'Don't worry so much. They don't expect you to be here yet.'

She tugged at my arm. I allowed her to lead me back through the office towards the stairs. What choice did I have? I couldn't stay here. Not with everyone's gaze fixed upon me. I felt like an animal at the zoo. One that was strange and unfamiliar.

I thought I'd finally started to find my place here. To be one of them. But I was still the outcast.

I snorted and Karen cast a sideways glance at me.

'So, how was your weekend?' Karen asked as she wriggled out of her fluffy white coat.

'Fine, thanks,' I smiled, as she draped her coat on the back of her chair, before dropping down on the seat.

She wheeled her chair closer to me, crossing the boundary where our desks joined. 'Come on, Jess. You always say that.' She rolled her eyes. 'I need details.'

My hands tensed as they hovered over my keyboard and I tried not to edge my chair away from her.

'There's nothing to say. It was just a quiet one this week.'

The words slipped easily from my lips. It was true. It had been a quiet weekend. All my weekends were.

'You must have done something exciting, even just a little bit.' She nudged my arm. 'Or at least watched a good TV programme?'

I stared at her.

Lie.

The instruction sprang into my head. I wanted to comply. I needed to. I grasped frantically for something plausible. But my mind went blank.

What did people do with their weekends? Other people. Normal people.

I swallowed. I liked things the way they had been before Karen started working here. She was different. Cheerful. Talkative. Inquisitive.

Too inquisitive.

Before her arrival I'd been allowed to slip through the work day with relatively little interaction. Everyone was courteous and polite. We exchanged good mornings and how are yous, but no one really paid any attention to my replies, or lack of them.

We were just moving through the motions. It worked that way.

I worked that way.

But Karen...

'Right, that's it.' Karen clapped her hands together and I jumped. 'We're going for coffee next weekend.'

I stared at her and drew back. 'What?'

'Co-ff-ee,' she said slowly as though I didn't understand the word.

It wasn't the word I had issues with, but the context. 'We?'

'Yes.'

'Why?'

She laughed. 'Because then at least we will have something to talk about next Monday.'

Karen wheeled her chair back to her own desk. I stared at the back of her head, my mouth hung open.

I should tell her I was busy. That I didn't want to go.

But I couldn't.

Neither was true.

'Will you be okay to drive home?' Karen asked as we reached my car.

'Of course.' I nodded. 'I'm fine.'

She shook her head. 'I've heard that before.' She gave me another hug. 'You've always been a rubbish liar.'

I studied her as she pulled back. Part of me wanted to correct her. It was surprising how proficient at lying I had become recently. But I bit my tongue. She didn't need to know that side of me. No one did. Especially someone who actually seemed to like me, even if I still couldn't figure out why.

'Why don't I call round tonight? I'll bring a bottle of wine. We can talk.'

My chest tightened. I shook my head. 'I don't want to talk about it. About him.' Karen's suggestion made me feel nauseous, yet at the same time I couldn't help feeling a little envious. I admired her confidence, her ability to make a suggestion and invite herself into someone else's home, someone else's life.

'You've said that every time I've called or messaged you over the last three days since...'

Since Adam died.

This is why I didn't want to talk. Not because of the words. But because of the silences. The lulls where the words that weren't said screamed at me so loudly.

'It'd help to talk about him.'

I shook my head again. 'Not yet.'

Karen took a deep breath but nodded.

I'd been so wrong about her when we'd met. She'd seemed pushy and intense. She was, but she also knew when to back off and give me space. I gave her a hug. I was grateful to her for that.

12

THEN

'You're different,' Stacey said as she washed her hands in the club's bathroom.

I paused as I reapplied my lipstick. 'Am I?'

Karen nodded. 'Very.'

I looked at her and arched an eyebrow. 'How?'

She stared at me in disbelief. 'Don't you see it?'

I turned back and examined my reflection. I adjusted my tight black skirt and straightened my glittery scooped red top. 'It's just new clothes.'

'No, it's not just the clothes. It's everything. It's you,' Karen said as she hung her arm across my shoulders.

I squinted at the woman staring back at me in the mirror. Was she really that different?

Her clothes were more modern, her hair more stylish, and her make-up more flattering. But they were just tweaks to her appearance. Underneath she was still the same. She just had a better camouflage.

'It's not just how you look on the outside that's changed,' Karen said. 'It's how you are.'

'Adam is a good influence on you,' Stacey added. 'He's made a lot of improvements.'

Improvements.

I bristled. 'What was wrong with the way I was?'

'Nothing was wrong with it. With you.' Stacey glanced at Karen. 'At least not to us. But to you...' She bit her lip as her eyes met mine. 'You didn't seem to like yourself very much.'

My stomach dropped. A hollowness descended inside me. I wanted to laugh it off; to protest; of course I'd liked myself. But the lie caught in my throat.

'You just seemed a little withdrawn,' Karen added. But it felt like she was trying to pacify me; to cover up the truth of Stacey's declaration.

'You rarely came out with us and certainly not at night. You always blew us off, with some lame excuse about visiting your mother.'

Stacey laughed. 'Yeah, I mean, how many times did you come out with that one? You could at least have been more inventive when ditching us.'

'I wasn't—' I clamped my mouth shut. Maybe they didn't need to know it wasn't an excuse.

They wouldn't get it. Their relationships with their mothers weren't the same as mine and Mum's. They weren't as close. They didn't understand what was expected of them. They didn't understand what it meant to be a good daughter. Not properly.

Karen and Stacey were just like the girls at school who'd moaned about their mums when they told them not to wear so much make-up, or made them clean their bedrooms. They didn't understand that their mums were looking out for them. They didn't understand that they had a duty to be respectful and helpful in return.

'But now you actually seem keen, excited even, when we

suggest going out for lunch or for drinks after work,' Stacey continued.

'It's like Adam brought you back to life again,' Karen added, giving my shoulder a squeeze, before stepping away.

She opened the bathroom door and I followed her back into the club; the pounding beat couldn't drown out the thoughts in my head.

Had Adam brought me back to life? And, if so, when had I stopped living?

Adam smiled as I approached. Karen and Stacey slid straight back onto the dancefloor with their partners, but Adam nodded towards the bar. His hand met mine as we walked.

I liked the feel of my hand nestled in his. I liked the way he reached for me without hesitation. I liked the way he always walked on the outside of the pavement closest to the road whenever we walked together. It wasn't planned, it was instinctive, protective.

Like him.

'You look like you could use a drink,' Adam whispered in my ear, his warm breath blowing my long hair.

'Do I?'

He nodded. 'Yeah, actually, you look kind of pale. Are you okay?'

I pasted on a smile. 'I'm fine.'

He studied me, uncertainty etched into his heavy brow.

'Really.' I nodded enthusiastically, determined to convince him.

I was fine. Preoccupied, but fine. However, I didn't want to explain that to him right now. I wasn't even sure I could explain it.

Karen and Stacey's comments had hit a nerve. They'd seen through my façade. It was eerie and unnerving. I'd thought I'd hidden it so well. I thought *I'd* hidden so well.

I'd always felt a little out of step. As though everyone else knew how to fit in and belong, while I stood on the outside feeling out of place.

It wasn't that I hadn't wanted to participate. I'd wanted to join in with Karen and Stacey's nights out, but somehow I couldn't. Some part of me wouldn't allow it.

There was a voice in my head that told me the same thing would happen with them as had happened in the past. I wouldn't belong. I'd be present, but somehow just a little removed from their reality. I'd try to join in, I'd smile and laugh, but it would feel more and more fake. It would eat away at me inside.

They'd ask questions I wouldn't answer. Or more accurately, I couldn't answer. Not without shattering the carefully constructed illusion I had created.

I'd been there before.

They'd want to know why I was single. They'd ask what had happened with my last boyfriend, and why we'd broken up. They'd talk about dates and places they'd been. They'd want to know about me, about my life.

It was how it was, how it should be, with friends. You shared things about yourself and listened while they did the same. I had the listening part mastered I was good at that. I could offer sympathy and understanding whenever they were down. But it was always one sided.

Then again, it wasn't as though we were really friends. Even now Karen and Stacey were just work colleagues who invited me out sometimes. I went along. I joined in. But I was still an outsider. Always a little out of sync. They didn't want to be bored by my stories.

I nibbled my lip. Of course, there was another reason I kept quiet. I couldn't face telling them. I couldn't tell anyone. Not even Adam.

No one needs to know.

I ground my teeth as Mum's voice penetrated my thoughts.

They'll ask what you did wrong.

Adam handed me a glass of white wine and I took a large swig.

'I guess I was right.' Adam laughed. 'You did need that.'

My face flushed. 'You know me so well.'

He thinks he does.

I shook my head.

'Hey, seriously, are you sure you're all right? Do you need some air or something?'

I hesitated. He was giving me an out. I could tell him I didn't feel well and he would drive me home. The old *me* would have done.

But maybe the girls were right. I wasn't that person any more. I belonged now. I fitted. I didn't want to slip back into isolated oblivion. I didn't want to be obsolete any more.

I took another swig of my wine.

'Actually, what I need is a dance.' I grabbed his hand and tugged him up to the dance floor, laughing at the stunned expression on his face.

13

NOW

I pushed the door open and stepped inside the pub, squinting as my eyes adjusted to the dim electric lighting. My nose twitched at the smell of fried breakfasts. I'd never been in here in the morning. It was different. Wrong.

I ordered an orange juice at the bar and then I walked instinctively to the corner with my gaze locked upon the familiar table.

Our table.

I took a deep breath as I pulled a chair out and sank into it. I set the orange juice down and my fingers automatically traced a circle of worn varnish on the wooden tabletop.

I screwed my eyes closed tightly. If I could block out the scent of greasy bacon and the sound of young children laughing as they ate with their parents, I could almost pretend it was nine months ago and I was waiting for Adam for our first date.

I could practically feel the nervous anticipation, the fear that he wouldn't show up and the desperate hope that he would.

But it wasn't real. I let out a deep breath and opened my eyes. I didn't carry any hope any more, only the heavy weight of resignation that things would never be the same.

I'd never been one to hold onto wistful fantasies. I was too practical. Too sensible. Or maybe just too jaded.

Adam had been different. He'd been something to hope for. Someone to put my faith in again. For a while at least. I'd tried to make it work. To make us work. But I'd failed. I'd always failed. I'd failed to make Adam happy, just like I'd failed...

I took a swig of orange juice and attempted to stop my mind from finishing that thought, but it was too strong, the truth wouldn't be denied any longer.

Just like I'd failed to make everyone else in my life happy. The list of my failings was long; past boyfriends, Susan, my parents...

'You talk as though we were better off before.'

I hesitated at the sound of Mummy's voice as I approached the kitchen. There was something about her tone that deterred me from entering.

'We were, Abigail.'

'We were broke.'

Daddy chuckled. 'We were hardly broke. Money was a little tight, but we managed. We were happy.'

'And now you're not?'

I set my school bag down quietly in the hall and edged closer to the kitchen door.

'No.'

I heard Mummy's sharp intake of breath.

'No one's happy. Not here. Not now. How can we be when you're so...'

'What?' There was a hardness to Mummy's voice. It was a tone I was becoming more and more accustomed to. 'Angry? Upset?'

'Yes,' Daddy said softly, as though he didn't really want to admit it. 'I understand why you feel like that. I really do. But that doesn't make it any easier to live with.'

'So I'm the problem. Not the money. Not the house. Me.'

'You know that's not what I meant.'

'You and Jess seem to be quite happy together here. It's only being around me that brings you down.'

'No, Abigail.' Daddy shook his head.

'I keep watching you two sitting at the end of the garden with your backs to me. Shutting me out.'

'You know it's not like that. Jess loves to watch the ocean waves.'

'She loves to watch them with you.'

'She'd love to sit and watch them with you, too.'

Mummy snorted.

'Have you ever thought about joining us there?'

'It's your thing. Something that's just between the two of you.'

Daddy reached for her hand. 'It could be between the three of us.'

Mummy yanked her hand away. 'The three of us. I always have to share you with her.'

'Abigail—'

'I won't compete with a seven-year-old for your attention.'

'What the hell are you talking about?'

I flinched. I'd never heard Daddy say hell before. It was a bad word. That's what Mummy always said whenever the neighbour said it in the garden.

'She's the centre of your world.'

'She's my daughter. Our daughter.'

Mummy scoffed. 'Ours. You wouldn't know it. She barely even talks to me.'

'Because she doesn't know what to say to you that won't upset you or make you cross.'

I shifted my weight from foot to foot and bumped the door. It creaked as it swayed on its hinges.

Daddy turned and his gaze met mine.

I drew back, waiting for him to tell me off. I was being naughty. I shouldn't listen to grown-up conversations.

'How long have you been there, Jess?' I studied Daddy's expression as he walked towards me. He didn't look cross. Just worried.

'Not l-long,' I stuttered. 'I didn't want to be late.'

He glanced at his watch and his eyes widened. 'Right, come on then, let's get you to school.'

Daddy picked up my bag and ushered me out to the garage.

'You forgot your briefcase,' I realised as we reached the car. 'I'll go and get it.'

I started to turn back, but Daddy stopped me. 'No, Jessie. That's okay. I'll get it later.'

Daddy opened the car door and I clambered in, frowning. 'Aren't you going to work today?' Daddy always went to work after he'd dropped me at school.

'Not straight away. Mummy and I need to sort some things out first.' He slid into the driver's seat and started the engine.

'Won't you be in trouble if you're late?'

Daddy chuckled. 'I think it will be okay, just this once.'

I shrank back in my seat. Everything seemed odd this morning. Daddy was never late for anything. Mummy didn't permit it.

'Can we still go to the library on Saturday?'

Daddy winked at me in the rear-view mirror. 'Of course, we have a volcano project to finish, don't we?'

I smiled. At least something hadn't changed.

I screwed up my nose, as an idea formed in my brain. 'Do you think Mummy would like to come with us?'

Daddy's reflection paled and he stared at me silently for a moment.

'Tell you what,' he said finally. 'Why don't you ask Mummy tonight?'

I nibbled my bottom lip.

'It'll be okay, Jess. I promise.'

I smiled and nodded.

The three of us.

My smile slipped away. Somehow, I wasn't sure Mummy would want to go.

14

THEN

I clung tighter to Adam's arm. The pub was rammed full of people. Music blared from tinny speakers, couples laughed as they danced, groups gathered with half empty glasses in their hands, shouting to one another above the ever-increasing din.

I was back where I'd started.

I swallowed. I could do this. I was better at it now. Adam and I had been to pubs and clubs together and I'd been fine. I'd survived. Enjoyed it, even. This was just the same.

I screwed up my nose. Except this wasn't just a crowd of random strangers, whose opinion of me was irrelevant. These were all people that Adam knew. People that mattered to him.

And I barely knew any of them.

Their curious gazes bore into me. They were judging me. My clothes. The way I stood. The way I spoke. Everything about me was being examined. It was though I had walked into a room full of microscopes, all focused directly on me. Who was I to be dating their Adam?

I glanced back at the door. I didn't belong here. Adam and I had been dating for two months, but I was still just on the outskirts of his life. Everyone else already knew one another, and from the way they greeted him, it seemed they had been part of his life for years. How could I ever measure up to that?

Maybe I'd never really belonged anywhere. I was still the same misfit I had been when I was a kid.

'You're here! I can't believe you actually came.'

Susan rushed towards me and engulfed me in a tight hug.

I gazed at the sea of multi-coloured dresses amongst the flashing disco lights that looked out of place in the school hall. 'Neither can I.'

'But what are you doing at the back here?'

I shuffled from foot to foot, my eyes fixed on my black school shoes. Even my feet didn't fit in here. All the other girls had pretty sandals or sparkly shoes.

'It's a disco, we should be out there dancing like everyone else.'

I shook my head. 'No one's going to dance with me. Everyone thinks I'm weird. The boys won't even talk to me at school, why would tonight be any different?'

Susan shrugged. 'Who cares about them? We don't need a partner to join in; we can just dance and chat like we do at home.'

But this wasn't home.

'I can't believe I let you talk me into this. You even got me to persuade Mum to let me come.'

Susan gazed at me in awe. 'I still can't believe you actually managed it.' She leaned closer to me. 'How did you do it?'

'I begged.'

'And it worked?'

She looked as stunned as I had been when Mum had finally caved. Mum never caved. Her word was final. It never changed. It didn't matter how reasonable or persuasive my argument was, her answer was always no. Until tonight.

The weirdest part was I hadn't even had to plead that much. It had been so easy. Too easy...

'Perhaps she's finally easing up on you.'

'Perhaps,' I said as my gaze met Susan's and I knew that neither of us believed it.

I shrugged as we moved further into the middle of the hall. It didn't matter why Mum had changed her mind, all that mattered was that she had. I was here. I was finally part of things.

A group of girls started sniggering beside us.

'Have you seen what she's wearing?'

'Ignore them, Jess,' Susan's reassuring voice was right beside me.

I nodded. She was right. I should just block them out and not let them spoil my evening.

'Are those her school shoes?'

The laughter grew louder.

'She's so boring.'

I glanced around. Everyone was staring at me now. I squirmed as they pointed at me and laughed.

They were messing everything up. My body shook as I fought back the tears. This was my night. The one evening where I finally got to be a normal kid and join in with the fun. I deserved that, didn't I? I was a good girl. Why wasn't I was allowed to be happy for once? And this time it wasn't even Mum keeping me from it.

I ran to the door, pushing my way through the crowd as the laughter echoed in my head.

'Jess!'

I heard Susan's voice above the music, but I didn't turn back. I'd been so stupid to think I could do this. Perhaps it had never been Mum that had been holding me back. Perhaps the problem had always been me.

I clambered into the passenger seat beside Mum. I should thank her for rushing out to pick me up early when I called in tears, but I couldn't. I was too mad.

'Why did you let me go?'

She took a deep breath as she flicked the indicator on and pulled out. 'Sometimes you have to find things out for yourself. I can't protect you from everything.'

'Why not?'

Mum glanced at me. 'Because you won't let me.'

I frowned.

'What did I say when you first asked to go to the school disco?'

'That it wasn't for me. I wouldn't belong there.'

'And what did you say?'

I hung my head. 'I said you were being unfair and begged you to let me go.'

'You thought you knew better. You thought I was being mean and stopping you from having fun.'

I squirmed.

'So I let you go. And what happened?'

'I didn't belong there.'

Mum nodded, a firm sharp nod. 'You see, I don't prevent you from doing things to be cruel. I do it to protect you. I'm your mother. It's my job.'

Mum had been right then and she was right now too. Adam and I were too different. This was his world and it was a place I would never belong. I didn't even have Susan here to make it bearable.

'Jess, there are some people I want you to meet.' Adam started walking forwards. My hand was still gripping his arm, I had no choice but to follow him.

He stopped in front of a couple. 'Happy birthday, son,' the woman said, as she kissed Adam's cheek.

'Jess, these are my parents.'

I stared at the couple in front of me. Their smiles were warm and welcoming, but their gazes tore into me, I could practically feel them trying to unearth my secrets and determine if I was worthy of their son's attention.

'Jess, we're so happy to meet you.' Adam's mum reached forward and squeezed my arm. 'I'm Helen, and this is Graham.'

I plastered a smile onto my face.

'We've been so curious about this mysterious woman Adam has been keeping from us,' Graham added.

'Mysterious?' My throat felt tight and constricted. Did Adam know I was keeping things from him? Could he tell I was holding back?

'I haven't been keeping her from you.' Adam rolled his eyes. 'I've just been keeping her to myself.'

The three of them laughed.

I tried to join in, but I couldn't. I was too nervous to laugh about anything.

'Adam tells us you're a lawyer?'

I swallowed. 'Well, not exactly—'

'So impressive,' Helen continued, oblivious to my objection. 'It takes real hard work and dedication to have a career like that. We're so happy Adam has found himself a decent girl this time,' she winked at me, before turning her head towards the bar.

I followed her gaze, but there were so many people I couldn't tell who she was looking at.

I felt Adam's arm tense beneath my hand and I glanced back at him. His face was pale and taut. His attention was fixed on something in the direction of his mother's gaze.

'Adam, what's wrong?'

He shook his head. 'Nothing, just an uninvited guest.' He turned to his parents. 'I should go and...' He levered my hand from his arm and strode towards the bar.

'Who is that?' I tried to see who Adam was heading towards, but they were obscured by the crowed.

'No one important,' Graham said as he pivoted me towards a table. 'Let's sit and chat while Adam is busy.'

'But—' I twisted around, straining my neck to find Adam.

'Don't worry, I'm sure he won't be long.'

'That's such a stunning dress on you,' Helen said. 'I wish I still had a figure like yours.'

My cheeks grew warm, no doubt matching the shade of my red dress. 'Thanks, it's...' I bit my tongue. They didn't need to know it had been Adam's choice, just like most of my wardrobe was these days. 'It's new.'

I adjusted the thin strap on my shoulder and tugged at the hem. My dress was a success. Everyone always admired the clothes Adam picked for me, even if they were a bit tighter and shorter than I was comfortable with.

But they were just clothes. And not even they could make this moment less stressful.

I smiled at Adam's parents as I searched my brain for something to say. I should compliment them too. Or would that look like I was trying too hard? I could ask them something about themselves. But would that seem like Adam didn't tell me anything about them? Or that I hadn't listened if he had?

My face was starting to ache. My smile was growing weary and it was still early. How was I going to get through the rest of the evening?

Despite my beautiful dress, despite the compliments, I still didn't fit in here. Maybe Adam hadn't changed me as much as Karen and Stacey thought. Perhaps his presence and attention had just given me more confidence for a while. He'd made me a better actress.

What I wore wasn't the problem. It was me that was wrong.

It always had been.

'So, a lawyer, huh?' Graham said.

I should correct him. I should explain that I wasn't really a lawyer. But maybe that's what Adam wanted them to think. Maybe he wanted me to be a bit more than I was.

'Do you enjoy it?'

I froze like a rabbit caught in headlights. I was exposed with nowhere to run. 'No, not really.' The confession slipped from my lips. It was the wrong answer. Honest, but wrong.

'Then why do it?'

'Because...' I stared at him as my reasons evaporated before reaching my tongue. Why did I do it? It was a good job, a decent salary, a solid, dependable, respectable career. But was that enough?

'You should do something you love.'

I nodded instinctively, but it was only slight. His simplistic philosophy was flawed. Life wasn't that easy.

Graham's attention shifted over my shoulder. 'All sorted?'

I turned and saw Adam approaching behind me. He nodded, but he looked serious.

'Who was that?' I asked him.

'So, who wants a drink?' Adam avoided my gaze.

I stared at him as his parents made their requests. Maybe he hadn't heard me. It was noisy in here. It wasn't as though he would intentionally ignore me.

Was it?

15

NOW

I turned the key and pushed the door open. I stood in the doorway, listening to the silence.

'Adam?' My voice was barely a whisper. I willed him to answer, to poke his head around the living room door and greet me with that broad grin of his.

But he didn't.

I hadn't really thought he would, and yet my shoulders slumped.

I kicked off my shoes and walked to the bedroom.

Adam's clothes were heaped in a pile where they had been since Friday night. It felt wrong to see them like that. Discarded. Unwanted.

Laundry, I'd told PC Davidson when he and his colleagues had asked to have a look around the apartment. He wanted to gain a sense of Adam's world, his mindset. At least that's what he'd said. But I couldn't shake the feeling there was more to it.

I bent down, scooped up his clothes in my arms and dropped them on the bed. I tugged a shirt, untangled the sleeves from the pile and slipped it on a hanger from the wardrobe. I hung it in place and returned to repeat the process.

It was therapeutic. I was doing something.

I refused to allow myself to think about anything else as I worked, I just kept focused on the task. I couldn't let my mind drift. I couldn't reminisce about the last time he'd worn his favourite sweater, or how good he looked in his black jeans.

I stared at the bed. There were no more clothes left.

Without a job to do I felt lost. Helpless.

I pulled my phone from my pocket and the screen sprang to life: 9.42 a.m. I took a deep breath. It was going to be a long day.

The date below the time caught my attention.

My chest tightened. With all that had happened I hadn't even thought about the date. Guilt engulfed me. I should have realised. I should have remembered.

I dropped to my knees, opened the drawer underneath the bed and pulled the spare bed linen out of the way. I reached to the back and my fingers traced the edge of an old biscuit tin. I lifted it out and placed it beside me.

I stared at it for a moment, before tugging the lid off. I pulled out an old hand-drawn birthday card. I'd made it when I was seven. It was the first card I hadn't been able to give him.

Susan and I scampered up the stairs, giggling. We reached her room and dropped our bags on the floor as she shut the door behind us.

'Do you want to watch TV?' Susan asked, as she reached for the remote control.

I shook my head as I glanced at the closed door.

'I keep telling you, it's okay.' Susan shrugged. 'As long as I get my homework done Mum doesn't mind us watching TV.'

'Yeah, I know, but it still feels weird.'

'Nah, your mum is just crazy strict.'

I laughed nervously. 'She's just looking out for me. She says too much TV is bad for my eyes.'

Susan rolled her eyes, but dropped the remote down on her bed. 'So, what do you want to do instead?'

I shuffled on the spot.

Susan frowned. 'Jess?'

'It's February.'

'Yeah, so?'

I nibbled my lower lip and stared at the soft pink carpet.

Susan's eyes widened. 'Of course, your dad's birthday is this month.' She opened a drawer beneath the little white desk in the corner of her room and pulled out some paper. 'Come on then, you know where the crayons are.'

I hesitated. 'Are you sure you don't mind?'

'Are you kidding?' Susan rolled her eyes. 'It's our tradition, we always make birthday cards for our parents.'

'Yeah, but my dad's not even around.'

'So you'll keep it for him.'

'Just like the one from last year.' I sighed as I sank onto the bottom of Susan's bed. 'And the year before that.'

She shrugged again. 'So, you're making an awesome collection of cards. It just shows how much you love him.'

'How much I've missed him.'

Susan sat beside me. 'Yeah, that too.'

'What if Mum's right? What if Dad's never coming back?' My voice cracked as I played with the hem of my grey school skirt. 'I mean, she's Mum. She's always right.'

Susan shuffled. 'Don't you want to make him a card this year?'

I stared at the blank sheets of paper in her hands. It was pointless. Dad would probably never see it. And yet...

'If I don't make him a card then that would be like giving up on him.

Maybe if I stop making them, if I stop hoping, if I stop believing, then...' I swallowed, unable to put my fear into words.

Susan nodded once. A short sharp definite nod. 'Then it's settled. We make a card again this year.'

'Every year,' I added quietly.

'Every year,' Susan repeated with certainty. I glanced at her and our eyes met. 'It'll be okay, you know.'

I nodded, but it was weak and hesitant. I no longer believed with unwavering certainty. I hoped he would return. I would always hope. But hoping for something wasn't always enough to make it real.

'Happy Birthday, Dad,' I murmured softly. 'I miss you.'

This was my tradition now. I no longer made a card each year, but I still wished him a happy birthday.

Another one spent apart.

I examined the cards one at a time. I remembered making them all. Susan had always helped. Always encouraged me. Always consoled me when I cried.

Susan.

There were moments when I felt her absence just as strongly as the day she'd walked away from me. Dad's birthday was always the worst.

Susan's accusation had been a betrayal of our friendship. It had shaken everything I believed in. She was the one person I had thought would always trust me, no matter what the circumstances.

Mum viewed me as fallible; wrong, but Susan...

I reached for my phone and went straight to her Facebook profile. Aside from Mum, Susan was the person that knew me better than anyone. She knew my past. She knew my pain.

And yet she had still turned her back on me. How could she do that? Was I really that bad?

I scrolled through her latest updates. What was she doing today? Did she ever think about me?

I bit my lip as an idea formed in my head.

There was one way to find out...

* * *

I stood on the unfamiliar doorstep and tried to summon the courage to ring the bell. It was a place I never thought I'd be. It was a bad idea, the knots in my stomach and lump in my throat told me so. And yet I was here.

My hand trembled as I pressed the bell. I flinched as it chimed loudly. Perhaps I should leave. I glanced over my shoulder at my car parked by the kerb. It was my escape route. It was waiting for me. All I had to do was walk away and I could return to...

I hesitated. Return to what?

I swallowed. That was the problem. I no longer had Adam to return to. All I had left were unanswered questions. Maybe Susan held the key. Maybe she had the answers that could help me discover what was real.

The door clicked as the catch lifted.

But would they be the answers I wanted to hear?

The door swung open and a woman my age smiled slightly in acknowledgement. 'Can I help you?'

My lips parted but no words came out. She was taller than the last time I'd seen her, but otherwise she looked almost the same. A little older, of course, but she still had the same curious blue eyes and cheery manner.

Susan's brow creased as she studied me. I watched as uncertainty morphed into surprise and her eyes widened as recognition dawned on her. Perhaps she wasn't the only one who looked the same.

'Jess?' Susan took a step back into her hallway.

I cringed. Was her reaction shock or fear?

'Hi, Susan. It's been a while.' I cursed the wobble in my voice. I sounded weak and afraid. But then that's exactly what I felt. I was scared she would slam the door in my face without hearing me out, without providing the answers I needed. But equally afraid she wouldn't, because there was a strong probability I wouldn't like the answers she had for me.

I silently willed her not to ask how I'd found her. I couldn't tell her the truth. I couldn't tell her that I'd followed her life just as closely as if we had still been friends. I'd stalked her Facebook profile along with her Instagram and Twitter accounts. I knew every detail of her life that she made public.

I don't know why I did it. Watching from the outskirts of her life didn't make me feel better about my own.

And it was never enough.

Every time I'd seen Adam with his friends it had been a potent reminder of what I'd lost. If things had been different, that could have been Susan and me.

She hadn't been that difficult to find. It wasn't as though she had tried to hide from me. If she hadn't wanted me to know about her life she would have made her Facebook profile private. I wouldn't have seen her wedding photos. I wouldn't have known her married name. I wouldn't even have known to focus my search still in Bournemouth.

Maybe some part of her was hoping that one day I would find her so we could put the past behind us.

But I'd hesitated.

As much as I wanted to reconnect with her, I knew that she posed a threat to everything I had with Adam. Mum kept my secrets out of loyalty and love. But Susan...

Now, though, I had nothing left to lose. Adam was gone. Susan couldn't hurt me now. At least not in that way.

'I can't believe you're here!'

I wrinkled my nose, trying to judge her tone. Was she just surprised to see me, or perhaps 'one day' wasn't today.

She lunged forwards and grabbed my arm. My body tensed.

'Come on.' She tugged my arm. 'Let's get you inside out of this cold. We have so much to catch up on.'

I allowed myself to be pulled into the warm hallway, too stunned to say anything.

This was the woman who had vowed never to speak to me again. And now she wanted to catch up as though we were still friends. It was almost as though the last thirteen years hadn't happened.

She hung my coat on a peg and ushered me into the kitchen. 'Coffee?' she asked with a beaming smile.

I nodded mutely and watched as she filled the kettle.

'So, what brings you here after all these years, Jess?'

'I want to talk about what happened with us, Susan.' I took a deep breath. 'I need to know if...' I bit back the words. I couldn't voice my doubts. Not now. Not ever. I'd been right back then. I had to have been.

Deep creases dug into her forehead as she stared at me. 'What happened?' She shook her head. 'We went to different unis, Jess. It happens.' She shrugged. 'Kids grow apart.'

'You went without me.'

Susan snorted as she reached into a cupboard. 'You mean you didn't come with me.'

'You didn't want me to.'

Susan froze, with a mug in each hand. 'That's true. I was so mad at you back then.' She arched an eyebrow. 'Do you remember why?'

'Tim.'

Susan nodded. 'I'm glad you overcame your problems, Jess.' She smiled warmly. 'I'm glad you finally remember the truth.'

I shivered. 'The truth?'

'About Tim. You made a pass at him. He was my boyfriend and you kissed him.'

'I didn't do it. You have to believe me.' My words tumbled out in a hurry. 'Whatever Tim said was a lie. It didn't happen that way.'

Susan's smile withered instantly. 'I thought you remembered.'

'Tim turned it all around. He was the one who tried to kiss me. I pushed him away. I told him no.' I edged forwards as I pleaded for Susan to believe me. 'I tried to tell you this back then, but you were so mad you wouldn't listen. You wouldn't believe me.'

'Oh, Jess.' Her voice was full of disappointment.

I stared at her in disbelief. I'd never understood how she could take the word of some guy over her best friend. I'd told myself she was just lashing out, that in time she would realise the truth and beg for my forgiveness. But it never happened.

However, we weren't kids any longer. She wasn't loyal to Tim any more. She had a husband now. Tim was nothing more than a distant memory. An adolescent crush. It was time she acknowledged his flaws.

'Susan, he lied to you.'

'Jess, it's in the past—'

She was right. It was the past and it had been silly of me to come here to dig it up. I'd known what she would say; known what she believed. But I couldn't help hoping after all this time she would be more willing to listen; more willing to realise I wasn't that person; I wasn't capable of hurting her like that. Because if I could make her believe me, then maybe I just might finally believe it too.

'I should have persevered. I should have made you hear me out at the time, but I was so hurt. I know he was your boyfriend, but I was your best friend. How could you believe him over me?'

It was the question that had taunted me for years; after all we'd been through; how close we were; how much she knew I needed her, how had she believed a boy over me?

'I didn't.'

I blinked and stared at her. 'What?'

'Tim didn't tell me. He confirmed what you'd done later when I confronted him, but it didn't come from him initially.'

'I don't understand. If Tim didn't claim I kissed him, who did?'

Susan winced. 'Your mother.'

'My mo-th-er?' I repeated slowly. The word felt strange and alien as I formed the syllables. That couldn't be right. I must have misheard her. It was a mistake. A weird nonsensical mistake.

But Susan didn't correct me. She just stared at me.

'Why would my mother tell you such a thing?' It was crazy. Mum wouldn't accuse me of something like that. She knew me better. She knew the truth. She knew what had happened.

I slammed the front door closed and threw my rucksack on the floor. 'Stupid boys.'

'Jessica!'

I swung round and my eyes met Mum's as she scowled at me.

'That's no way to enter the house.'

'I'm sorry, Mum.' I hung my head. 'But I'm just so angry. He ruined everything.'

'Who?'

'Tim.'

Mum's expression hardened. 'Who is Tim?'

'Susan's boyfriend.'

'Susan's?' Mum stepped towards me. 'Not yours?'

'No, not mine. I wouldn't want to go out with him.' I shuddered.

'Besides, I don't want to go out with anyone, not after Matt.' I tried to shrug off the loneliness that had descended upon me at the thought of him. Did it hurt so much because I still missed him, or because of the way he'd ended it, as though I'd never mattered? We'd never mattered?

Mum nodded, a sharp short nod of approval.

I frowned. Was there a sense of satisfaction in her expression? She'd never really liked Matt, I'd always known that, but she'd been so supportive when he'd dumped me. She'd seemed sad for me. Whatever her feelings had been towards him, I was her daughter and the last thing she wanted was to see me hurting.

'So why are you so worked up about someone else's boyfriend?'

'He's not just someone else's boyfriend. He's Susan's boyfriend. And he tried to kiss me.'

Mums eyes widened.

I paced the hall in a frenzy. 'Why would he do that? How could he? Susan is crazy about him.'

'What did you do to encourage him?'

I stopped dead and stared at Mum, my mouth hung open in disbelief. 'Nothing. I didn't do anything.'

'You must have done something, Jessica. A boy wouldn't just kiss you without a reason, especially when he has a beautiful girlfriend like Susan.'

'But I didn't do anything. We were just talking. That's all.'

'You were talking to Susan's boyfriend? Without her there?' Mum raised an eyebrow.

'We were waiting for Susan. The three of us always meet after college and walk to the bus stop together.'

'So you meet him every day?'

'Well, yes, with Susan.' I had an unnerving suspicion that Mum thought I'd done something wrong.

'A proper friend would have left them to be alone together.'

'But Susan wanted to walk with me. We've always done that.'

'Hmmm.'

I swallowed. I didn't like the sound of Mum's hmmm. It was the noise she made when she disapproved but was refraining from comment. She was casting judgement, letting her disapproval be known but without putting her thoughts into words. It was worse in a way; words I could at least try to defend against. I couldn't form a rational argument against hmmm.

'I don't know what to do now.'

'There's nothing to do.' Mum shrugged. 'Just stay away from that boy.' She turned and walked back to the kitchen.

I stared after her. 'But I have to tell Susan. I can't let her keep dating a jerk like that.'

Mum stopped and turned back, her eyes narrow and accusing. 'You want to destroy their relationship. You want to break your friend's heart.'

'No, of course not.' I shook my head frantically. That was the last thing I wanted. 'But I can't just let her keep thinking Tim loves her. Susan needs to know the truth. She deserves to know.'

'And who do you think she'll believe?'

I frowned. 'What do you mean?'

'Assuming she listens, assuming she believes you even for a moment, when she asks him about it, what will Tim say?'

'Why wouldn't Susan believe me?'

'He'll deny it, of course. He'll say you made it up, or you encouraged him, or maybe even that you kissed him.'

'But I didn't. Susan would know that I would never do that.'

'Would she? Are you sure?'

'Yes,' I replied, but there was a wobble to my voice.

'Sure enough to risk your friendship?'

I leaned against the stair rail as Mum walked away. What if she was right? What if I lost Susan over this?

'But if Tim had tried to kiss you, why not just tell me straight away?' Susan leaned back against the counter.

'I couldn't risk our friendship, not over some boy.' I edged forwards, my eyes pleading for her to believe me. 'Tim wasn't even applying to the same universities as us. By the autumn I figured he'd be out of your life.' It had seemed so sensible. The ideal solution. I didn't need to deprive Susan of a few more months of happiness with him. Time and distance would solve the problem naturally. I didn't need to get involved.

She chuckled. 'Seems kind of convenient, Jess.'

'It's the truth.'

'Is that why you came here? To dig up the past about a boy I dated for a few months thirteen years ago? Seriously?'

'He's the reason everything fell apart. He's the reason you left without me. The reason I got stuck here.'

'Oh, Jess. Is that really why you didn't go to UCL?'

'How could I go? Without you I'd have been completely alone.'

'You'd have made new friends. That's the point of going away to uni, Jess. It was a fresh start. Besides, I got over you and Tim in the end.'

'There never was a "me and Tim".' I shook my head. 'You still don't believe me, do you?'

'Jess, you know your memory is faulty.'

I swallowed, but my mouth was dry. 'Why would you say that?' It was one thing for Mum to say it, but now Susan as well...

'There were always things that didn't add up, things that didn't seem to have happened the way that you claimed. I couldn't understand it at first, but then your mum explained it to me. Just like she explained what had really happened with Tim.'

I shook my head. 'But I don't understand why she would do that. You must have misunderstood. Mum knew what happened. Mum knew it wasn't my fault.'

'She knew everything, Jess. She thought I did too. Your mum

thought you'd told me. She said she was so happy that we'd worked things out; that I'd forgiven you.'

I stared at her. I heard the words; she was speaking English and yet it may as well have been a foreign language. Nothing Susan was saying made sense.

'She even apologised for you.' Susan shrugged again. 'Which is more than you ever did.'

'Why didn't you tell me?'

'Back then I didn't want to talk to you. I didn't want to hear your lies or your excuses. I just wanted you to tell me the truth. I'd have forgiven you instantly if you'd just told me yourself.'

I reached for the wall. Everything looked hazy and dim. My head span, my knees felt weak. 'Why would Mum do that? She must have known it would destroy us.'

'Susan hates me, Mum.' Tears streamed down my face as I stood in the kitchen the next day, my rucksack still on my shoulders, but I didn't notice its weight. It didn't matter. All that mattered was that my best friend hated me.

'You told her?'

I shook my head. 'No, Tim must have done. But he couldn't have told her the truth. Susan thinks it was me.' A sob escaped my lips muffling my words. 'She blames me. She won't even talk to me now.'

It couldn't have been Mum. She wouldn't have done that to me. Susan was wrong. Just like she was wrong about my memory. I knew what Tim had done. I knew it now just as clearly as I had known it back then. It was Susan who had allowed him to ruin everything.

'We had so many plans.' I looked at Susan through watery eyes. 'We were going to go to UCL together. We were going to be Londoners. We were going to do all the touristy things together between classes. We were going to have an adventure. A life.'

'We still had adventures, just not the way that we'd planned.'

'You still had adventures.' A strange sensation burned inside me. I was angry with her. Angry that she'd believed the worst about me. Angry that she'd abandoned me. 'Without you I stayed home, I went to Bournemouth University. I didn't need to live on campus there. You went off without me and my world shrank.'

'That was your doing, Jess. Not mine.'

'But... but...' I tried to protest, but I couldn't form an argument. If what she said was true then I'd given everything up for nothing. We could have salvaged our friendship. I could have gone to UCL. I could have been free.

I'd let Susan's reaction define my life.

Without her I'd been too scared to take a chance and follow my dreams alone. I had Mum to remind me of my weaknesses, and no one to remind me of my strengths.

Maybe I would have hated it. Maybe I would have struggled.

But maybe I should have tried.

'Jess, I'm sorry, if what I said back then...'

I backed out of the kitchen into the hall. All this time I'd blamed Susan for failing me, but maybe the truth was I'd failed myself. I'd given up my plans; my hopes. I'd given up on myself.

'You don't have to leave. Not like this.'

I grabbed my coat and pulled the front door open.

'You still don't believe me, do you?' I asked, turning back to face her. 'You still think I betrayed you.'

'I forgive you, Jess.'

Her words stabbed at my heart. The years had extinguished her anger, but it hadn't changed her opinion of me.

What would Adam have thought if he'd known? Who would he have believed? Me, or Susan, a complete stranger to him? The answer should have been simple and obvious. He knew me, loved me, and trusted me. But so had other people once; Mum, Dad, Susan, boyfriends who had come before Adam. Somehow none of that mattered. Whatever the situation they never believed me; they never chose me.

I was unreliable and irrelevant. It was as though my existence in their lives came with an expiration date. At some point I ceased to be useful, I ceased to be relevant.

They chose to believe the worst about me. Perhaps they saw something I couldn't. Or perhaps I just didn't want to see it. I didn't want to accept it. I didn't want to be the person they all came to see me as eventually.

You know your memory isn't reliable.

Maybe Mum was right. Perhaps it was easier to ignore it, to forget it, that part of me, the bad part. The part that made bad decisions. The part that hurt people. People I loved. People like Susan.

But the accusations jarred against me. Somehow they never felt real. No matter how much evidence there was to the contrary, something inside me proclaimed my innocence. It was a voice that wouldn't be silenced, but it was a voice even I wasn't sure I could believe.

'I couldn't have done that. Not to you. Not to us. I would have remembered...'

Tim confirmed it.

It wasn't just Tim's accusation. He'd supported what Mum had said.

I was outnumbered; two to one.

What if they were right?

I turned and ran down the path to my car. It had been a mistake to come here. The past was too far gone to be changed, but it still had the power to hurt.

16

THEN

I stood at the edge of the ocean, with icy cold waves washing over my feet.

'Come on, Jess,' Adam called to me from further out. The water came up to his waist, but he didn't seem to care. The blue and white surfboard bobbed in front of him as though impatiently waiting to get out to sea. 'Just give it a try.'

I bit my lip and shuffled forward another two steps. The water was at my ankles now.

I saw his tanned chest heave as he took a deep breath. I was trying his patience. I didn't intend to, somehow I just seemed to manage it.

I missed our usual Sunday ritual. He would go for an early morning surf while I had a lie in. It was my one luxurious lazy indulgence. An 8 a.m. start just one day a week. By the time he arrived home, hot coffee was waiting for him and we ate breakfast together.

I didn't mind him slipping out early. I didn't resent him having a hobby that didn't include me. We could be independent and still work.

Couldn't we?

Clearly Adam didn't think so. He wanted to involve me. He wanted me to share his excitement of paddling out to sea, scrambling to my feet to perch precariously as the waves buffered against the surfboard. He wanted me to like what he liked.

He wants to change me.

I shook my head. No, he just wanted me to be part of his world. His whole world.

I clenched my fists, digging my nails in to the palm of my hands. I could do this. It was just a surfboard. Nothing to be afraid of.

It had seemed so simple when he taught me what to do on the sand. I'd practised over and over. The surfboard lay flat on the beach as I lay on my stomach. I pushed myself up on Adam's command and stood as he'd showed me. It was so easy. But on the beach there was no momentum, no unpredictability, and no deep blue depths lurking beneath me...

I glanced at the ocean that expanded before me. It was huge. Fierce. Unrelenting. What if I lost control? I would make a fool of myself. I'd screw it up somehow. I couldn't do that, not in front of Adam. He'd think less of me. He'd see me for myself. My flaws. My weaknesses.

Adam waded towards me, dragging the surfboard behind him. 'Why do you always freeze up? Why can't you just let go and have a little fun?'

I stared at him blankly. 'I don't know.'

He shook his head at the feebleness of my answer.

It wasn't even true; I did know why. I was scared. That's all there was to it. I wanted fun in my life, but I was terrified of it. How ridiculous was that? I didn't know how to just kick back and enjoy the moment. All I knew how to do was over-analyse things and scare myself out of them.

I'd spent a lifetime being cautious and responsible. They were attributes I hated. I wanted to be different; to be free; adventurous. And yet when presented with the opportunity to be just that, I froze.

What you want doesn't matter.

I screwed my eyes closed. I desperately wanted to disprove those words, but somehow all I ever did was find more evidence to support them. I wanted to be different, but wanting it wasn't enough. I wasn't strong enough to change who I was.

I needed to be good enough. To be perfect.

Practice makes perfect.

Mum's voice echoed in my head and I cringed at the phrase that had followed me through my childhood. It hadn't mattered what it was, or how good it was, it was never good enough.

I let out a long slow deep breath as my hands rested on the piano keys, the final notes still lingering. I'd done it. I'd played the whole sonata from beginning to end without a single mistake. My fingers had glided over the keys. There were no fumbled notes, no hesitations. Just beautiful accuracy.

I beamed with pride as I turned to my audience. Mum sat on the sofa behind me and nodded slightly. 'Play it again.'

My smile slipped away in an instant. There wasn't even a momentary celebration of my success, just a demand to repeat it as though to prove it wasn't a stroke of luck.

Fear lodged in my stomach, making me nauseous. I knew what would happen. The same thing that always happened. I would fail.

Nerves would cause my fingers to be heavy and uncooperative. They would stumble across the keys, sending jarring clashes straight to Mum's ears. She would hate it.

Mum strove for perfection. It was her measure of success. Anything that fell even a little short equated to failure. It wasn't good enough. I wasn't good enough. But even success wasn't enough. It had to be repeated. I had to prove it wasn't a coincidence.

It's how I viewed everything now. Every achievement was undermined. Success was a fluke; an accident; something that couldn't be repeated, rather than an accomplishment and the result of my hard work.

'Maybe I should go.'

Adam stared at me. 'We came in my van.'

I nodded. 'Right, of course.' Adam was my ride home. The only way I could leave was if he did too.

I mustered a smile. 'So, I'll just watch from the beach and you can show me how it's done.'

Adam's expression softened. 'No, you'll be bored. I should drive you home.'

My heart soared. He cared.

'I'll be fine.' I smiled again. Brighter this time.

He looked doubtful.

'Really.' I rested my hand on his arm. 'I want to stay.'

He hesitated for a moment longer. His gaze drifted back to the waves. I could see the wistfulness in his expression. 'Well, if you're sure...'

He didn't wait for any further encouragement. I watched him wade back out and clamber onto the surfboard. I settled down on the soft warm sand as he paddled further away from the shore. Away from me.

I ran my fingers through the soft sand beside me. I was sitting on the side lines again. It was where I was comfortable. Where I belonged.

'There's a concert at school at the end of term.' I smiled as I gave Mum the leaflet. 'My music teacher wants me to pick a piece of music to play on the piano.'

'She wants you to be in the concert?' Mum stared at me, her eyes wide with disbelief.

'Y-e-s.' My voice wobbled.

'Do you think that's a good idea?'

I scrunched my nose up as I debated how to answer. Mum clearly thought the answer was no, but why? 'I'd like to. It could be fun.'

'Fun?' Mum shook her head. 'Playing in front of all those other students and parents? They'll notice when you make a mistake. It wouldn't be the same as playing just for me.'

'I'd practise a lot. I promise.'

'You need to be realistic, Jessica. Stick to things you know, things you're good at.' Mum screwed up the leaflet in her hands. 'Don't set yourself up for failure and embarrassment.'

I nodded slowly as Mum's advice echoed in my head. It was safer on the side lines. It was foolish to take risks.

17

NOW

'You're home, then.'

I glanced round at Mum as I hung my coat in the hall. I couldn't answer. To acknowledge her statement would be like admitting that this was home; that it was where I belonged.

I frowned as I turned away. Where did I belong? Had I ever belonged anywhere?

I glanced at the door. I always returned here. It was like a magnet, always pulling me back.

This time was different, though. I had a purpose.

I needed clarity.

Susan's claims made no sense. Mum wouldn't have told her I'd kissed Tim. Mum knew the truth. And Mum never lied.

And yet Susan had been so convinced.

I nibbled my lip. I needed to hear Mum's explanation. There had to be one. A perfectly logical reason, one that I just couldn't see for myself.

'Come on, I'll make you a cup of tea. You look like you could use it.'

I nodded and followed Mum to the kitchen. It was funny how

tea was always the first thing that people thought of; as though it was a magic cure for all ailments.

'I wondered where you'd gone when I woke up this morning. You didn't tell me you were going out.'

I twisted my hands together in my lap as I sat at the kitchen table. It was the same seat I had sat in since I was a child. It was my seat. My place.

'I was worried,' Mum added.

The kettle popped and whirred in the background, filling the empty space between us.

'I'm sorry.'

She nodded. My apology pacified her. I could feel it. Her mood lifted as the frown dissipated from her brow.

Except, was I sorry? I tilted my head to the right. I hadn't wanted to make her worry. I never wanted to do that. But an apology implied I had done something wrong. Had I?

I rubbed my eyes. The truth was becoming harder and harder to distinguish these days. Until recently everything had always seemed so simple. Lately I was questioning everything, even things that I had simply accepted before.

I frowned.

Had I really accepted them? Or had I just chosen not to think about them?

I rolled my eyes. I was doing it again. More questions. More doubts.

Mum clanged cups behind me. 'So where did you go?'

This was my chance. I could tell her where I'd been; tell her what Susan had said. I could ask Mum why she had betrayed me.

I hesitated.

Did I really want to know?

Was my curiosity about something that had happened so long ago really worth risking my relationship with Mum? If Susan was right about Mum's involvement, then it meant Mum had lied to Susan. She'd destroyed my only friendship. And she'd done it intentionally.

Or perhaps Mum hadn't betrayed me. Maybe Mum really thought I had already confessed.

We don't have secrets, Jess. Not between us.

What if she didn't have secrets from me? What if I simply couldn't remember the truth?

Was I ready to face that? It wasn't just Mum's theory now; Susan had made the same accusations that my memory was faulty. What if they were right? What if...?

I gripped my hands together and my nails dug into my skin.

What good would knowing the truth do now? It couldn't change the past. It couldn't give me a second chance at the life I had lost; the opportunities I had let slip away. All it would do was risk my present.

Taking risks was foolish. It was dangerous. I belonged on the side lines, where I had always been.

'Just for a drive.'

The vagueness of my statement surprised me. It wasn't a lie. But then it wasn't the whole story either.

It was a half-truth. Not wrong. But not entirely right.

'I guess you just needed to clear your head a bit.'

I nodded, but my stomach twisted inside. Somehow Mum's acceptance of my explanation made my deception worse. She was always suspicious, and yet for once she didn't question my answer.

'This whole situation has been most unsettling.' Mum set cups of tea on the table and sat opposite me.

'Situation,' I repeated her word as I stared at her. That's all Adam was to her. A situation.

'You know what I mean.' Mum shrugged.

Her shrug was another dismissal.

'The whole thing is a bit distasteful.' She picked up her tea, took a sip and winced from the heat.

'It's more than distasteful. It's...' I floundered for the right word to sum up the magnitude of how I felt. But every word I thought of somehow fell short.

'Yes, well, true,' Mum conceded, saving me the trouble of finishing my search.

'I just don't understand how it came to this.' I heard the whine in my tone and braced myself for Mum's disapproval.

She blinked. 'Don't you?'

The surprise in her voice grated on me. It was as though she thought I should have seen it coming; that I should have expected it.

Mum shrugged. 'Well, you never manage to keep them, do you?'

I stared at her. 'Adam *died*.' I could not believe even she could be that callous.

'He still left, didn't he?' She nodded, as though answering her own question. 'Just like the others.'

Tears brimmed in my eyes and I blinked them back frantically as the past resurfaced in my mind.

'Look, Jess. I'm sorry. We had fun, but...'

'But what?'

Matthew stared at the ground as he kicked a stone with his mud-encrusted trainer. 'I couldn't turn it down.'

'Turn what down? I don't understand.' I shifted the textbooks that weighed heavily in my arms.

'I'm sorry.'

'You said that already.'

Matthew shrugged. 'It's all I can say.'

'What does that even mean?'

'It's true, though. Jess. I am sorry.' He slung his rucksack over his

shoulder. 'I gotta go. If I'm seen talking to you...' Matthew looked up and down the road nervously.

I glanced at the other students who surrounded us, seemingly unaware of our presence. 'Seen by who, Matt?'

He pulled a car key from his pocket. He clung to it as though it was a lifeline. I stared at the key, my eyes widened in surprise. 'Your mum finally let you borrow her car?'

The colour drained from his face. 'No, er, it's, er, mine.'

'Yours?' I blinked. 'You have your own car?'

Matthew rammed the key back in his pocket as though he wanted to hide it from me. But why? It didn't make sense. None of it did.

'You gotta stay away from me, Jess. You deserve better. You really do.'

I watched as he walked towards a shiny new red Golf. 'I don't want better. I just want you.'

'It's not the same. Adam didn't have a choice.'

Mum arched an eyebrow. 'Didn't he?'

I shuffled. 'He didn't intend to leave. It was an accident.'

Mum leaned towards me. 'Then why was he drink driving?'

My heart raced.

'I...' Words slipped away. I didn't have an explanation. Not one I could share. Not with her. Not with anyone.

'Did he have a problem with alcohol?'

'No!' My response was instinctive. Her question sliced through me like an accusation, not just about him, but about me too, about us. Adam didn't drink, not really. He didn't need that escape, he was happy, we were happy. Or at least we had been.

'Maybe he didn't before, but perhaps more recently?' Mum persevered. I should have known she wouldn't let the subject drop. She never did. 'Had something happened? Were you two having any problems?'

I froze. My breath caught in my chest. Did she know? Could

she sense it from me? Could she tell from my manner, my tone, that I wasn't as heartbroken as I should be?

'Of course not.' The lie slipped from my lips so easily. Too easily.

Guilt chafed against me. I shouldn't lie to her, not to my mum. She deserved better. I licked my dry lips, summoning the courage to come clean.

It felt wrong to lie to her. I wanted to take it back. I wanted to tell the truth. But to do so would be to admit that I had lied in the first place.

The lie was out there now. The sin had been committed. My confession wouldn't make it right, it would just highlight my deception. Everything I said from that point on would be questioned more thoroughly. I had the capacity to lie. The ability to deceive Mum, and she had believed me. My confession wouldn't lead to my redemption, but to my destruction.

I never used to lie. Not to her. I told her everything. She was involved in everything. Too much so perhaps. It didn't mean she trusted me. She had always been suspicious and doubtful, even though she had no cause to be.

Now I was hiding something from her. But then if I was truly honest with myself, I'd been lying to her for months. I'd kept things from her; pretended everything was fine; that I was fine. It was wrong of me. I was deceptive and bad. But maybe I wasn't entirely to blame. Maybe I shouldn't have had to lie because she shouldn't be that involved. She shouldn't demand to know every detail of my life. She shouldn't have a say in all my decisions. She could give advice, of course. But with Mum it was more than that. It was always meant to be her way.

'Really?'

I stared at her. There was something about her tone, the incredulousness of it and the way her gaze locked upon me, studying me intently, as though searching for a crack in my armour. Indignation bubbled inside me. It was almost as though she wanted us to have had problems. She wanted to be proved right. She wanted Adam to have been bad for me, for our relationship to have been flawed.

My confession withered from my lips. My desire to be honest was outweighed by my stubborn pride that refused to admit she'd been right.

I gritted my teeth. Anger surged through me. Not just at her, but at Adam too. He'd put me in this position. He'd let me down. He'd made Mum's predictions come true. He'd made her right about him.

I sat up straighter. Adam had failed me, but that didn't mean I was ever going to let Mum have the satisfaction of saying 'I told you so'.

18

THEN

My phone beeped with a text message.

'Your mum?' Adam asked as he placed a vanilla latte on the table in front of me.

I nodded, feeling a surge of pride. He'd picked this café to meet at as he knew I loved their lattes. We'd only been dating for a few months and he already knew so much about me. He cared enough to notice the small details of my life. He remembered things that I didn't even recall telling him. He knew what I liked and what I didn't. Maybe this time I'd finally found a decent guy.

I glanced at the screen. 'She's just checking in.'

He snorted. 'Checking up on you again, you mean.'

My fingers froze mid-way through typing my reply and I stared at him, stunned. He'd never snorted at me like that before. His voice had never had that callous tone before either.

'What's that supposed to mean?' I cursed the hurt that echoed in my voice, making me sound small and feeble.

Adam winced, but said nothing as he slid into the seat opposite me.

'Adam?'

'She's always messaging you, Jess.'

I shrugged. 'Of course, she's my mum. We talk all the time.'

'But that's just it.' He took a deep breath. 'You shouldn't.'

I blinked. 'I shouldn't talk to my mum?' I must have misheard him, that couldn't be what he meant.

'Not all the time, no.'

'Why not?'

He glared at me as though he couldn't believe I'd asked that question. 'Because it's not normal.'

My skin prickled. And the café around me slipped out of focus.

It's happening again.

I fought to steady my breathing, ignoring the voices that tormented me in my head. Voices from another time. Scathing. Hurtful. Afraid...

'You're nuts, Jess.'

'Stay away from me.'

'I don't want you here.'

Adam shook his head. 'Your relationship with your mum, the hold she has over you, it's not right.' He sighed. 'You need to find your own way, not keep running back to your mother all the time.'

I scowled at him. 'I don't run back to her, I help her. She's my mother and she needs me.'

He scoffed. 'Not as much as she wants you to think and not as much as you need her.'

I drew back, his words stung.

He made me sound like a scared little girl who still needed her mother. Was that really how he saw me? Was it what I was?

I frowned. Most people needed their mothers, didn't they? Not in the same way as they had when they were a child, of course. But that connection, that bond, didn't just evaporate. Or at least it shouldn't.

'She's my mum, of course I love her. Of course I value her thoughts and opinions.'

He stared at me, his eyes were wide as they gazed into mine. 'You really don't see it, do you?'

The sudden change in his tone threw me. The scathing harsh critical condescension had gone and in its place was a softness that made my breath catch in my throat.

'You value her opinions more than you value your own.' He reached for my hand and I could feel pity transmitted through his touch. 'You are so desperate to be a good daughter that you can't see what you have given up.'

I shook my head, trying to shake away the confusion, but his words made no sense. I hadn't given up anything. Had I?

I wanted to protest, to deny his claims, but the words wouldn't come. My mouth felt dry as doubt lodged itself in my head until it was all I could think about. He was wrong. He had to be wrong. And yet somewhere deep inside me I felt the truth resonate.

I'd always had the feeling that I'd been biding my time, waiting for my life to start. Waiting to have the things I longed for; a husband, kids, a job I liked. I was waiting to be happy.

The café seemed louder. There were so many people. The espresso machine whirred and popped, cups clanged, incessant chatter rose above it all. I felt like it was closing in on me; the noise, the people, the heat...

I pulled my hand away from Adam's and grabbed my bag. 'I need to...' My words trailed out as I scraped my chair back and stood up.

I froze as my gaze fell upon the obstacle course of people and tables that separated me from the door. My breathing quickened. I had to get out.

I felt Adam's hand gently press against the small of my back.

'It's okay,' he whispered as he edged me forwards, guiding me through the maze.

He pulled the door open and the warm summer air hit me as I stepped outside. I leaned against the wall and closed my eyes as I took long deep breaths.

I felt Adam's presence beside me. He didn't speak but I knew he was watching me. I glanced at him and saw concern etched into his creased forehead.

My face flushed. Not from my panic, but embarrassment.

'Sorry,' I murmured.

The corner of his mouth curved upwards in a lopsided half smile. 'You don't need to apologise, Jess.'

He reached for my hand again and this time it felt comforting and safe.

'I should be the one to apologise,' he said, lowering his gaze. 'I shouldn't have said all that.'

I waited for him to tell me he was wrong. To admit that he hadn't understood my relationship with my mother. Maybe even to confess that he was jealous.

He'd grown up in a big family. He didn't know what it was like to be an only child or have a single parent. His family had scattered, reuniting only for special occasions, whereas Mum and I were still close all year round. Every day.

But he didn't say anything. He just looked at me with his dark brown sorrowful eyes and I knew he still meant every word he'd said. He didn't take them back because he couldn't. He was so sure he was right about Mum; about me.

'Come on, let's go for a walk on the beach.'

I nodded as I fell into step beside him, my hand still nestled in his. We crossed the road and ambled through the lower gardens in silence. Laughter rippled through the air. The gardens were always busy when the weather was warm. They were the pathway to the seafront, a green oasis separating the town from the ocean. After a lifetime of living here I never grew tired of them, their beauty, their life.

But today I barely noticed them. I followed blindly as Adam led me down the familiar path. He was trying to make amends, to mollify me with a walk on the beach. He knew it was my favourite place. The place where I could lose myself and my troubles. But it wouldn't work. Not today. His words had cut too deeply for even the sea to wash them away.

His accusations were flawed, though. I couldn't blame my problems, my failings, on Mum. It wasn't her that drove my boyfriends away, it wasn't her that caused me to feel bored and unsatisfied by a successful career. It was me. It was always me.

There was something about me, something faulty, that I couldn't seem to fix. Something that left me feeling empty, no matter how full my life was.

Why wasn't I happy? Why did I feel so out of place?

Adam was giving me an out. A way to blame my trouble on someone else, but I couldn't take it. It wasn't fair. I wasn't perfect, but one thing I never did was shy away from my responsibilities.

The pier came into view ahead and we veered left to the promenade. It was our usual route. It was like we were guided by autopilot now. In just a few short months this had become routine. We stepped down on to the sand and dodged a group of kids playing football as we strode straight to the shoreline. We stopped at the edge of the dry sand and watched the waves crash towards us, almost touching our toes. It was a game. Our game. Sometimes we misjudged it when the tide was coming in and we'd leap back, laughing, as we tried not to let our shoes get wet.

Today, though, the tide was going out. There'd be no laughter or games. Just Adam and me and a gulf between us.

'Don't call her. Don't reply to her messages. Just be here

with me.'

'What?' I stared at him. 'I can't do that. I can't cut her off.'

'Not forever. Just for a week.'

I shook my head.

'A couple of days, even.'

'That would be so mean, so rude.'

'She has your attention 365 days a year, Jess. All I am asking for is a little of your time.'

His voice sounded so forlorn, so lost, my anger ebbed away. He wanted me. Despite his disapproval, he still cared, still loved me.

'You have my time and attention. I'm here with you.' I snaked my arms around his waist. 'Just you and me.'

He shook his head and pushed my arms away. 'I don't have your full attention. I never do. You're always checking your phone, answering her questions.'

'I type a quick reply to her texts, that's all. It only takes a few minutes out of my day, if that.'

Adam raised his eyebrows. 'You still don't see it, do you? Jess, if you're not talking to her or texting her, you're thinking about her.'

'I am not.'

'When you go shopping you pick out things she'd approve of instead of choosing what you like. If we try a new restaurant, you comment how much your mother would enjoy it or hate it there. Everything is about her, even when it's not.'

I recoiled and turned away to face the sea.

'You don't need her approval to live your life.'

'I know that.' I bristled with indignation. I resented the way he thought he knew me. He didn't. How could he? We'd barely been together a few months, whereas Mum had known me my whole life.

I froze. That thought circled in my brain.

Oh, my God.

Did he actually have a point? Hadn't I just done the very thing he'd accused me of?

It wasn't like I actually needed her approval. Of course, it was always nice to have it. Positive reinforcement of my decisions was reassuring, calming. I valued her input. But I didn't always adhere to it.

I squinted, racking my brain, trying to think of an occasion where I had gone against what she thought. My frown deepened. There had to be something. Lots of things, even. Didn't there?

Random thoughts popped into my head, but none of them fitted. I'd listened to her each time.

I shook my head. It didn't mean anything. Just because I couldn't think of anything right now, it didn't mean I'd never gone against her. It would be impossible for me to have agreed with her all the time.

Unless Adam was right.

A queasiness stirred in my stomach.

Did he have a point? Was it possible that I'd missed it? My life was about control, every moment was planned, every choice was thought out. But whose plan was I following? Mine or Mum's?

I'd thought I was good at assessing things; of looking for flaws and issues. My entire career was about analysing the fine print, looking for the bit that didn't make sense. Had I missed the part that didn't make sense in my own life?

'What do you want from life, Jess?'

'I don't know.' I dismissed his question. It was irrelevant. 'I'm too busy doing what I'm expected to do to think about that.'

'Do you realise what you just said? You should only do what Jess expects. It's your life and that's the only thing that matters.'

He was right, of course. My answer was a cop out. I was just avoiding the question. Of course, what I wanted should matter. Shouldn't it?

'I want...' I paused. 'I...' My mouth felt dry. It was crazy, why couldn't I tell him what I wanted?

Because I don't know.

I shook my head. 'I know. I must know.' But I could hear doubt creeping into my voice. 'It would be stupid not to know.'

'Why?'

I blinked. 'Everyone knows what they want. They have to. I have to.'

Adam reached for my hand. 'Not if you've never been asked. Not if you've never been allowed to want something of your own. Something independent. Something that's you.'

I pulled away. I didn't want to think about it any more. 'I'm just so confused.'

'Of course. You've never made a decision only for you before. That's why you're confused. You're so worried about the outcome and how it will affect other people that you get yourself stuck and end up listening to everyone else.'

'But isn't that what you want me to do too? You want me to listen to you. To cut Mum off. To do what you want.'

Adam put his hands on my shoulders and twisted me round to face him. 'No, Jess. I'm not trying to make you do what I want. I'm just trying to make you realise that you have a choice.'

I frowned as I stared at him. Was he trying to help me or control me?

'Your mum is holding you back.'

'She's protecting me.'

'From what? From life?'

I rolled my eyes. 'Don't be ridiculous.'

'Then what is it, Jess? What do you need her protection from?'

'From myself.'

I froze. A voice in my head screamed at me, but it was too late, the words were out there. Adam had heard them.

I stared at him, watching as his expression shifted from surprise to confusion.

'From you? Why do you need protecting from you?'

'I—' I swallowed. 'I always mess things up.'

'What things?'

I shrugged. 'Everything.'

'Such as?'

'Mum looks out for me.' I avoided his question. Adam didn't need to hear the details of my failures and I certainly didn't want to talk about them. It was bad enough they had happened, but to say them out loud...

It would be like admitting they were real. Secretly, some part of my brain still denied their existence; it still proclaimed my innocence despite all of the evidence to the contrary.

Something inside me still held onto the childish hope that I was a good person. That I was better than that. I wasn't capable of...

I shook my head. But that was the problem, I was capable.

Mum knew it. She had always known it. With her I didn't have to hide who I was. I didn't have to pretend to be normal.

But was that enough of a reason to stay? Why hadn't I broken free? Had I ever really tried to? I'd had hopes; plans, even. But they were always reliant on someone else. I never tried to make it alone. I never believed I could.

What did that make me? Foolish? Weak? Too scared of my own mother to make a stand; to live my own life?

It's what Adam believed.

But somehow it didn't feel right. I respected Mum; I obeyed her; but I wasn't afraid of her.

I took a shaky breath. The truth was I was afraid of who I was without her.

That was one thing that Adam must never know.

19

NOW

'Take a seat, I'll be right back,' PC Davidson said as he showed me into a small square room. The door clicked shut behind me and it felt as though the oxygen had suddenly dissipated. I took a shaky breath and paced back and forth by the door. I knew I should do as he said and sit down at the table to wait, but I didn't want to. I felt too restless. I had ever since his phone call.

His request had seemed so simple. 'We'd like you to come down to the station, we have a few more questions for you.'

Of course he had questions. Everyone did. I was the logical choice to direct them to. I was Adam's girlfriend. I knew him best. Or, at least, I should have done.

His mother had had questions too. She'd rung nearly every day. We'd spoken more since Adam had gone than we had in the entire time we'd been dating.

'How could this happen, Jess?' Helen's voice wavered as I pressed the phone to my ear. 'How could it happen to Adam? Why him? Why now?'

I shook my head, momentarily forgetting that she couldn't see me.

'Adam is too young, too good, to have his life snatched away like this.'

'I know.' My voice cracked.

But did I know? Had Adam ever been good? Or was he just not good enough for me?

For Helen, Adam was her son. He was perfect.

Even his imperfections were irrelevant to her. She couldn't see them. She loved him unconditionally.

What did that feel like?

My pacing halted. It felt like a question I should know the answer to.

But I didn't.

Unconditional love was just a vague concept. Alien and unfamiliar. Love always had conditions. It had boundaries that mustn't be crossed.

The door opened behind me and I swung round to face PC Davidson and another man.

'This is Detective Constable Fisher,' PC Davidson said.

I nodded at the man in a faded crumpled suit and PC Davidson gestured to one of the chairs.

Reluctantly, I sat down and they sat opposite, with the table dividing us.

All the way here I'd tried to imagine the questions they might ask. I'd rehearsed my answers. Short and simple. Open and honest. I needed them to trust me. To believe me.

This time.

They'll ask what you did wrong.

I swallowed, forcing down the nausea, as I desperately tried to silence the voice in my head. Now wasn't the time for this. I needed to focus on the situation at hand. I needed to act normal; *be* normal.

Except holding conversations with myself was normal. At least for me. It had been for years. Without Susan to talk to, I'd withdrawn into my own head. There were things I couldn't talk to anyone else about; only myself. A debate raged inside me. Everything was questioned, analysed, repeated. My life was on a well-played loop as I searched for clues; evidence of my innocence or guilt; reminders of things I may have forgotten. Not that I would ever admit it to anyone else…

'Did you know Adam was having financial difficulties?'

I frowned. 'What?' PC Davidson's question caught me by surprise. 'No, that can't be right. He had a bit of a cash flow issue a few months ago, but that was only temporary.'

'We're going through his finances now, but on the surface it would seem he was almost broke.'

'Adam would hate that.'

PC Davidson raised his eyebrow.

'Adam was a very private man. He'd hate that strangers are looking through his stuff, prying into his life.'

'He never told you about his problems?'

'It's nothing for you to worry about,' I murmured Adam's phrase under my breath.

'Pardon?'

I blinked. 'It's what Adam used to say whenever I asked him if something was wrong.'

'So, he never opened up? Never confided in you?'

I took a slow deep breath. 'Adam could be evasive.'

'About more than just money?'

I kept my expression neutral. I was heading into treacherous ground. They didn't need to know what he wouldn't talk to me about. They didn't need to know Adam's secrets. Or mine.

'He was very proud. He always paid for dinner when we went out. He liked to spoil me. To treat me. He was always buying me things; clothes, flowers—'

'Flowers? For no reason?' DC Fisher asked.

I could see the scepticism on their faces. They were probably the kind of men that only thought to buy flowers for special occasions, or as an apology, to ease their consciences and make peace. But Adam was different. 'He bought them because they made me smile.'

'That's all?'

'That's enough of a reason, isn't it? To do something for someone else because you know it will make them happy?'

Or to ease his guilt.

I pushed that thought away. It wasn't true. Adam had bought me flowers long before he'd had anything to feel guilty for.

As far as I know...

'Miss Harper?'

I froze. PC Davidson had seen my doubt. I searched for an explanation, but I couldn't find one. Only one thought circled my brain.

'I miss him.'

PC Davidson nodded slightly, as though accepting my response, but questions still lingered in his eyes.

I knew that expression well. I'd seen it in the mirror for months.

That niggling doubt that loitered under the surface, always present, but not quite strong enough to put your finger on. Just a feeling. An instinct. And yet it was real.

I'd thought it was Mum's influence at first. Her doubts and insecurities had rubbed off on me. Perhaps her distrust of Adam had made me paranoid. Adam wasn't perfect. No one was. But he was close enough. And most importantly he was mine.

Except he wasn't. Not fully. I wasn't sure if he ever really had been.

20

THEN

'What are you wearing?'

I followed Mum's gaze to my skinny jeans. My fingers instinctively ran to the hem of my T-shirt and I tugged downwards, trying to stretch the fabric to hide behind it. 'They're just jeans.'

'They're so tight!'

I tried to shrug; to brush off her disapproval. 'They're supposed to be. That's the fashion.'

Mum's gaze didn't waver. 'They aren't *you*.'

I frowned. Did I look that bad? I shuffled in front of the long mirror that hung in the hallway. I liked what I saw. I was different. Taller. Younger. More vibrant. Why couldn't that be *me*?

'You look cheap.'

I recoiled from the mirror. I'd felt so good on the way here. Modern. In keeping. Just like everyone else. But now...

'Whatever made you buy those?'

'I didn't.' I bit my lip, but it was too late. The words were out there.

'Adam bought you them, didn't he?' Disdain oozed from each word.

I nodded. 'He couldn't believe I didn't already have any…'

'Of course you don't have any.' She rolled her eyes. 'You have more taste and dignity than parading around in skin-tight clothing that leaves little to the imagination. I don't know why you listen to that man.'

That man.

I bristled. 'He's my boyfriend.'

'First it was those ridiculous red high heeled shoes, now these.'

Images of my growing wardrobe flashed in my head. I'd lost count of how many clothes Adam had bought me now. Colourful clothes. Tighter. Shorter. Not overly so. Just more flattering. More youthful. More… normal.

'He's trying to change you. To make you into something you're not.' She looked down her nose. 'Someone you're not.'

I looked at my reflection again. Why couldn't I be? Adam thought I could. He saw something in me. Potential. Beauty. Something more than I was.

'You should take them to the charity shop in the morning.'

My eyes narrowed as I glared at her. She wanted me to throw them out. A gift from Adam, and she wanted me to discard it like it didn't matter. Like he didn't matter.

'Did your mother make you take your mini-skirts to the charity shop?' I'd seen the photos from when she and Dad were dating. It was the eighties and mini-skirts had come back in style, she said, when I'd teased her about them.

Mum stared at me, her mouth hung open.

I could feel my body trembling. Was it shock? Exhilaration? Or perhaps fear? I'd never snapped at her before. I'd never been disrespectful. Never answered back.

I started to open my mouth. I needed to apologise; to make it right. But the words wouldn't come. Why wouldn't they? Why couldn't I take it back?

Because I'm not sorry.

The realisation hit me like a wave of cold water. I wasn't sorry. I didn't want to take it back. I liked my jeans. I liked how they made me look. I liked how they made me feel. And for once, not even Mum could take that from me.

21

NOW

Mum was waiting for me in the car park. She'd insisted on driving me to the police station. I could have driven myself, but she didn't think it was a good idea. According to her, I was too emotional to be driving.

I took a deep breath of the warm afternoon air and tried to steady my breathing.

Maybe she was right.

I saw her steer the car towards me and took another breath. Yet somehow driving myself here still felt like it would have been the better option.

But then it never really had been an option. That would imply I'd had a choice.

I'm just trying to make you realise that you have a choice.

Adam's words sprung into my brain. Even now I still hadn't accepted them. I was still abiding by someone else's expectations.

Usually.

Mum pulled her silver Ford up beside me and I tugged the door handle.

‘What did they want?’ The question was out of her mouth before I’d even got the door fully open.

I clambered in silently, playing for time, debating how to answer. Telling her about Adam’s financial situation didn’t seem wise. It would only strengthen her belief that all he’d seen in me was my bank balance.

‘Well?’

She stared at me. Her hands were poised on the wheel, but I knew we weren’t going anywhere until she got an answer. Not just any answer. A satisfactory answer.

‘They just wanted to know a bit more about Adam. What he was like. That kind of thing.’ I was being evasive. I knew it and from the strained look on Mum’s face, so did she.

‘Such as?’

‘I don’t know. Just little things.’ I kept my head down, focusing my attention on fastening my seat belt. ‘Like him buying me flowers.’

‘Why on earth would they be interested in that?’

I shrugged. I didn’t dare meet her eyes. The police had been very interested in that. Too interested, in fact.

‘Unless they’ve realised he was trying to buy your affection.’

I faced forward and dug my fingernails into the car seat. ‘He wasn’t buying anything. Just flowers.’

‘And clothes.’

I shrugged again. ‘He liked to buy me gifts. He liked to spoil me.’

‘He liked to change you. The way you are. Even the way you dress.’

I could feel her gaze boring into me. Even now she was critically appraising my choice of clothing. My skinny jeans had become her enemy. A physical reminder of Adam; even though he’d gone, his influence still lived on.

Perhaps she'd thought I would revert without him. I would retreat back to my quiet little life of sensible clothes and evenings at home with her. Part of me had thought I would too. But I hadn't.

Not yet.

I shook my head. Trying to shake myself free of the doubts that were still my constant companion.

Some things not even Adam had been able to change.

'Are you a suspect?'

I bristled at her question. 'Why would I be a suspect?'

'You were Adam's girlfriend.'

'So?' I shrugged, but my shoulders felt heavy.

'So, don't the police always investigate those closest to the victim in these kind of cases?'

'Victim? These kind of cases?' I stared at her. 'You make it sound like something sinister happened to Adam. It was an accident.'

'Are you sure?'

I blinked. 'Well, no, not entirely sure. I mean, the whisky...'

I never touch the hard stuff. I'm such a lightweight.

Adam's voice echoed in my head. The image the police portrayed of Adam jarred with everything I knew about him. He wouldn't turn up to a job drunk. He wouldn't drink-drive either. He was responsible and careful.

But if it hadn't been a reckless accident, then what did that mean?

'I'm not talking about Adam's drinking.'

I ran my hand through my hair feeling flustered and confused. 'Then what are you talking about?'

'Where were you that morning, Jessica?'

My hand froze, my hair entangled around my fingers. 'What?'

I tugged my hand free and jerked forwards, but the seat belt jarred against me. 'I can't believe you just asked me that.'

'Well?'

'I was at home.'

'You mean at your apartment?'

I gritted my teeth. 'That's what I said. At home. My home.'

'Are you certain?'

I glared at her.

'You choose to forget the bad things, Jessica.'

'What's that supposed to mean?'

'Maybe you only think you were at your apartment.'

'I only think I was? And where do you think I was, then?'

I cringed inwardly. Why had I asked that question? I didn't want to hear the answer, it was already clear where Mum thought I was.

Mum shuffled. 'The men in your life tend to encounter difficulties when things aren't going smoothly in your relationships.'

'I told you before, I had nothing to do with any of that.'

'You don't *remember* having anything to do with it.'

My body tensed.

'You always block out the bad things; the things you don't want to think about; things you don't want to deal with. You have ever since Dad left.'

Dad.

The memory of him crushed against me.

'Perhaps it was my fault; I encouraged you to forget.'

Somethings are best forgotten.

Mum's words, from the day after Dad had left, echoed in my head.

'I thought I was helping you; protecting you,' Mum continued. 'I didn't want you to carry that pain, that responsibility, with you for the rest of your life.'

'Responsibility?' Bile rose in my throat. 'What had I done?' My voice shook, but I persevered. 'You never really did tell me why he left.'

Mum shook her head. 'What good would it do to open up old wounds now? It's in the past. You have enough demons to contend with in the present.'

'But I want to know,' I urged. 'I need to know.'

'Do you?' Mum raised her eyebrows. 'Really?'

'I...' My voice faded away along with my conviction. Truthfully, I wasn't entirely sure. If I did, wouldn't I have asked before? We'd never talked about why Dad left, not since that morning. The question had lingered in my mind, constantly tormenting me.

They'll ask what you did wrong.

I'd wanted to ask what I'd done. I'd had years to do so. But something always stopped me. Maybe it was a childish desire to hold onto what remained of the fragmented picture I still held of him. Perhaps I wanted to preserve the image of the doting father who loved me; the one I adored; the one I would never do anything to hurt. Or maybe it was the expression I'd seen on Mum's face that day when her eyes refused to meet mine...

'Given the things that have happened,' Mum interrupted my thoughts. 'We have to consider the possibility that you could have had something to do with—'

'You think I killed Adam?' I snapped at her, I couldn't stand her tentative side stepping. I was making her face that question head on. I was pushing her. Testing her. Challenging her belief; her loyalty. I wanted to hear her deny it. I wanted her to reassure me that it was impossible for her to consider even for a second that I could have been involved. I wanted her to say it, because I needed to hear it. I needed her to convince me that I wasn't capable of killing my boyfriend. That despite everything else I had done, I hadn't fallen that far.

'I got you through it last time, Jessica, and the time before that.' Mum took a deep breath. 'But this is different. This is bigger. I'm not sure I can protect you from this.'

I sank back into the seat. She really thought I had done it, my own mother believed I had killed my boyfriend.

I fought back the tears that were brimming in my eyes. I felt betrayed. She'd failed me. She thought the worst of me.

And yet, part of me couldn't help wonder if maybe she was right.

What if there were two sides to my character? The one I knew; the one I saw each day in the mirror. Quiet. Compliant. And another... Rebellious. Vengeful. Yet her existence was an enigma. I never saw her. Never felt her. The only trace of her were the repercussions she left in her wake.

I was always the one to deal with the fall out.

22

THEN

'He thinks you have money.'

I shifted the phone by my ear as I walked to my car. 'Then he'll be sorely disappointed, Mum.'

'He's seen your apartment.'

I rolled my eyes, glad she wasn't able to see my disrespectful reaction. 'But it's not mine, is it? At least not completely.' I laughed. 'In fact, I own the smallest share. You and the bank own most of it.'

'But he doesn't know that.'

I paused beside my car and rummaged one-handed for the keys in my bag. It had been a long day at work, all I wanted to do was go home, put some music on, slip into a hot bath and unwind. Debating my boyfriend's motives with my mother was not part of my plan.

My boyfriend.

I smiled as those two little words repeated in my head. I loved the sound of them. They were special. He was special. And he was mine.

At least for now, but that would soon change if Mum got her way.

I found my keys and jabbed the remote. 'Why can't you give him a chance?'

'What has he done to prove he deserves a chance?'

I opened the driver's door and flung my bag across to the passenger seat, before clambering in. 'What has he done to prove he doesn't?'

Silence resonated on the line.

I blinked. I'd stumped her. For the first time in my life I'd made a point she couldn't argue with.

A smile tugged at the corner of my lips. I was right and she was wrong. It felt momentous. Satisfying. Comforting, even. It could happen. Occasionally, I could trust my own instincts. My own choices.

'Just because we haven't caught him out yet, doesn't mean there's nothing to catch.'

My smile withered. Her cynicism was never ending. But it wasn't her scepticism that bothered me. I was used to that. I expected it. It was her wording that caused my stomach to feel empty and hollow.

We.

It was as though she saw it as some strange new mother-daughter activity to trip up my boyfriend, to expose him, to destroy our relationship.

It was a challenge to her; or worse still, a game. One she thought we played together.

23

NOW

Mum pulled the car up to the kerb in front of my apartment block. 'I don't know why you want to stay in that empty apartment, when you have a perfectly good room waiting for you at home.'

'*This* is my home, Mum.'

I heard her sharp intake of breath. 'Your *home* is at our house, just as it has always been.'

I shook my head slowly. It was pointless to argue with her. She would never accept my view on it. My opinion didn't count. Not unless it conformed to hers.

'I should never have lent you the money for it.'

Lent.

I swallowed.

That word had never been mentioned before. The apartment was mine, that's what she'd said. She'd just been helping her daughter out. It was what mothers did. It's what she did.

She'd never understood why I'd wanted it. It was the only thing we'd ever really disagreed on. Until Adam, of course.

'What do you need a flat for?'

'I want my own space, Mum.'

'You have your own space here. You have your own room. You can take one of the spare rooms too if you need to spread out more. You could make it your own living room. We could put a TV in there—'

'It's not the same thing, Mum. This house is yours.'

'It's ours. Your grandparents wanted us to have this house. It's their legacy.'

'They wanted you to have it, Mum.'

Mum shook her head. 'They wanted us to have it. They wanted it to be our home, for us to be as happy here as they had been. They left it to me and someday I'll leave it to you.'

'Mum,' I groaned. I didn't want to think about inheriting it from her. It was morbid and depressing. It would mean she'd be gone. I'd be alone.

She rolled her eyes. 'Don't be oversensitive, Jess. I'm just being pragmatic. I won't be around for ever, but thanks to your grandparents you'll always be taken care of. You'll always have a home here. A life here.'

The hairs on my arms raised as a chill ran through my body. My destiny was tied to that house. My past. My future. My life.

I had to change it. I had to break the cycle before I was entrenched in it forever.

'But I want something of mine. I go to work every day. I sit at that desk, reading document after document and for what?'

'It's a good job.'

'It's a boring job.'

'You're just working your way up the ladder. You'll get promoted and then things will be better. More interesting.'

'But it's still pointless. I have a job to earn money, but I rarely ever spend any of it. I just put it in the bank and leave it there. What's the point?'

'You're saving. It's an investment.'

'A flat would be an investment. It would also be a purpose. A reason to go to work.'

'It would be wasteful. You'd spend it on bills and maintenance charges. Then you'd wish you'd stayed here. With me.'

'I found a lovely little one-bedroom flat. It's modern and energy efficient. It won't cost too much to run.'

'You really don't want to be here, do you?'

I let out a slow breath. How could I answer that? 'It's not about not wanting to be here. It's about wanting something more.'

'Something more than me?'

'I...'

'Am I really that bad?'

'No, Mum. It's not like that.' Guilt twisted and churned in my stomach. Why did I always hurt her? I didn't intend to. Somehow, I just managed it. Asking for something for myself was always deemed to be a reflection of dissatisfaction with her.

She reached out and took my hand in hers. 'Then stay here. With me.'

My chest tightened and my mouth felt dry. My conscience was screaming at me to say okay. I should apologise and drop the idea. It was too painful to her. Too insensitive of me.

And yet...

I licked my lips. I couldn't say it.

I was terrified of hurting her. But I was more terrified of what would happen if I caved. If I stayed now, something told me I would never leave.

It wasn't that I wasn't happy here. It wasn't about wanting to leave her. In fact, it wasn't really about her at all. But I needed to find my own path. And something told me I needed to leave to do that. Just like every other son or daughter did at some point. The longer I stayed, the further away my dream of creating a family of my own seemed to get.

I squeezed her hand. 'I need to do this.'

The money had been a peace offering. Or at least that's what I'd thought. Her way of telling me she'd finally accepted my decision. Not that it was entirely my decision by that point. My cosy little one-bedroom flat, which I could afford with my savings, had been deemed to be unsuitable.

It was too small. Too cheap. The area wasn't good enough. Or safe enough. I couldn't argue with her logic. But it would have been mine. Just mine.

My flat morphed into a three-bedroom executive apartment with a concierge. It was stunningly gorgeous and luxurious. But somehow it never really felt like mine.

24

THEN

I pulled open my front door and my smile froze on my face. 'Mum.' I gripped the door catch. 'What are you doing here?'

She rarely came here. I'd given up inviting her months ago. She always declined. It was as though she thought visiting me in my apartment would be some form of acceptance of my decision to move here.

'I came to visit my daughter. Or is that not allowed?'

I flinched at her tone. 'No. Yes.' I let out a nervous laugh. 'I mean of course it's allowed.'

There was a time that her presence here would have filled me with joy; now, though, it just made me nervous. Why was she here? Why now?

She nodded, but her expression didn't soften. 'Are you going to invite me in, or just leave me standing in the corridor?'

I laughed again. 'Yes, sure. Come in.'

I hesitated for a moment before stepping back to let her pass. I hurried to the living room while she slipped off her shoes in the hallway.

My gaze darted around the room, seeking out the incriminating evidence that I knew would be around. Adam's sweater was draped over the back of the sofa. I grabbed it and screwed it up in a ball in my arms, before my gaze fell upon the stack of his DVDs beside the TV.

I cursed silently. I wouldn't be able to move them in time. They would have to stay where they were and hopefully she wouldn't notice that they weren't things I would buy, or for that matter even watch if I had a say in it.

'Whose shoes are those on the shoe rack?' Mum asked as she came in behind me.

I couldn't answer, I just clung tightly to the sweater, wishing Adam was here with me, instead of just his belongings.

'Adam's?'

I cringed and turned slowly to face her. She already knew the answer. There was no point trying to deny it. 'Yes.' I tried to keep my voice calm and steady.

'Why are they here?'

I shrugged. 'I guess he left them here.'

She strode towards me. 'So I suppose you're telling me he left here barefooted?'

'Of course not.'

'Then wouldn't he need his shoes?' Her gaze dropped to the sweater in my arms. 'And his sweater?'

She was testing me. She knew the answer already. It was obvious. She just wanted to make me squirm. To know I was in the wrong. To feel guilty.

'He left some of his stuff here.' I turned to walk past her, but Mum side-stepped in front of me.

'Why?'

I lifted my chin and met her gaze. 'Because he stays here sometimes.'

Her eyes narrowed. Even though she'd known the truth, it was as though hearing my confession had somehow lowered her opinion of me.

'I thought you had more sense.'

The back of my neck prickled at her insult. 'I do have sense.'

'Obviously not. Otherwise you wouldn't have let that plumber move in.'

'He's not *that* plumber.' I glared at her. 'He's *my* plumber.' I felt a tingle of warmth surge through me, but it wasn't embarrassment, it was pride.

She scoffed. A condescending sound that grated against me.

'And his name is *Adam*,' I added haughtily.

Her eyes widened slightly. She looked as taken back by my tone as I was. I was being disrespectful. Snapping at her. Answering her back. It wasn't like me.

'You've only known him five minutes.'

'I've known him four months.'

'That's nothing.'

'It's *everything*.' The certainty of my voice surprised me. I'd been hesitant when Adam had first started leaving his things in the apartment. It hadn't been much. Just a toothbrush and a change of clothes. Little things. But somehow, they'd looked out of place in my bathroom and my wardrobe.

It was a strange in between place. He didn't live here. And yet he sort of did. Sometimes.

It wasn't that I hadn't wanted him here. I had. But it was in my nature to be nervous and doubtful. Half of me was terrified that it was too much too soon. But the other half of me wanted him here all the time. I wanted my home to be our home; our lives to be combined.

I wanted certainty. Permanence.

I *needed* it.

I saw Mum's shoulders sag. 'I just don't want you to get hurt. Not again.'

Guilt stabbed me in my heart. She was only looking out for me. She was concerned about my welfare. She'd been there for me through everything. The one constant in my life. No matter how bad it had got. She'd stayed.

When everyone else left. She'd stayed.

I reached out and squeezed her hand. 'Adam is different, Mum. I'm different.'

'Because of him.'

I nodded. 'Yes.' I stood a little straighter. 'He helps me to see that I am better than I think I am. I'm stronger. Happier.'

'I'm glad, Jess. I really am.' Mum took a deep breath. 'But what if you're wrong?'

'I can't keep living my life with "what ifs", Mum. I can't keep second guessing every decision, just in case I make the wrong one again. It was driving me crazy.' I laughed, a feeble hollow sound. 'Or at least crazier.'

'Oh, Jess.' She wrapped her arms around me and enveloped me in a hug.

I stayed there, frozen, not really sure how to respond. She wasn't a hugging sort of mother. Not since I was little. The memory of her hugs had faded, and I often wondered if they had ever been real. I couldn't even recall what they had felt like. The idea of it had seemed so warm and comforting. But the reality just felt disconcerting and strange.

She pulled back and studied my face. 'I just don't trust him.'

I nodded. 'I know.' She didn't trust anyone. She couldn't. I smiled slightly as I gazed at her. It wasn't her fault. Life had been cruel to her. Losing her parents, then Dad. The past had eaten away at her. Her ability to trust had been its first casualty.

It was an infliction I was familiar with. I'd suffered the same fate. Different circumstances, but the same result. My ability to trust, to love, had diminished.

Dad had been the one constant in my life. The one person I'd counted on. We'd always been close, but after Mum's parents died, he became my lifeline. Then he'd left.

No explanations. No goodbyes. No contact. Just an emptiness that consumed me.

It was the not knowing that tormented me. The whys. The wondering what I'd done wrong, or could have done differently. But mostly it was the endless waiting for him to come back... that frail hope which dwindled a little more each day, but never entirely went away.

If it had been Mum who'd left I would have been less surprised. I would still have been hurt. I'd still have missed her. I'd still have had questions. But in many ways she had left already. Her departure had been slow. She'd pulled away gradually, until the Mum I'd known had disappeared. Physically she was still there, still going through the motions of living, present but not really there.

Dad's departure had been such a stark contrast. The suddenness of it had jarred against me. It shook the foundations of everything I believed in. If he could leave me, then how could anyone else ever love me enough to stay?

And then I met Adam.

He'd changed me. I hadn't even realised it was happening. But I trusted again now. I trusted in him. I trusted in us. Maybe not fully. Not yet. I was still a work in progress. But I had potential. I could see it now.

Whereas Mum...

'I don't want him getting my money when I'm gone.'

I flinched at her words. There was no hope that Adam would be genuine, just an expectation that he wouldn't. It wouldn't last.

It couldn't. It didn't really matter who the guy was. It wasn't really about him.

'He stays here occasionally, Mum. That hardly qualifies him as raiding my inheritance.'

'It's the first step. This week it's a few of his things here, next week he'll be moving in boxes of his stuff, then it'll be a ring on your finger.'

My left thumb ran across my empty ring finger. If only...

'It's part of his plan.'

'Maybe. If he loves me enough.'

She snorted again. 'If you're gullible enough, more like.'

I bristled. 'What's that supposed to mean?'

'You're too nice. You let people walk all over you. Give them an inch and they'll take a mile.'

I cringed at the age-old cliché. She never grew tired of saying it. It was her mantra in life. She always assumed everyone was only out for themselves.

'You let everyone take advantage of you.'

It seemed wrong hearing it from her. She was the person who'd encouraged me to be helpful. It's what she'd taught me when I was a child. It's what she expected from me even now.

But then perhaps she wasn't being contradictory at all. It wasn't my personality and helpfulness she wanted to change; only the scope of it. It should be more focused – on her.

* * *

I lay cocooned in Adam's arms, staring at the clothes he'd tossed carelessly on the chair in front of my dressing table. He never folded his clothes. He said it was a waste of time, they would only have to be unfolded in the morning to put them back on.

I tilted my head up to look at him. 'Why don't we ever go to your apartment?'

'You wouldn't like it there. I don't even like it there.' He snuggled closer to me. 'It's not what you're accustomed to.'

'How do you know what I'm accustomed to?'

He opened one eye and peered at me for a second before closing it again. 'It's not this.'

I stared at the wall. 'I didn't always have this. I didn't even want it. This was Mum's choice. Mum's money.'

Adam pulled away as he propped himself up on his elbow and stared at me. 'She bought it?'

'Most of it. I couldn't have afforded it on my own. I'd wanted something smaller.'

'Why?' His eyebrows knotted together. 'This apartment is amazing.'

'But it's not mine. It's too perfect. It's fake and artificial.'

Like my life.

'It *is* perfect. Believe me, when you don't have money you appreciate things like this more.'

'I appreciate it. I do.' I felt chastised. He thought I was spoilt and ungrateful. I wasn't. I just had smaller dreams. 'Besides, we didn't always have money.'

'Really? I mean, I have seen the house you grew up in, Jess.'

'It was my grandparents' house. It was their money.' I shuffled up in bed, and tugged the duvet up higher as the cool air chilled my shoulders. 'Before they died we lived very differently.'

'You're lucky.'

My body went rigid. 'Lucky?'

Adam rolled his eyes. 'They gave you a way out.'

I frowned. Had it been a way out? Or had it just been an expensive trap?

25

NOW

I leaned against the sink, surveying my immaculate kitchen as I waited for the kettle to boil. It was flawless. Just like the rest of the apartment. I'd inherited my mother's compulsion for cleanliness and order.

I ran my fingers along the edge of the granite worktop and glanced around the open-plan apartment. It was modern and gleaming, simplistic and minimalist.

I shivered and rubbed my hands over my arms. Was that its appeal or its necessity? Was my lack of statement pieces and personal touches a style preference or a reflection of my identity?

I turned and opened the fridge. I reached for the milk and paused as my gaze fell upon the six pack of lager Adam had left. I slammed the door shut quickly, my desire for a cup of tea instantly dissipating. The few reminders of Adam looked out of place. His lager in the fridge. His phone charger on the breakfast bar. His car magazine that was out of date and yet still sat on the end of the sofa.

Adam didn't have the same obsessive need for everything to be put in its proper place. To him it was perfectly reasonable to leave things lying around. It had grated on me at first. I'd tried not to comment. I just subtly tidied up his things for him when he wasn't using them.

It was an endless job. I'd thought about asking him to put things away himself, but I never did. Partly because I didn't want him to think I was being fussy. But mostly because, weirdly, I really didn't mind.

My desire for neatness seemed to be outweighed by the surge of joy I felt at seeing his belongings in my home. It was a physical reminder of him when he wasn't in the apartment with me. It was a reminder that he was mine; that we were together; I wasn't alone.

Except I was.

I frowned and pushed that thought away. I should get rid of his things. I should move on. And yet for some reason I couldn't. My friends would tell me it was too soon to think about such things. Adam's mother would undoubtedly be horrified if she knew I was contemplating casting out her son's belongings before they had even found his body. But the truth was, it wasn't Adam's disappearance that had ended our relationship. His death had just given me closure. Or at least it would when they found him.

What if they don't?

I froze as the unwanted thought sprang into my head. What if he was never found? What if his body had been washed out to sea? Or maybe – I shook my head, shunning that thought from my brain. I wouldn't allow myself to think of the gruesome things that could have happened to him. He would be found. He had to be. It was the only way I would finally be able to put this behind me and move on.

I wandered into the living room and flicked on the TV. It wasn't as though I still loved him. Not the real him, anyway.

But I still missed his presence in my home; my life. I missed feeling a part of something.

I stared at the images that flashed on the screen, but barely even noticed what they were. They were just meaningless blurs. Just like my life.

Adam had given it meaning. He'd given me purpose. At least for a little while.

I picked up the remote and pointed it at the TV. My thumb hovered over the power button. I wasn't in the mood for watching TV, but without it the silence would return.

I put the remote back down on the coffee table, the button unpressed. Silence never used to bother me. Not for a long time. I'd grown used to it.

I sat on the damp grass at the end of the garden, staring out to sea. There was something comforting about the way the waves rose and fell; a constant flow that never ended.

'Jessie?' I turned at the sound of Daddy's voice behind me. 'What are you doing out here? It's freezing. You'll catch a cold.'

I shrugged. It wasn't so bad. Not if I didn't think about it. 'I was watching the waves.'

Daddy leaned towards me and held out his hand. 'Come on, let's get you inside in the warm.'

I glanced at his hand and then at the house behind him. 'Do we have to go back in there?'

'It's our home now, Jessie.'

I screwed my nose up. 'But it doesn't feel right to be here. Not without Granny and Grandad.'

His shoulders hunched and he knelt beside me. 'I know, sweetie. Everything feels a little strange right now, but they wanted us to be here. That's why they left Mummy the house, so we could carry on their dream now that they're not able to. They want us to be happy here, just like they were.'

'Mummy isn't.'

Daddy's gaze dropped to the floor and he shook his head slowly. 'No, she isn't.' He turned back to me. 'But she will be.' He smiled, but although his lips moved upwards his eyes still looked sad.

'When?'

He held his arms open and pulled me towards him. I snuggled against the warmth of his chest. 'I don't know, Jessie. I don't know.'

Daddy picked me up and carried me towards the house. I clung tighter to him with every step.

'I don't want to go back inside,' I whispered in Daddy's ear. 'It's like the house is sad and still, like it's waiting for Granny and Grandad to come home.'

Daddy squeezed me in his arms, but didn't speak. He opened the patio door and stepped inside. He set me down on the coconut mat and we kicked off our shoes.

Mummy stood by the hob; her head was bent forwards, her gaze fixed on the pan in front of her as her hand stirred a wooden spoon. She never even looked up.

The prickles of the mat dug into my feet. I wanted to move; to do something, but I didn't know what.

My arms ached to wrap themselves around Mummy's waist. She looked so sad, I just wanted to hug her until she smiled again.

But she wouldn't.

She never did.

She just brushed me away, saying she was too busy.

She was always too busy. Even when she sat on the sofa starring at a blank wall, she was still too busy for a hug.

Daddy nudged my back. 'Why don't you go and play in your room until dinner time?'

I nodded silently and retreated to the hall. I glanced back through the open door and saw Daddy standing beside Mummy.

'Honey, I'm worried about you. We both are.'

'I'm fine.'

I cringed. It was Mummy's usual answer now. She was always fine. Yet somehow she never seemed it.

'No, you're not. You're grieving.'

I glanced at the stairs. I should go up to my room like I'd been told to.

'Then leave me alone and let me grieve.'

'It's been six months.'

'I didn't realise there was a time limit.' Mummy sounded cross.

I crept back down the hall and peered around the door frame.

'You know that's not what I meant. I just think that maybe it's time that we thought about finding you someone to talk to.'

'I have you to talk to.' Mummy turned away from him and started to walk to the window, but Daddy caught her hand.

'But you don't talk to me. You won't.'

'I'm not ready,' Mummy whispered.

I blinked, trying to dislodge the tears that were forming in my eyes. Mummy sounded so sad.

'I know.' Daddy reached out and stroked her cheek. 'That's what worries me.' He took a deep breath. 'And it worries Jess too.'

Mummy pulled away. 'Jess is too little to understand.'

'She's not too little to notice how sad her mum is. She's not too little to not be hurt that her mum won't talk to her, or hold her.'

Mummy leaned against the sink. 'I can't.' Her voice sounded strange, all cracked and broken.

'I don't know if we did the right thing moving in here.' Daddy looked around the kitchen and I ducked back out of sight. 'This house is a constant reminder of them; of what you've lost.'

'They wanted me to have it. It's their last wish...'

'I know. But maybe we should at least move some of our things in. Our furniture is still in storage. Maybe with our sofa and—'

'No.'

'Honey, it's like a shrine to them.'

'I said no!'

I jolted back from the doorway. Mummy had sounded so mad. I'd never heard her snap like that before.

I crept back to the stairs. I shouldn't have been listening. I wouldn't have heard her then.

I tiptoed up the stairs, praying they wouldn't creak. I didn't want Mummy to catch me. I didn't want her to be mad at me, too.

26

THEN

I perched on the arm of the sofa, my toe tapping on the floor as I stared out of the window, waiting for Adam's familiar white van to come into view. I leapt up as soon as I saw it pull into the car park. I rolled my eyes as I watched Adam amble up the path to the building. He was hopeless.

I held the front door open, listening as he thudded up the stairs. I resisted the urge to shout to him to hurry up. This was a night for celebration, not for nagging.

Adam stopped at the top of the stairs as his eyes met mine. 'Wow, you look amazing.' A coy smile formed on his lips as his gaze travelled slowly down my body.

My desperate need to hurry evaporated. So what if we were late? It didn't matter. Not when he looked at me like that.

Adam walked towards me. 'I could get used to coming home to this.'

I laughed. 'Then maybe you should come home a little earlier.'

Adam winced. 'I would if I could. You know that, right?'

I cursed myself silently. 'Of course I do. I didn't mean to make you feel bad.'

Liar.

The word resounded in my head as I ushered him inside. It was exactly what I'd intended. I'd wanted him to feel guilty; to feel remorseful. I wanted him to be on time, to pay more attention to me.

It felt as though he was getting more and more distracted over the last few weeks. The newness had worn off our relationship now. I was old news. Unimportant. He'd stopped trying to impress me with his attentiveness and his gifts. He could come home late because he knew I would still be here waiting for him when he arrived.

'So, what's the occasion?' Adam asked as he slipped off his trainers.

I stared at him blankly.

'Are you off somewhere with the girls tonight?'

I blinked. 'No.'

He frowned. 'Oh, Jess. You weren't hoping we'd go out, were you? I'm knackered.'

My eyes narrowed suspiciously. 'You're teasing me, aren't you?' He had to be. He played a convincing part. I could quite easily believe he had forgotten, but I knew him better than that. Adam never forgot anything. Especially not things that mattered.

Confusion passed over his face and my stomach sank. He wasn't pretending. He really didn't remember.

'Did we have plans?'

I closed my eyes and tried not to let the hurt show on my face. 'We had reservations.'

'We did? Where for?'

I opened my eyes and stared at him. 'Level Eight.' We'd talked about it for weeks. A classy restaurant and cocktail bar with views of the coastline. Somewhere special to mark the occasion.

Adam closed his eyes. 'Our six-month anniversary.'

'You forgot.' My accusation was pointless, we both knew it now.

'I'm so sorry.' Adam reached for my hands. 'I'm such an idiot.'

I didn't respond. I couldn't think of anything to say. I should tell him it was okay, shrug it off and say it didn't matter. But it wasn't okay. It did matter. To me at least.

'You're mad. I can see it in your eyes. You're so mad at me.'

'No, I'm not mad.'

'I don't blame you. You have every right to be. Heck, I'm mad at me.'

'I said I'm not mad.' My voice came out louder and sharper than I'd intended.

Adam studied me dubiously. To be fair, I actually did sound pretty mad now. But I wasn't, or at least I hadn't been, until he insisted on repeatedly telling me how I felt. Up to that point all I'd really felt was disappointed and overlooked.

'I'm not mad, honestly,' I told him, grateful that my voice sounded calmer this time. 'But we should hurry if we're going to make our reservation.'

Adam licked his lips. 'You sure you want to go there? I mean, we could just have a quiet night in, just the two of us.'

My shoulders sagged. 'These days all we have are quiet nights in. I want to go out for a change.'

'But,' he glanced down at his faded jeans. 'I'd have to shower and get all dressed up.'

I raised my eyebrows. 'You mean like I did?'

He cringed. 'You look amazing.'

'Thank you.' I smiled at him, the best, most encouraging smile I could muster and twizzled in my short black cocktail dress. 'I'm a little bit too dressed up for just staying in, don't you think?'

'It's just...' Adam shuffled and stared at his feet. 'Things are a bit tight right now.'

My eyes widened. 'But you've been working flat out. You're late home almost every night and you're always so exhausted.'

'Yeah, of course.' A red tint crept into his cheeks. 'I'm busy. I've got enough work. It's just...' He frowned. 'A timing thing.' His voice was hesitant.

'A timing thing?'

Adam nodded. 'I have a couple of big jobs with a lot of upfront costs.' His voice grew more certain as he spoke. 'As soon as they pay up everything will be fine.'

I let out a deep breath and felt the tension in my shoulders ease. 'You should have said.'

'It's not a big deal. It's nothing for you to worry about.'

'But if you need some cash to tide you over—'

'And have your mother thinking I'm sponging off you? No way!'

'You wouldn't be sponging off me. I'd just be helping you out until you get paid. I want to help. And Mum wouldn't need to know.'

'She'd know. She always knows everything.'

'Not from me.'

'Not intentionally.'

The curtness of Adam's words cut through me. 'What's that supposed to mean?'

'Your mum has a way of wheedling information out of you without you even realising.'

I bristled and glared at him. 'You make me sound weak and gullible.'

'I didn't mean it like that.'

I studied him carefully. His words sounded sincere, but his shrug implied otherwise.

'I get it, Jess. She's your mum. She has a hold over you. She always will.'

I opened my mouth, but clamped it closed again. Was Adam right? Did Mum still have a hold over me, even now? I'd moved out, I was making a life with Adam, and yet she still influenced my decisions and my way of seeing things. Was that never going to change?

Or maybe I just shared her values. It's what I'd been taught. The way I'd been raised. Our beliefs were still aligned but I was independent now, wasn't I?

Maybe it was about time that I proved it.

'Come on,' I said as I straightened my back, put my hands on his shoulders and turned him round.

'What are you doing?' Adam asked as he twisted back to look at me over his shoulder.

'I'm hungry.' I pushed him down the hall to the bedroom.

'Ok-ay, but in that case shouldn't you be leading me to the kitchen?'

'Nope, you are going to shower and change and then we are going out as we'd planned.'

Adam stopped and turned to face me. I frowned, frustrated. He was too strong for me steer without his compliance.

'I told you I can't afford it right now.'

I shrugged. 'But I can.'

'Jess—'

I glared at him. 'All I wanted to do was help.'

Adam blinked and looked confused.

'You have a little cash flow issue, so I offered to help. It's what couples do. But instead of accepting my help you turned it into an opportunity to criticise me and my ability to take control of my own life.'

'I wasn't—'

I held my hand up, cutting his objections short. 'So this is me taking control, Adam. I'm hungry and I want to go out and celebrate our anniversary just as we'd planned. And if you are too stubborn to join me, then I will go alone.'

Adam blinked and then the corner of his mouth twitched. 'You're going to celebrate our anniversary alone?'

I scrunched my nose up as the ridiculousness of my plan sank in. 'If I have to.' My voice sounded less certain now, but I'd committed to this path, I couldn't backtrack, not without looking as weak as he'd made me sound. I would have to go through with it. 'So, tell me, do I have to?' I willed him to say no. I'd feel a fool sitting alone in a fancy restaurant. It wouldn't be a celebration, just an uncomfortable sign that maybe we weren't right for each other. I wasn't good enough. Again.

'No,' Adam said. 'You don't have to go alone.' He slipped his hand in mine. 'I'm sorry. Sometimes my stupid pride gets in the way. This money situation really isn't a big deal, though. It's just temporary, I swear.'

I nodded, as my heart softened. 'It's okay, I get it.'

We smiled at one another and I felt calm and light. We were going to be okay.

I gave him a nudge. 'Now go and get ready.'

Adam leaned forwards and kissed me, a long passionate kiss where I almost forgot to breathe. I smiled as he stepped back. He hadn't kissed me like that in weeks. If that's what happened when I took control, I was going to have to be bossier.

'What time did you make the reservation for?' Adam asked as he started to walk towards the bedroom door.

'Me?'

Adam froze and turned back.

'You made the reservation last month.'

He didn't speak, he just stared at me.

My stomach sank. 'You did make the reservation, didn't you?'

Adam's face looked pale and pained. 'I...'

I closed my eyes. 'You forgot that, too.'

'We could just go, maybe they have a table free.'

I shook my head. 'They'll be too busy by now. It's too late.'

'It's not too late,' Adam said as he pulled his sweater off over his head. 'I'll grab a really quick shower and then we'll go. I won't take long. I promise.'

I squeezed past him into the bedroom. I stood with my back to him as I unclasped my necklace. 'We'll just stay in, like you wanted. It's fine.'

'No, Jess. It's not fine.' Adam wrapped his arms around me. His musty aroma engulfed my nostrils, but there was something else, a sweetness I couldn't place. 'I screwed up. I'm so sorry.'

I shrugged and pulled away. 'It doesn't matter.'

'It does matter. You matter.'

I placed the necklace back in my jewellery box and closed the lid. Did I really matter?

I used to matter. I was certain of that. But recently I'd begun to wonder. Begun to doubt.

'We could go somewhere else. Anywhere you fancy.'

I shook my head. 'I don't really feel like going out any more.'

'I'll take you there one day, Jess. I promise.'

I glanced back at him over my shoulder and forced a small smile onto my lips. 'It's fine.' But it wasn't. Nothing was. It hadn't been for a while. I'd tried to ignore it. To pretend nothing was wrong, but he was different. We were different.

Adam didn't move. 'Are you sure you're okay with this?'

'I'm fine.' The word stuck in my throat. Fine. Again. I caught myself saying it more and more these days. It had become my catchphrase. There was a degree of normality to it. It was meant to be reassuring, but it carried with it a sense of pretence. It wasn't really an answer. I wasn't good or happy, but it didn't betray the sadness I felt inside either. It was a no-man's land trapped somewhere in between. Just like me.

I pulled my jeans out of the wardrobe. 'Have your shower and I'll go and see what we have in the freezer.'

'I'll make it up to you, Jess. I promise.'

I nodded as I watched him retreat into the en suite. He sounded so sincere, so believable, and yet a strange emptiness in my stomach told me he wouldn't. He couldn't.

* * *

I rolled over and my hand fell against the cold empty space beside me. I opened my eyes and peered at the indented pillow next to mine. I pushed myself up on my elbow and blinked as my eyes adjusted to the sunlight trickling in through the gap in the curtains.

Footsteps padded in the hallway and I turned towards the bedroom door.

'Great, you're awake.' Adam beamed at me from behind a cluttered tray. 'Sit up and make yourself comfortable.'

I shuffled up in the bed obediently. 'What is all this?'

'Breakfast in bed,' Adam replied proudly.

'You made me breakfast?' I couldn't keep the disbelief out of my voice. Adam had never made me breakfast before. I was lucky if I could get him to make me a cup of tea.

'Yep, scrambled eggs on toast with a glass of orange juice,' he announced as he set the tray on my lap.

My gaze fell upon the scrambled egg and my stomach heaved.

'I just wanted to show you how sorry I am for last night.'

I nodded, unable to take my eyes off the egg. I should smile, thank him, something. This was big. He'd been thoughtful and sweet.

I swallowed.

He wasn't to know.

'I told you I'd make it up to you.'

My head jolted up and I stared at him. This wasn't just his apology, this was his solution. He thought scrambled egg and slightly burnt toast was a suitable substitute for our romantic evening of cocktails and fine food.

Adam snuggled under the duvet. 'What are you waiting for? Dig in.'

My gaze dropped back to my plate. I glared at the scrambled egg. I hated it. Even the sight of it took me back to that moment when my world had changed.

He's never coming back.

I picked up my knife and fork and tried to push the memory away. I fought not to grimace as I shoved a fork full of toast and scrambled egg into my mouth. I chewed silently. The cold rubbery texture churned my stomach.

Maybe I should just tell Adam I didn't like them. I swallowed. He'd understand, wouldn't he?

I glanced at Adam. He was watching me expectantly. He was so pleased with himself. He thought he'd done something special. Something thoughtful.

It wasn't his fault he'd picked a food that made me heave just from looking at it. He wasn't to know what memories a simple meal could hold. I'd never told him that Mum had made me clear my plate and eat every mouthful as silent tears ran down my cheeks, knowing my dad was never coming home.

I prodded the egg with my fork. Perhaps he should know. It

was the kind of thing a couple should have talked about, wasn't it? I loved him. He was my boyfriend. My partner. We shared a life together. And yet he knew so little about me.

I'd lived a lifetime of secrets that he didn't even know existed. That couldn't be good.

I was hurt that he'd forgotten our anniversary. Hurt that I didn't matter enough to him to be remembered. But perhaps my sin was worse. How hurt would he be if he knew I kept secrets from him?

Perhaps on some level he did know. Maybe he could feel it. Maybe the gulf between us wasn't his fault. Maybe it was mine.

It was time I changed that, for him, for us.

'Adam?'

'Yes, Jess?' He looked at me expectantly.

'I have to tell you...' I bit my lip, searching for the courage to continue.

They'll ask what you did wrong.

My throat seized. What if the truth didn't save us? What if it destroyed us?

I forced a smile onto my lips. 'You're a really good cook.'

27

NOW

I glanced out of the window. It was dark outside. The corner of my mouth curved upwards. It was the first time I'd ever been grateful for the dark February evenings. It made it feel more acceptable to have crawled fully dressed into bed at 5 p.m. Not that I had anywhere else to be.

It felt warm and safe snuggled under my duvet. I could lie still, close my eyes and pretend that nothing had changed. Time was an illusion here.

My phone rang, pulling me back to reality. Its cheerful, upbeat tune grated on my nerves. I rolled onto my side, flicked the bedroom light on and glared at the phone as it vibrated on the bedside cabinet.

I didn't want to answer it. I didn't even want to know who was calling me. It wouldn't be anyone I wanted to talk to. It would probably be Mum with her endless questions about Adam, and her missing notebook. Or Karen to ask for the hundredth time if I was okay, despite knowing that was the one thing it was impossible for me to be right now, or maybe ever again. Or maybe the police with news I didn't want to hear, or more questions I didn't want to answer.

I wasn't sure how much more I could take. The questions. The accusations. At some point I'd fall apart. The irony was that Adam wasn't even here to help me through it. I was alone.

With a sigh I picked up the phone and glanced at the screen. I rolled my eyes as I hit the green button.

'Hi, Mum.'

Well, maybe I wasn't entirely alone. I still had Mum.

Checking up on you again.

Adam's voice lodged itself in my brain. I shook my head, trying to shake free of him and his cynicism. Mum was just concerned.

I took a deep breath. The problem was that with her incessant questions she was almost as bad as the police. I knew what was coming, before she even spoke. What did they ask you? How did you respond? Did they believe you?

'So, have you had any more questions from the police?'

I cringed. Maybe I shouldn't have answered the phone.

'No, Mum. Not since you took me to the police station yesterday.'

'Do you think they have made any more progress with the investigation?'

'I don't really want to talk about it tonight, Mum.'

'But I want to know. I'm worried about you.'

'I know you are. But I don't kn—'

'Don't keep me in the dark, Jessica.'

Memories of Adam drifted into my head.

'You need to make some changes.'

I nodded. 'I know. The problem is I don't know what, though...'

Adam shook his head. 'Yes, you do. You're just afraid to.'

'That's not—'

'You avoid confrontation. You always do what she wants you to do.

You always say yes. See? Your bottom lip is trembling at the thought of disagreeing with her. Of disappointing her.'

'But the point of an argument is to win or to make yourself feel better. Mum gets so mad and upset if I disagree with her that I feel bad. There's no victory in whatever I gain from it and I always end up wishing I hadn't bothered. I'd have been better off and the discomfort of doing whatever it was is over quicker than the fallout from avoiding it.'

Perhaps there was another way; a way that avoided confrontation but still brought me some peace.

'When things have settled I'm going to take some time off.' I needed to get away from here for a while. I needed to reassess my life. 'I think I'll take a look in the travel agents tomorrow.'

'I'll come with you.'

I shook my head. 'No need.'

'But you need me there to help you avoid making any mistakes.'

I heard it then. That one sentence summed up our entire relationship. She wanted to pick out the trip for me. She would probably want to go away with me too. If I went away alone she wouldn't be there to tell me what to think.

A cold calmness descended on me.

'Then I'll just have to make my own decisions.' There was no hostility in my voice, just a flatness. That surprised me. I should feel angry, shouldn't I? I finally realised what Adam had been telling me all along. I relied on her. Her thoughts were fact. Her opinions didn't just override mine, they overwrote them. She'd been the voice in the back of my head for so long that her views had become mine.

'I was only trying to help.'

Mum's hurt quiet voice tore at my heart. I hadn't needed to be so abrupt and dismissive. Mum was right, she was only trying to help. Maybe her methods weren't always ideal, but her intentions were good.

'I'm sorry, Mum.' I needed to fix my blunder, atone for my rudeness. 'I didn't mean to snap. It's just been a long day. Well, several days really.'

'Of course.' Mum was instantly forgiving. 'I doubt you've slept properly since all this began. You must be exhausted. Maybe you should have an early night.'

I glanced at the duvet wrapped around me. 'Yes, I think I might do that.'

'Well, I'll let you go. You can tell me everything first thing in the morning.'

'Hmm, tomorrow.' Another day. Another call. Another inquisition.

'But Jess, before you go...'

'Yes, Mum?' I braced myself.

'Are you sure you haven't seen my notebook?'

I rolled my eyes. 'No, Mum, I told you. I've not seen it.'

'Maybe I dropped it last time I was at your apartment. Maybe it could have fallen under the sofa, or something?'

'I'll take a look.'

'Tonight?'

I clamped my jaw closed. 'Sure,' I muttered through clenched teeth.

I hung up and put the phone back on the bedside cabinet. I pushed the duvet away and swung my legs out of bed. I may as well go and look for the notebook now, she was never going to relent until she found it.

My gaze fell upon the wardrobe facing the bed. The door was partially open, revealing a neat row of colours inside. I stepped forwards, opened the door wide and ran my hand across the soft materials. My fingers lingered on a short tight black skirt that

Adam had encouraged me to buy. I pulled it out and laid it on the bed along with the glittery scooped red top he'd loved seeing me in.

I turned back to the wardrobe and this time pulled out a loose-fitting pair of grey trousers and a smart dark blue shirt. They were Mum's choices. I laid them on the bed beside the skirt and top.

I studied the two sets of clothes. It was as though I was two people, one old and one new. But the irony was that neither was really me. I was who they told me to be.

I picked up the short skirt and held it against me as I studied my reflection in the mirrored wardrobe. Did I even like it? Or did I only think I liked it because that's what I was supposed to like? Because it's what Adam liked? Or because my mother didn't?

What was my style? Or for that matter, who was I without other people's input? Adam's tastes were younger, colourful and more flattering. The clothes he picked out were more my own age, but did that mean they were more me?

Were either really me? Perhaps I was neither one nor the other. Perhaps I lay somewhere in the middle; a mishmash of conflicting influences that formed something unique. I was none of it and I was all of it.

I'd rejected Mum's style for Adam's because he had made me feel different; vibrant and beautiful. But mostly he made me feel like I fitted in. I was no longer on the outskirts of everything, of fashion, of friendships, of life. I was part of it. I belonged.

But maybe it wasn't the new clothes that made me belong, maybe it wasn't even Adam, perhaps I would always have belonged, but I'd never tried to find out before. Perhaps neither of them were wrong. Their choices were based on what they believed were best for me. Perhaps the problem was only that I had listened too much. I hadn't just listened to their advice, considered it and made up my own mind. I had followed their opinions to the letter. I had let them guide me, steer me even. I was an extension of them because I'd never tried to be me.

I reached for the photo of Adam and me that sat beside the bed, we had taken it in the summer when we went hiking in the New Forest.

'You were right,' I told him, as I stared at his tanned face. 'I'd twisted myself up trying to be the person I thought I needed to be. But I didn't realise I was sacrificing myself to achieve it.'

I dropped down on the bed, still staring at the photo. It was the closest thing to Adam I had left.

'I've strived all my life for accomplishments that I didn't even want, all in some misguided effort to prove my worth. But what have I proved, besides how hard life is and how miserable it's made me?' My words gushed out in a torrent.

My successes hadn't made me feel like less of a failure, because success wasn't measured by what you achieved, but by how you lived. I could see that now. My qualifications; my career, it was all meaningless. A certificate was just a piece of paper when what it represented held no value to you.

'I'd been looking for a Prince Charming to come and save me.' I ran my finger across his face. 'I'd wanted you to be my hero and carry me off into my happy ever after. But maybe that was the problem. There are no Prince Charmings. There are no fairy-tales. The past should have taught me that.'

I brushed away my tears with the back of my hand. I knew the truth now. People were unreliable. Fallible. Adam was the same as the others after all. A disappointment.

I'd wanted Adam to love me. But maybe no one could. Not fully. Not properly. Perhaps this was the life I made for myself. A half-life. I'd cut myself off. How could I expect people to let me in, to love me, for me to be enough to occupy their interest and attention fully? How could anyone love me completely when I wasn't complete myself?

I needed approval, from Mum, Adam, my boss, even my colleagues. It was the only measure I had of my own self-worth. It was faulty thinking. I could see that now. I shouldn't need anyone's approval but my own.

The problem was I still didn't approve of myself.

I didn't even know how to start.

It was like hating sprouts your whole life, and then being told you should make yourself like them. They were still sprouts. They hadn't changed. I could cook them differently, hide them with gravy and sauces, attempt to mask them with flavours I did like, but underneath they were still sprouts.

28

THEN

I took another sip of wine as I sat on the sofa. It was the most relaxed I'd been all day. Christmas dinner was always hard work, but this year... I glanced at Adam beside me and then at Mum, who sat in the armchair opposite. I took a deep breath. I'd doubted the sanity of my bold idea to invite Mum to join Adam and me for Christmas. I was even more surprised when she'd actually accepted.

The day had gone surprisingly well so far. No arguments. No thinly veiled insults, well, not many, anyway. Now everyone was too sleepy from overeating to bother bickering. We'd survived.

'So, are you living here all the time now, then?'

I cringed. I was wrong. This had just been the lull before the storm.

'Not all the time, no,' Adam replied.

I lifted my glass to my lips. I was going to need more wine to get through the rest of the afternoon.

'I assume you're sleeping together.'

I coughed and spat the wine back into my glass. 'Mum!'

'Well, you are living together.'

'That's not really any of your business, Mrs Harper.'

I stared at Adam in awe of his polite restraint.

'I just want to make sure you know what you're getting yourself into, Jess. What if you get pregnant? What kind of mother would you be?' She shook her head.

I tried to speak; to voice my objections. What made her so certain I'd be a bad mother? I'd love to have kids, maybe not just yet, but someday. I could do that, couldn't I? I could look after them and love them. I could be a good mother. It was possible, wasn't it?

'I just don't want you making more of a mess of your life.'

'More of a mess?' I glared at her. 'Is that how you see my life? How you see me?'

'You know what I mean, Jess.'

'What I know is that Adam loves me and we want to have a future together.'

Mum scoffed.

'Why is that so hard to believe?' It was possible, wasn't it? He could love me? Really love me?

It was as though my dream of being in a relationship, of being married someday, was somehow an insult to her. Why was it so wrong for me to want someone to love me, to be with me? It wasn't mutually exclusive to loving her. It was just different.

'There was a time you wouldn't even contemplate speaking to your mother with that tone. You've changed.' Mum glared at Adam. 'He's changed you.'

'I'll walk you to the door,' Adam said, rising to his feet.

Mum glared at me. I could read her expression; her eyes questioning if I was really going to let him kick her out.

I didn't move. Apparently, I was.

She grunted and picked up her bag from the floor by her feet.

She always kept it with her when she visited, especially if Adam was home. She carried it around with her, never letting it out of her sight, as though she was afraid he might steal her purse. Another way of showing me that she didn't trust him.

She marched into the hall. Adam followed at her heels. He didn't trust her either.

Guilt gnawed at me. I hated being on bad terms with Mum. She was my mother. She deserved better from me. With a sigh, I walked towards the hall. Apologies were whirling in my head. I needed to smooth things over. I needed to fix it.

'You won't split us up, you know,' Adam said as he opened the front door. 'She loves me.'

Mum shrugged and smiled. That coy gloating smile that I'd seen thousands of times when she knew she'd won. 'Don't be too sure about that. I will get rid of you. Even if I have to do it myself.'

She slipped through the open doorway. My planned apologies slipped away with her. There was something about her tone, the sheer venom of it was bad enough, but the certainty of it sent a chill through my body.

Adam closed the door. As he turned, his gaze met mine and he smiled. 'She really doesn't like me, does she?'

I shook my head. 'You're dating me.' That was all the explanation that was needed.

He shrugged. 'Come on, let's go watch Netflix and forget about it.'

I nodded and we ambled back into the living room. Adam put the TV on and I watched as he scrolled through the films, searching for one he liked.

I couldn't get their conversation out of my head. It wasn't just Mum's words that bothered me. It was Adam's, too.

She loves me.

It felt one sided. I loved him, not we love each other.

I shook my head. I was being silly and reading too much into it. Adam loved me. I studied his profile, his gaze was locked on the TV screen.

Of course he loved me.

Didn't he?

29

NOW

I sighed at the sound of someone knocking on the door. It'd be Mum. It had to be. No one else ever came here. Except for Adam.

I grabbed the arm of the sofa, feeling as though the air had been sucked from my body.

Adam.

An image of his smiling face lodged itself firmly in my mind.

My Adam.

Except he wasn't mine. Not now. Not for a long time.

I shook my head, dislodging his presence, at least temporarily. He'd be back. Adam might have gone, but in some ways he was never far from me.

I swung my legs down off the sofa, rammed my feet into my slippers and shuffled to the hall. Why couldn't Mum believe me when I told her I was fine? I wanted to be alone. I needed to be. Why did she have to keep checking up on me?

I unlocked the door, already knowing the answer. Because I wasn't fine. Far from it. I sighed again and pulled the door open.

'Helen.' I stared at Adam's mother standing in front of me. My breath caught in my chest. Did her presence mean… I dug my nails into my palms, refusing to allow myself to finish that thought. 'Adam?'

Helen shook her head, her brown curls bobbing around her pale face. 'No, there's no news.'

I let out a deep breath. Part of me felt relieved. Part of me felt disappointed. The absence of news meant the waiting was prolonged. It was just delaying the inevitable. Maybe it would have been better to get it over with.

'I just...' Helen's voice cracked. 'I needed to talk to you.'

'Oh.' My chest tightened and I felt nauseous. 'Okay.'

I stepped back, opening the door wider so she could pass.

Talk.

It sounded so innocuous; so simple.

Helen stepped inside and I glanced through the open doorway at the now empty corridor outside my apartment. It seemed so inviting. I could just slip out...

My shoulders slumped and I closed the door, shutting us inside.

It felt strange having her there. I'd only met her and Adam's dad, Graham, once. That had been Adam's choice.

We don't live in each other's pockets, Jess.

I gritted my teeth. Even now, I could still hear the criticism in his voice. The unspoken 'I'm not like you' had hung between us.

He'd deemed my closeness to my mother to be a character flaw; a weakness.

'Would you like a cup of tea?' I asked, as I headed towards the kitchen without even waiting for her reply.

'All I want is my son.'

I froze. My legs seemed to forget how to walk. My knees felt weak and unsteady. All I could do was stand there like a statue. Waiting.

I heard Helen shift behind me. 'What happened, Jess?'

I turned slowly. I kept my eyes fixed on the floor, I couldn't bear to look at her. I dreaded to see the hatred in her eyes; the blame.

'Jess?'

I lifted my gaze and our eyes met. Her watery brown eyes stared at me.

A lump formed in my throat. All I could see in her expression was heartbreak and confusion.

'I don't know.' I forced the words out. They were true. At least partially.

She walked towards me. 'Why would he have been there?'

'He was working at the holid—'

'No.'

I jumped at the forcefulness of the word.

'Adam had finished that job.'

'Maybe they called him back. Maybe there was a problem.'

She shook her head. 'I called the company that operates the cottages. There weren't any issues. No one had called Adam back there.'

My stomach lurched. 'So there was no reason for him...'

I couldn't finish the sentence. I couldn't even finish the thought. Without a work-related reason, that meant...

'He stopped by on Friday evening,' Helen said.

'You saw him?'

Nausea churned inside me. If she'd seen him that night then... I swallowed. Adam could have told her we'd fought. She could know what I'd said. What I'd yelled at him. What if she'd told the police?

She nodded. 'He seemed different. Not himself.'

My hands trembled and I clasped them together. 'What do you mean?'

'Adam kept apologising for something that had happened

years ago. Something we didn't talk about. He told us how much he loved us, how sorry he was for his mistakes. It was as though he was saying…'

'What?'

Helen's lips parted, but then she shook her head. 'It doesn't matter.'

I edged forward, my heart pounded against my chest. 'You think he could have…' The words lodged in my throat. I swallowed again. 'You think he was saying goodbye.' I edged forwards. If he'd been saying goodbye then that meant he'd known he wasn't coming back. 'Could Adam have taken his own life?'

It was a bad thing to hope for. It wasn't that I wanted him to feel that lost, that desperate, but if it had been his choice…

The colour drained from Helen's face. 'I…' Her eyes glazed over. She turned away and stared at the pristine white wall ahead of her. She was probably reliving that moment, that goodbye. How many times had that memory already played in her mind? How many more times were still to come? It would be like an old movie, faded and worn but constantly with her.

Sympathy tugged at me, willing me to step forward and show support. A gentle hand on her arm, a hug, something, any small gesture that would let Helen know she wasn't alone.

But I couldn't.

She was alone.

I didn't share in her grief. Not in the same way. Adam's disappearance wasn't a loss that crushed against me. It was… I frowned as I searched for a word that fitted how I felt. Freedom.

The question was what lengths could I have gone to in order to achieve it?

I shook my head. If Adam had said goodbye, then maybe I hadn't killed him. Relief washed over me like a wave knocking me off balance. I reached out to steady myself against the wall.

I glanced at Helen, praying she hadn't noticed. I had to pull myself together. I couldn't let her know that there was a possibility that I could have been involved. No one could ever know.

Guilt churned my stomach. It felt wrong to be excited by the prospect that my boyfriend had killed himself. I should be mourning his death, not celebrating his sorrow.

I might not be a murderer, but I was still a bad girlfriend. Even if I hadn't physically pushed him off that cliff, perhaps in some way my actions had driven him there. At the very least I hadn't stopped him. How could he have reached such a dark, desperate place where suicide had been the only way out without me even noticing?

'Maybe...' I clung to the only possibility that could fully redeem me. 'Maybe Adam is okay. Maybe he survived.'

Helen turned and stared at me as silent tears trickled down her face.

'We don't know he's dead.' I closed my eyes, willing it to be true. 'Not for sure.'

'But he might be.'

The hollowness of Helen's voice made my eyes fly open.

'A mother shouldn't have to bury her son.'

The refrigerator hummed in the background as we stared at one another in silence.

'What I don't know is why.' She squinted as her gaze locked on to mine. 'But you know, Jess.'

I couldn't move; couldn't think.

'You must know something. You're his girlfriend. He talked to you; he confided in you.'

She turned away and walked towards the sofa in my open-plan living room. Her hand rested on the back of it as though she needed its support to hold her up.

'His dad and I didn't even know Adam was having money issues again.'

Again.

'Why didn't he come to us for help, Jess? I know we were tough on him last time. It had been a shock. We'd been disappointed. Too much so.' She hung her head. 'Perhaps we were too hard on him.' She swung back to face me. 'But we still loved him. He was still our son.'

I nodded as though I agreed. But agreed with what?

I should just ask her what she was talking about. What had happened in the past? How had it changed him?

But I couldn't.

It would be like admitting I'd never really known him at all.

'You think his money issues are the same as before?' I asked cautiously.

'No, that was all over. It ended when he met you.' She smiled at me, full of tenderness and admiration. 'He changed when he met you. You were so good for him, Jess.'

I shifted awkwardly. She was grateful to me; glad that her son had met me. It felt wrong. I felt wrong.

'How did he change?'

She tilted her head to the side. 'Didn't you see it?'

I shook my head.

'No.' She nodded slowly. 'I suppose you wouldn't. Adam always said you only saw the good in him.' She smiled again. 'I think that's what inspired him. He wanted to live up to the vision you had of him. He wanted to be the man you saw him as.'

I walked to the sofa in a daze and sank onto the leather seat.

'He was good.'

In the beginning.

Wasn't he? I rubbed my forehead. From the way Helen spoke,

maybe he hadn't even been good then. Maybe everything had been a lie. An act.

I tried to shake that thought away. I needed to believe he loved me so I could redeem the image I had of him in my head. So I could still hold onto the notion that despite his flaws and the knowledge that we'd have never worked, he did love me once.

Because if it was all a lie, if he never really loved me at all, then maybe no one ever would. Maybe no one could.

Helen put her hand on my shoulder. 'Which is why none of this makes sense. That police officer said Adam was on the verge of having his van repossessed. His rent hasn't been paid in months either. I've been to his flat; most of his stuff has gone, there's barely anything left.'

'Where did it go?'

'It's not here?'

I shook my head.

'You were living together.'

'Not really. Not yet. Adam had only brought a few things over. We were planning on making it permanent, but then...' My voice failed me.

But then things changed.

'Didn't you notice his stuff was disappearing from his flat?'

I stared at her blankly. 'I've never been to his flat.'

'Never?'

I shook my head. 'He didn't want me to.'

'Oh.'

There was something about the way she said that word that spoke volumes. She thought it was strange.

It *was* strange. He had a separate place that I'd never been to. A secret.

'Were you two having problems?'

I didn't answer. I couldn't. I waited for the accusations. The questions. Why was Adam drinking? Why whisky? Something must have triggered it. Something between us. Did she'd know that we rowed? Or that the last words I'd spoken to him had been fuelled by anger and hurt?

'Jess, I know it's not something you'd want to discuss with me but,' she shrugged 'the police asked me yesterday.'

'What did you say to them?'

'I said no, Adam was the happiest I'd seen him in a long time. But...'

The hairs on the back of my neck bristled. 'But what?'

'Something was wrong, Jess.' Helen stared at me. Her brown eyes boring into my soul. 'He was almost broke, his apartment cleared out, the bottle of whisky in his van...'

'You think he was drunk?'

'Do you?'

I licked my dry lips. 'I don't know what to think.'

'Why whisky, Jess? It wasn't like him.' She took a step towards me. 'None of this is like him.'

I swallowed. 'I know.' Nausea rose in my throat. 'I failed him.'

Helen's eyes widened.

'He needed help and I let him down. I hadn't been there for him. I couldn't have been.' I shook my head. 'Otherwise I would have noticed, I would have realised there was something more going on. Something wrong.'

Had I been too preoccupied by his betrayal that I had missed the real issue?

It felt as though Adam was slipping from me. I'd started to lose him weeks ago. He'd told me I was wrong, I was paranoid.

Like before.

But maybe the affair had been a cry for help, a desperate plea for attention. Had I neglected him so much that he'd felt he had to go elsewhere for comfort?

'I'll make us that tea.' I leapt to my feet, hurried to the kitchen and filled the kettle with water. I needed to keep moving; keep busy. It was the only way to keep my mind from straying. It made sense now; that compulsion Mum had to make cups of tea when anything was wrong. It wasn't about the tea. It was about having something to do.

'Jess?'

I swung round.

'Are you all right?'

I nodded. I didn't trust myself to speak.

'I'm sorry.'

Her apology threw me.

'I forgot how hard this must be for you. You must miss Adam so much.'

'I do.' The revelation startled me. 'More than I expected.' But then I hadn't expected to miss him at all.

You can't keep doing this to me, Adam. I won't let you!

The words I'd spat at him the night before his disappearance seeped into my brain. I'd hated him in that moment. That hatred had carried me through the last few days. But what if I was wrong? What if I'd judged him too harshly? What if there was more to his actions? An explanation? A reason?

Helen wrapped her arms around me and pulled me into a hug. I froze. Every muscle in my body tensed. I didn't deserve her sympathy; her compassion. I'd failed her son. I'd given up on him; on us.

A sob escaped my lips as I gave up the fight to hold back my tears. Helen hugged me tighter. 'It's okay, Jess. Let it out.'

* * *

I lay on my bed after Helen had left. Her visit had been exhausting. Or perhaps it had been my tears. They'd seemed endless. It was the first time I'd allowed myself to cry properly in years. I'd cried for Adam; for us; but mostly for myself.

Being the centre of Adam's attention had been amazing, like being seen for the first time in years. Seen and admired. But his attention had wavered. I couldn't keep it.

The spotlight went out and I'd become invisible again.

I'd tried to keep him; to make him see me. But I'd known I was failing. I wasn't enough. Somehow, I'd fallen short. Just like always.

I stared at the photo of us on my bedside cabinet. I should move it; put it away somewhere in a drawer, out of sight. But I couldn't. It was a reminder of what we'd had. It was a perfect memory of an imperfect life.

'What did I do wrong, Adam?'

Silence was the only answer.

Perhaps that was the answer. Nothing.

I frowned. Was that even possible? Had the failings in our relationship not been my fault? Or at least not entirely?

I'd always assumed it was me that was wrong. Somehow.

But what if it wasn't me? What if it was him?

I shuffled up in bed and picked up the frame.

Why did my visibility and relevance depend on him?

I had so many restrictions on my life. I thought they'd come from me; from my fears; my inadequacies. But what if they'd come from Mum's insecurities? She'd repeated them; undermining my confidence until her fears and priorities had become my own. And I'd let her.

It wasn't that I wasn't important. Just that everything else was more important. I could wait because that's what I'd always done.

I put myself last because that was my place. I wasn't good enough to be first.

I'd spent years feeling trapped; like I was biding my time getting though life, waiting for it to get better, instead of actually living it and doing what I wanted.

And then Adam saw me. For the first time in so long, someone had seen through my invisibility and liked me for who I was. I was good enough. I was better than just good enough; I was beautiful and wanted.

For a little while.

30

THEN

I studied my reflection in the beauty counter mirror and fluttered my heavily outlined eyelids. 'Are you sure about this colour?'

The beauty assistant kept her head down as she cleaned her brushes after applying my shimmer silver eyeshadow and black eyeliner.

'Absolutely,' Adam replied beside me.

'But it's so shiny.'

'It's striking.' Adam kissed my forehead. 'Like you.'

I stared at him. I wasn't striking. I never had been. I'd always been subtle and understated. I turned back to the mirror and frowned. They were two things this new shade of eyeshadow definitely couldn't be described as.

'How do you even know the names of eyeshadow colours anyway?'

'Huh?'

'You asked the assistant for this particular shade.'

'Did I?' Adam shrugged. 'I must have seen it on the display over there.' He nodded towards the counter beside us.

Funny, I hadn't even noticed him looking at it earlier. I took a step towards the display.

'Come on, Jess.' Adam slid his hand in mine and tugged me towards the till. 'Let's pay for your new make-up and then get some lunch. I haven't got long.'

'What do you mean?' I asked as the assistant scanned the eyeshadow and liner through the till. 'We're spending the whole Saturday afternoon together, aren't we?'

'Sorry.' Adam shrugged. 'Another job cropped up.'

I pouted. 'Oh, Adam. You promised you wouldn't take any more jobs at weekends for a while.'

'I know, but...' He shrugged again.

I tapped my card against the card reader, and tried not to cringe at the price. Adam's insistence on upgrading my image was getting expensive. In the beginning he'd have paid for the make-up himself. His treat, he would have called it. Now he just stepped back and waited for me to swipe my card.

I didn't mind, it was for me after all. I frowned. Wasn't it?

I rolled my eyes. Of course it was. Just because it wasn't something I would usually have bought for myself, it didn't mean anything. Adam was just helping me find a better style, a better me, the same as he'd always done.

'We barely spend any time together these days,' I told him as I waited for the receipt.

'We spend nearly every night together.'

'True, but it's not exactly quality time, is it? You're so exhausted you sit in front of the telly until it's time to sleep.'

Adam glanced at the assistant and steered me away from the counter, before I'd barely taken the receipt out of her hand.

'I've got a lot of work on at the moment. In my line of work, you take what you can get.'

'I appreciate that, but—' I clamped my mouth closed. I

sounded whiny and needy. I didn't mean to be. I fully understood the pressures of obligations. He was self-employed. Of course he would take work when it was offered. He couldn't guarantee that the work would still be there tomorrow, he had to take it while he could.

But it still didn't make me feel any better. Rational explanations weren't enough to shift the disconcerting feeling I had that Adam was pulling away from me.

I was waiting for the inevitable. That moment when I ceased to be useful; when I'd served my purpose. The point at which I was no longer relevant and would become invisible again. It was the loneliest feeling. It always had been, but now it would be worse, because he'd actually noticed me. For the first time in so long, someone had actually treated me like I mattered. To go from that to irrelevant would be a much bigger and harder fall.

'But what?'

I screwed my nose up, contemplating how to answer.

'Jess, just tell me what you're thinking. You know you can tell me anything.'

'I guess I just can't help wondering if you still love me the same way.'

I'd given up on love a long time ago. It was safer. I had nothing, therefore I had nothing to lose. And then I'd met Adam. Now I had dreams again. I had hopes. I had love. But it was fragile and new. It wasn't strong enough to withstand rejections and setbacks. I wasn't strong enough.

Adam rolled his eyes. 'Why are you like that? Why can't you believe that you're special? Why can't you accept that I want to be with you? That I love you?'

I opened my mouth, but the words wouldn't come.

Adam's face looked pinched and pale. 'Just because other

people have let you down, just because they've left you, it doesn't mean I'm the same.'

His reminder dug into my heart. 'I didn't... I don't... I...' I ran out of words. I wanted to protest, to deny it. I wanted to reassure him that I didn't think that, not about him. But I couldn't.

How could I be sure that he wasn't the same?

'If I'm not being useful, I'm not relevant.' I fumbled for the words that would make him understand. 'So now I guess I question why people are in my life. I always wonder what they really want.'

Why would he be interested in you?

I screwed my eyes closed trying to block out Mum's voice.

'There's a reason we met. I see a lot of things in you that you don't.'

'Maybe. But to me it feels like you're talking about someone else. You just haven't realised it yet. But when you do...' I shrugged. 'Then you'll leave.'

He took a deep breath. 'What more can I do to convince you? You can't live your life being dubious and cautious all the time. It's impossible.'

Impossible.

The word repeated in my head. Was it, though? Really? It was how I lived. I had done for years. I'd proved it was possible. 'It's not good, but it's possible.'

Adam shook his head. 'But you're not really living.'

I stared at him as his words circled in my head. Was he right?

'Things are good, Jess. We're good.' He pulled me to him. 'Stop looking for problems where there aren't any. Just accept things as they are. We're happy, aren't we?'

I nodded. 'Of course.'

My response was automated. Expected.

But was it real? Was I happy? Really happy? We had been once, I knew that. Adam had moved into my apartment, into my life. It had been romantic at first. Everything I'd hoped for. And then...

Somewhere it had changed.

Hadn't it?

I nibbled my lower lip. Or maybe Adam was right. I was creating issues where none existed.

31

NOW

I sat in the chair PC Davidson indicated, as he sat down opposite. I was back at the station again. Back in this room. With him.

I didn't like him. He was too persistent. Relentless.

'This interview is being recorded,' DC Fisher said, as he pressed a button on the recorder at the side of him.

I stared at him, his words causing my stomach to lurch as he stated our location, date, time and our names. It was so formal.

His eyes met mine. 'You aren't under arrest and are free to leave at any time. You are entitled to have a solicitor present during the interview, if you wish.'

I shook my head. What could a solicitor do for me? They would just be yet another person with questions I couldn't answer.

'You do not have to say anything but it may harm your defence if you don't mention when questioned, something which you later rely on in court. Anything you do say may be given in evidence.'

I swallowed. How had it come to this?

Again.

'I see there have been issues in the past,' PC Davidson said.

I turned to face him. 'Not with Adam.'

'But with previous relationships...'

'There were some misunderstandings.' I shuffled. No, I really didn't like PC Davidson. His relentlessness was bad enough, but his knack of dragging up the past was worse.

'Thanks again for picking me up.' Paul smiled at me from the passenger seat, as I pulled up on the drive, but his face looked lined and drawn.

'No problem.' I pulled the handbrake on and rested my hand on his knee. 'You know I'm always here for you.'

'I know, babe.' Paul placed his hand over mine. 'I'm sorry things have been a bit strained between us recently.'

I cringed. I hated being called that, but I pasted a smile on my face. 'That's in the past.' I shrugged. 'We don't need to think about that now.'

'Well, I'm glad I've got you in my corner, especially on days like today.'

'Always.' I shook my head slowly. 'I still can't believe someone would do that to your car.'

Paul's eyes narrowed. 'Not just someone.'

I stared at him in surprise. 'You know who did it?'

He nodded slowly. 'I have a pretty good idea.'

My breath caught in my chest. 'Did you tell the police?'

'Not yet, I wanted to be sure first.'

'How?' I swallowed.

Paul laughed. 'I haven't worked that out yet. But I will.' He kissed my forehead. 'Don't worry.'

I tried to muster a smile.

'We should get moving. I know your mum hates it if we're late.'

'We don't have to do this tonight.' I glanced at the house in front of us. 'I could just drive you home, Mum would understand.'

Paul shook his head. 'Hey, I finally got an invite for dinner. I told you my charm would wear her down eventually. You think I'm going to blow it now by not turning up?' He winked at me as he smiled that cheeky smile of his.

I laughed. 'You're right, this is a good sign.' I spoke softly. Afraid to say the words too loudly in case I jinxed it. But Paul was right. Over the last few weeks Mum had gradually seemed less resistant to his presence in my life.

This time Paul's smile reached his eyes. 'Come on, then, let's not destroy my hard work by sitting in her driveway talking.'

I opened my door. 'I'll just get the groceries from the boot.'

'I'll give you a hand.'

Paul met me at the back of the car and smiled at me as I opened the boot and picked up a couple of bags.

He reached for the others but stopped and frowned. 'What's this?'

I followed his gaze and shrugged. 'I don't know. I noticed it earlier and wondered where it had come from.'

Paul stood up straight and glared at me. 'It was you.'

I shifted the heavy bags in my hands and glanced back at Paul. 'What was me?'

'How could you do it?' He ran his hand through his hair.

I blinked, stunned at the hostility in his voice.

'Do what? I haven't done anything.'

'You trashed my car.'

'What?' I stared at him, my jaw hanging open as my mind raced. His words didn't make sense.

Paul leaned into the boot and picked up the spray can. He waved it in front of my face. 'You put graffiti on my car.'

A bubble of nervous laughter escaped my lips. 'That's ridiculous. Why would you ever think that?'

'You have spray paint in your car.'

'It's not mine. I told you, I don't know where that came from.'

'It's in your boot, Jess.'

'Yeah, but—'

'It's the same colour that was used on my car.'

'What? You said your car had been damaged, you didn't mention anything about paint.'

'Gold paint.'

I stared at the can. 'Well, that doesn't mean—'

Paul slapped his forehead. 'How did I not see it? The word sprayed on my car, of course it was you. It's what you've been accusing me of all week.'

'Word? What word?'

'I thought it was a guy from work. He accused me of cheating him out of a deal. I thought it was just sour grapes. A bit of payback.' He shook his head. 'How could I have been so stupid?

'What word?'

'Cheat, Jess. They wrote cheat. You wrote cheat.'

I stared at him. My fingers were numb where the bag handles dug into my skin.

'How many times do I have to tell you, I'm not having an affair? There was no one else, Jess. Only you.'

'Paul, I—'

'No!' Paul flung the can back in the boot. 'I don't want to hear it.'

'But—'

'You're nuts, Jess.' He shook his head as he stared at me. There was something about his expression. It wasn't just anger. It was revulsion. 'I'm done.'

Paul took a step back and started to turn away.

'Paul!' The shopping bags tumbled from my hands as I grabbed his arm.

He yanked free of my grasp. 'Stay the hell away from me. I never want to see you again.'

Paul marched down the driveway. I stared after him. He was leaving. Another man walking out of my life.

My vision blurred. I felt dizzy. I reached out to steady myself but there was nothing there. I fell to my knees amongst dented tins of soup before everything went black.

'You were arrested for criminal damage.'

'Paul claimed I'd vandalised his car.'

'Because you suspected him of cheating on you.'

'I didn't do it. He dropped the charges.'

'Because your mother paid for the repairs.'

'No, because I was innocent.'

'But she did pay...'

I shrugged. 'She wanted to help. It's her way.'

'To help Paul, or to help you?'

I swallowed. Mum thought money could solve everything. She'd thought it would solve the 'Paul issue' as she called it. She was right. It had. In a way. But did she pay for the repairs just to make the problem go away, or because she believed I was guilty?

My memory of that day was clear. I drove to work, ploughed through endless emails, ate lunch alone at my desk, and stopped at Sainsbury's on the way home. Until I received Paul's phone call asking me to give him a ride, the day had been the same as any other. Normal. Routine. No detours to buy paint. No stalking my boyfriend to find out where he parked. No vandalising his car.

My protests about my innocence weren't just about the things I couldn't remember, but the things I could. I remembered that day. All of it.

And yet the can of paint had been in my car. How could Mum argue with that? How could I?

'And the restraining order?'

Stay away from me, Jess.

I winced. 'Mike accused me of stalking him.'

'Another mistake?'

'Yes.'

'So you'd never followed him?'

I shuffled. 'I did once.'

PC Davidson nodded. There was a smugness to his expression, as though he'd caught me out.

'But only once.'

'And that just happened to be the time that Mike caught you?'

'Yes.'

'That seems coincidental, doesn't it?'

I could hear the disbelief in his voice. But it didn't matter. It was the truth. I had only followed him once.

That you can remember.

I shook my head. It *had* only been once.

'And what about Adam? Was he a mistake?'

'Adam was different.'

'How so?'

'He stayed.' The admission slipped easily from my lips. That had been Adam's best quality. The thing I'd valued most in our relationship. He'd stayed. Even when he shouldn't. Even when it may have been better for both of us if he'd left. He'd still stayed.

32

THEN

I kicked my heels off as I closed the front door behind me. It had been a crazy day. Work was busy enough at the best of times without spending my lunch break with Mum at the bank. Of all days to have to help her open a new account, it had to fall on the same day as my interview for the promotion.

'Can't we go another day, Mum?'

'I've made the appointment already.'

'Surely they could rearrange it if you asked?'

'This is the best interest rate, Jessica. If we dawdle the rate may go down.'

'But surely one more day won't hurt—'

'I'm doing this for you. I'm investing in a bond that will be yours when I'm not around.'

'I know, Mum, and I appreciate that—'

'So, you won't mind coming with me then, will you?'

I swallowed. 'Of course not.' I was being selfish. She was doing something thoughtful for my future and I was grumbling about inconvenient timing. How petty was I?

'Good. I'm glad that's settled. Now, don't forget to bring your power of attorney documents and proof of ID.'

'Yes, Mum.'

I took a deep breath as I dropped my bag on the sofa and slipped off my grey suit jacket. It had felt strange having an interview where I already worked. With my manager on the panel, it meant he knew my skills and experience almost as well as I did. It was odd describing situations I felt I had excelled in while he sat there studying me, no doubt questioning my recollection and interpretation.

I pulled my phone from my bag and checked it for messages again.

Nothing.

There was a time when Adam would have asked. He'd have sent me a message. Just a line. 'How did it go?' It was all that it took to make me feel warm and wanted. He'd cared. He'd remembered. He'd asked.

But that was then.

I sighed.

Maybe he was busy. Maybe he hadn't noticed the time.

Or maybe he'd forgotten. Perhaps the information had slipped from his brain a split second after he'd nodded his acknowledgement this morning as I'd headed out in the smartest suit I owed.

How had we gone from where we were to this? How had I slipped from his memory with such ease?

I dropped the phone on the sofa beside my bag and the envelope with the power of attorney caught my eye. I pulled it from my bag and walked to the filing cabinet beside my desk.

'Adam doesn't need to know about this, Jess,' Mum had said as I met her in town outside the bank.

'Do you think he cares if you're opening a new account? It's not as though you're about to include him, is it?'

Mum stared at me. 'Absolutely not.'

'Well then.' I rolled my eyes and pushed the door open.

'Jess?' I turned back to see Mum still standing outside, her hand on her hip.

I held my hand up. 'Okay, okay, I'm not going to say anything.'

I heard the front door open. My hand froze with the envelope poised over the open drawer as I turned my head to the hall behind me. My heart soared. 'Adam! You're home early.' I beamed at him.

'Hey, Jess.' He dumped his tool bag in the hall and clunked into the living room in his trainers.

I glared at his feet. I hated it when he wore his shoes inside. Now I would have to mop the floor again.

He leaned towards me and kissed my cheek. 'What are you doing?'

'Oh.' I felt my cheeks flush as I followed his gaze to the envelope in my hand. 'Just some filing.' I rammed the envelope into an empty suspension file and slammed the drawer closed. 'What are you doing home so early?'

I couldn't keep the smile off my face. Obviously he hadn't forgotten about my interview after all. He just wanted to hear all the details in person instead over a text message.

Adam shrugged. 'I finished work early so I thought I'd go for a workout.'

My shoulders sagged. 'You're going to the gym? Now?'

'Yep, just dropped in to pick up my bag.'

'But...' I willed him to remember my interview.

He arched an eyebrow.

I could remind him.

'Aren't you... tired?' I asked lamely. It wouldn't be the same if I had to prompt him. I wanted him to ask; I wanted him to be interested, because he cared, not because he felt obliged to.

'No, I'm good. It was an easy day today.' He gave my cheek another kiss, and marched off to the bedroom.

I stared after him. 'Adam, your...' I sighed. 'Shoes.' He wasn't listening.

I shook my head. Well, it looked like I was going to be spending the evening alone.

'Bye, Jess,' Adam called as he headed out of the front door with his gym bag slung over his shoulder.

I picked up Adam's headphones from where he'd tossed them aside on the sofa last night. I might as well tidy up, at least it would be a distraction from the ache in my chest. I wrapped the wire neatly around the headphones and slid them into the cupboard beneath the TV. Everything had a place. Or at least it should. I just wasn't sure what my place was any more.

I turned back and frowned. Adam's sweater sat in a heap on the floor beside the sofa. I rolled my eyes as I picked it up. I folded it neatly and carried it to the bedroom where it belonged in a drawer.

I had the unsettling impression that Adam was starting to feel more at home in my apartment than I did.

I put his sweater away and picked up the laundry basket from the corner of the room. It weighed heavily in my hands as I carried to the kitchen. It was always full since Adam had started staying here. He never emptied it. He never used the washing machine.

It's not my apartment.

Adam laughed it off with a shrug, as though he didn't like to use something that wasn't his. Funny how he never minded using my TV.

I sighed as I pulled out a couple of his T-shirts and slung them into the washing machine. I reached back into the basket and picked up a pair of his black jeans. I shoved my hand into a pocket; a tip my mother had taught me. Always check the pockets for stray coins and tissues before washing. I moved onto the next pocket and pulled out a slip of paper. I smiled slightly. Mum's advice was always right.

I glanced at the paper. It was a receipt. I started to set it down on top of the washing machine but the words across the top caught my attention.

Level Eight.

The jeans slid from my hand as my grip tightened on the receipt.

I'll take you there one day.

Adam's promise echoed in my ears. One day.

I scanned the page for the date. It seemed one day had been yesterday. Except only one of us had gone.

I saw the price and my eyes widened.

Champagne.

The sound of my breathing filled the kitchen as I staggered to the breakfast bar. A bottle of champagne wasn't something you bought when drinking alone. It wasn't something Adam would buy with his friends, either. Champagne was expensive and special. It was saved for things that mattered. People who mattered.

I perched on the breakfast bar stool. I used to think everything would work out eventually. Life was bad right now, but I just had to ride it out and it would get better.

Adam was my 'better'.

I placed the crumpled receipt on the breakfast bar and ran my hand across it, attempting to straighten the creases.

I'd been wrong. He wasn't better. He was worse. A new level of bad that I hadn't seen coming. Perhaps I should have done.

Perhaps I had been negligent. Complacent. I'd never been good at keeping things I loved, or more accurately, people I loved.

One minute they were my world and the next... I closed my eyes and took a deep breath. No, I mustn't think about them. Not now. Not ever.

It was the past. I'd moved on. I'd kept going. What else could I do?

And this time?

I opened my eyes and glared at the receipt.

Adam had betrayed me. The worst part was Mum was right about him. She was always right. I hated that. It ate into me. I'd defended him. Fought for him. But in the end it had been for nothing. Mum had won. Again.

Perhaps I should listen to her more. Why did I go against her when she was just looking out for me?

I pulled my phone from the pocket of my jeans. I wanted to talk to her. She was the one person who had never failed me. I needed to hear her reassurances that everything would be okay.

I paused, the phone nestled in my hand, its screen still blank.

But with Mum there would be no reassurances. No sympathetic support. Only 'I told you so'. She'd demand I kick Adam out and stop taking his calls. My world would instantly shrink. It would be just her and I. Like before.

But it didn't have to be that way. I set the phone down beside me.

I had choices. I always had choices.

I could confront him.

Would he admit it? Or would he protest his innocence, deny the evidence and attempt to come up with a plausible explanation?

Which would be worse?

I could follow him. I could gather more evidence and confirm my suspicions. But did I want to? What good would that certainty do me?

I picked up the receipt. My hands trembled as I held it. It was strange to think how much power that one tiny slip of paper held. It could destroy everything, or…

I tore the receipt in half, then half again and again until white paper confetti fluttered down on the breakfast bar.

I'd made my choice.

Denial.

It probably wasn't wise. It certainly wasn't healthy. But it was done now. The evidence had been destroyed as though it had never existed. Except it had. I'd seen it and its image lingered in my memory. It wouldn't be so easy to remove it from there.

But I would try.

Practice makes perfect.

It had been an error. A moment of weakness. He'd stumbled, but that didn't mean what we had should be discarded. It just meant we had to start again. I would be better this time. I would be more attentive; more useful; more… everything. He wouldn't need to seek companionship elsewhere. I could be everything he needed. I would be.

I could do what I'd always done; act. My mask had slipped since I'd met him. I'd let my guard down. I'd confided in him. I'd shown him my fears; my insecurities. I thought he understood; appreciated it even. I'd opened up to him. Been honest about who I was.

Not completely.

I couldn't deny it. I hadn't told him everything. There was a boundary to my honesty. It was convenient, but it existed. Except perhaps it wasn't about my lack of honesty. Maybe it was more about my lack of trust.

I didn't have faith in him not to turn away from me if he knew my whole story. I couldn't count on him. I couldn't count on anyone.

In some ways it was as though I was testing him. If he didn't run away from the little things, then maybe in time...

I shook my head. Clearly, he had failed my test.

33

NOW

I took a deep breath as I fastened the seat belt in Mum's Ford. This was our routine now. First the police interrogated me, and then Mum.

'So?' She stared at me, waiting for the second-by-second replay.

'They've reviewed my police record.'

Mum took a sharp intake of breath. 'I wondered when that would come up.'

I shrugged. 'It's not a big deal. It's not like I was ever charged or anything.'

'But you were questioned a couple of times and even arrested once.'

'Thanks for the reminder.'

'We can't ignore this, Jess. It's too big. We should get you a lawyer.'

'I don't need a lawyer.'

'This is the second time you've been called in for questioning. You need a lawyer.'

'Maybe,' I admitted grudgingly. I crossed my arms across my chest. 'But I still don't want one. It would make me look guilty.'

Mum sighed. 'Do they know about the psychologist?'

'Probably.'

'What did they say?'

'Nothing. Yet. But it was part of the deal with Mike, wasn't it? He dropped the stalking charges if I agreed to see a psychologist. It must be in the records somewhere.'

Mum rubbed her head with her hand. 'Oh, Jess, how do you keep getting yourself into these messes?'

I nibbled the inside of my cheek. 'I wish I knew. I really wish I knew.'

Mum started the engine and we edged forwards. 'What else did they ask?'

I shuffled.

'Jess?'

'It's not what they asked...' I took a deep shaky breath. 'It's what they found.'

'What did they find?' The car veered as Mum's head jolted around to face me.

'Scuff marks.'

'What?' Mum glanced back at the road and slowed as we approached the exit.

'In the gravel. They said...' I closed my eyes. 'They said it indicated that Adam's van wasn't driven off the cliff. It was pushed.'

I jolted forwards as the car stalled.

* * *

'You should at least come home for some dinner,' Mum said as she pulled up in front of my apartment block.

'I have food here.'

Mum grunted.

'I'll be fine.' I reached for the door handle, but paused. 'If Gran and Grandad...' My voice cracked as I eyed Mum nervously. It was risky to mention her parents. It never went well. But something compelled me to voice the question that had been tormenting me for days. 'If they hadn't died the way they did, or when they did, we wouldn't have moved to Bournemouth, would we?'

Mum's eyes narrowed and she stared at me silently.

'I mean, we had our own home, our own lives. If we hadn't moved here then—'

'Bournemouth isn't responsible for your failed relationships, Jessica.' Mum's tone was sharp and disapproving.

I squirmed. 'I know.'

I hung my head. It was a betrayal for me to try to blame Bournemouth, to blame my grandparents. Logically I knew that nothing that had happened had been their fault. But some part of me still disagreed. If we hadn't moved here, I would never have met Adam. I'd never have met any of the men in my life.

'Thanks for the lift.' I slid out of the door and trudged towards the building and up the stairs. There was also the possibility that if we hadn't moved to Bournemouth, then maybe Dad wouldn't have left us. Maybe we would still be a family.

I unlocked the door to my apartment and pushed it open. My phone beeped in my pocket, I pulled it out and sighed at the low battery warning that flashed on the screen.

I kicked off my shoes and padded to the breakfast bar in my socks. My hand instinctively reached for the phone charger. I froze with my hand outstretched. It wasn't there.

I scanned the empty breakfast bar, before stepping back and checking the floor; perhaps it had fallen off the counter. I frowned. Still nothing.

I pivoted on the spot as my eyes scanned the open-plan

kitchen and living room. Had I moved the charger? I didn't recall moving it. It was Adam's. I hadn't moved anything of his yet. I couldn't.

The charger had sat on the breakfast bar just as it had always done.

'It's the perfect place for it.'

Adam's voice echoed in my memory from the one occasion when I had tried to persuade him to put it away in a drawer when it wasn't in use.

'There's no point putting it away today, when I'd only have to get it back out again tomorrow.'

So it had stayed.

Until now.

I shook my head. It was silly to be worried about something as insignificant as a phone charger, I had another. But its disappearance bothered me. It belonged to Adam. An eerie hollowness settled in my stomach. It felt careless to lose something of his. Like I had lost him.

What if I was starting to forget him? Forget us?

You know your memory isn't reliable.

It was one thing to forget the bad things, but with Adam it hadn't always been bad. There were good things too. Things I wanted to remember. Things I needed to.

* * *

The upbeat ringtone of my phone interrupted the silence. I glanced at the caller ID.

Karen.

I hesitated.

I didn't really want to answer. I didn't want to talk. Not to anyone. But at the same time, I was touched she kept calling.

Calling once would have been out of obligation, but Karen had called every day. She hadn't needed to. She had done her part as a concerned colleague. Yet she called anyway. She called because she wanted to. She cared.

I picked up the phone.

'Hey, Jess. How are you doing?'

It was always the first question she asked and I still didn't know how to answer. What was the correct reply in this situation? A standard 'fine, thanks', had got me through my whole adult life. At least until I'd met Karen. She didn't buy it. Not then and certainly not now.

'I'm…' I searched for the right words. 'I'm still here.'

My answer was too honest. It told her too much. I was hanging on; going through the motions; surviving each day.

'I know it doesn't seem like it at the moment, but it will get easier.'

I heard the compassion in Karen's voice. She was an eternal optimist. She always believed tomorrow would be better.

She thought my response was a temporary state. But the truth was, when I thought about it, my whole life could be summed up by that one sentence; I'm still here. Not necessarily living. Just existing.

Adam had been right about that, after all.

'I have some good news for you.' I heard excitement in Karen's voice.

I sat up straight. 'Adam?' He was my first instinct. My first thought. Even though it didn't make sense. Why would Karen have news about Adam?

'Oh, Jess, I'm sorry. It's not about Adam.'

'No, of course not.' I shook my head as I tried to keep my disappointment from my voice.

'It's about work.' Karen was more hesitant now; I'd killed her excitement with one single word. 'But maybe it's not the right time.'

'No, it's fine.' Guilt churned my stomach. She'd been trying to cheer me up and I'd made her feel bad.

'Well, the management team wanted me to talk to you. Normally they would have called you themselves, but under the circumstances they didn't like to intrude.'

'Management want to talk to me?' My head span. How could that be good news? Management only spoke to me if there was a problem. Had I done something wrong? Had I taken too much time off? It was only Friday. I'd been out of the office for the whole week, but I had holiday time accrued.

'They want to offer you the promotion.'

I blinked. 'Promotion?'

'You had the interview for it last week.'

'Right.' I chastised myself for my stupidity. 'Was it only last week? It feels like a lifetime ago.'

'I'm not surprised. You've had a lot to deal with.'

'They really picked me?'

Karen laughed. 'Don't sound so surprised. I told you you'd get it.'

'I know, but...'

'You didn't believe me.'

I cringed. 'No.'

She laughed again, before her tone turned more serious. 'I'm so proud of you, Jess.'

Something contracted in my chest.

I'm proud of you, Jessie.

Those were good words. Powerful words.

They were some of the last words Dad had said to me, as he dropped me off at school that morning before he'd left.

I squinted as I tried to catch hold of the memory, but it was fragmented and faded. I couldn't even recall what he'd been proud of me for. At the time it probably hadn't seemed that important. Only his pride in me had mattered.

'You should be proud of yourself too, Jess.'

I nodded instinctively to Karen's instruction.

Was I proud of myself? Had I ever been?

Besides Dad, no one else had been proud of me before. Perhaps I hadn't done anything to be proud of. Or perhaps the bar was always set too high. A passing grade should have been a distinction. An award was always greeted with a question of why it had taken so long.

'Jess?'

'Hmm?' I pulled myself back from my thoughts.

'Do you think you'll accept the promotion?'

'I...' my mind went blank.

'You don't have to decide right now.' Karen's words were hurried. 'I didn't mean to rush you. I was just curious. Management know you may need a little time to think things through.'

I nodded slowly. Time. Yes, I needed time to think.

'But personally, I hope you take it. You deserve it, Jess. You'd be so good at that job.'

I smiled. Karen had been my cheering section right from the start. She was the reason I'd submitted an application in the first place.

'Did Craig tell you he's leaving?' Karen whispered as we walked to the café next door to the office.

I nodded sadly. 'It's going to be weird having a new boss.'

Craig was okay to work for. He didn't hover. Didn't pester. He let me get on with my work uninterrupted. I liked that system. It worked.

Someone new meant change.

'They're going to advertise the role internally.'

I frowned. Was that a good thing? On the plus side it meant I would already know my new boss; I wouldn't have to get accustomed to working for a stranger. But was there anyone here that I would like to work for? Someone who wouldn't micromanage? Someone who wouldn't disrupt the flow?

'You should apply.'

I stared at Karen. 'Did you just say—'

'You should apply,' Karen repeated with a nod. 'You'd be perfect for the role. You've been here the longest. You know how everything operates. Heck, you're practically doing the job already, we all know Craig comes to you for help when he's stuck.'

'But...'

'What?' Karen glared at me as though daring me to challenge her.

'Management wouldn't promote me.'

'And why not?'

'Because,' I shrugged. 'They barely even know who I am.'

'Well, then, it's about time we changed that. It's about time you got some recognition around here.'

'But I like how things are. I like being...'

Karen raised her eyebrow. 'Anonymous?'

I cringed. I couldn't deny she was right, though it wasn't ideal that she had realised it. I liked being in the background. It was safe there. Secure.

Karen linked her arm through mine as we walked. 'Take a chance, Jess. You can do it.'

I'd filled in the application form, convinced that I wouldn't even get an interview, let alone actually get the job. It hadn't seemed so scary when I thought about it like that. It was just a form. A harmless form. Nothing would come from it. Nothing would change.

Except it had.

Maybe it was supposed to. Maybe it was time for things to change.

Was Karen right? Could I do this? Management obviously thought I could. Maybe it was time I started to believe in myself, too.

Maybe I didn't need Adam by my side to make me feel like I was good enough. Maybe I had always been good enough.

'You know, I thought Adam was the turning point. That when he'd walked into my kitchen that day it had been the pivotal moment when my life changed. His presence changed me. "I" became "we". I was no longer alone.'

'Oh, Jess. I can't even begin to imagine how much you must miss him. And here's me blabbering on about work and a promotion.'

'I went out. I socialised. I lived.' I carried on, almost oblivious to Karen's apologies. 'But was it really Adam that changed me? Or had I started to change before I even met him?'

Maybe that was the reason Adam had noticed me. The reason I wasn't just another customer. The reason he saw something in me that day that interested him, something that wouldn't have been noticed before.

I'd been single for two years before I'd met Adam. Dating was too hard. Too much pressure. Too much disappointment. And yet, I'd said yes when he asked me out.

If he'd flirted with me a few weeks earlier, would I have responded? Would I have smiled and laughed giving him the encouragement to ask me out? And even if he had, would I have agreed? Would I have turned up to a crowded pub on a Friday night convinced I was going to be stood up and yet still stayed?

'Jess, I'm not sure I'm following you.'

'You'd dragged me off for that coffee one Saturday a few weeks earlier, just so we would have something to talk about at work. You gave me something to do. Somewhere to go. Something to be.'

'Oh, Jess, I didn't do anything.'

'Yes, you did. You wouldn't let me hide.' I took a deep breath. 'You wouldn't let me remain anonymous.'

34

THEN

I twisted my hands together in my lap, my gaze locked on the road ahead as I sat beside Adam in his van.

Forget it.

The voice in my head was a mixture of a command and a desperate plea. It's what I'd intended to do. The receipt was gone. The moment to confront Adam had passed. I'd made my decision. And yet...

Who was she?

How long had he been seeing her?

Was it serious?

I couldn't forget it. The endless questions that circled in my brain wouldn't let me. They'd played on a loop all night. They were relentless. But worse still, they were unanswered.

He's here with me.

I took a deep breath. That thought was like dim light in the darkness that had descended upon me since my discovery. He'd invited me to join him today. He hadn't had to. He was working. He could have left me at home and met me later. But he'd wanted to bring me along, to show me somewhere he thought I would like to see: Anvil Point.

Maybe he was trying to make amends, a silent apology for something we would never discuss. He didn't know I knew, and I would never tell him. What good would it do? It would give it life, whatever it had been. Talking about it would make it real. Not just a mistake, but a problem. One that lingered in the midst of our relationship.

I didn't need him to confess. I didn't want him to. I didn't want to know. All I wanted was him. Just as I always had.

Maybe Adam sensed that too. This day trip was his remedy. Maybe it was exactly what we needed. A break from our usual routine. Something different. Something new.

'I can't believe you've never been out here.'

I blinked and glanced at Adam beside me as he steered his van through the one-way system around the car park.

I'd been so lost in my thoughts I hadn't even noticed we'd arrived. I shrugged, playing for time as I fought to make my voice sound normal. 'Dad used to say we'd do lots of trips after we moved here, but...'

'He left before he got round to it,' Adam finished for me.

I nodded as Adam pulled up in front of a wooden gate that blocked the road. 'It says no entry,' I stated bluntly, glad of the chance to change the subject, but disappointed that our adventure had been stalled.

'It's to keep the general public out,' Adam said as he turned and winked at me. 'But I'm special.'

I felt a bubble of pride swell in my chest. Yes, he was special. And he was also mine.

But not just mine.

I swallowed and clamped my teeth together. I couldn't allow thoughts like that to seep into my mind. I had to shut them out.

I could do it.

I'd done it before.

'Would you mind opening the gate for me?'

I glanced back at the gate and hesitated.

'It's fine, I promise.' He smiled. 'You're with me.'

I laughed and slipped out of the van into the sunshine. Adam was right; *I* was with him. Whoever his companion had been the other night, it was irrelevant. Maybe it was a mistake. A momentary lapse of judgement. He didn't feel anything for her. He couldn't. He loved me. It was just lust. A physical attraction. A moment of weakness.

He would be regretting it now. Guilt would be tormenting him. I knew him. I knew how he felt. Didn't I?

He had come back to me. That had to mean something.

I was with him now, not her. All I had to do was make sure that it stayed that way.

I walked towards the gate. There was no lock, just an old metal catch. I lifted it and pushed the gate open slightly. I glanced around, half expecting someone to appear demanding to know what I was doing. Even with Adam's assurances it still felt wrong.

I opened the gate fully and waited as Adam drove through. It was crazy. I was so accustomed to following the rules, the idea of breaking them churned my stomach, even when I wasn't actually doing anything wrong.

The van stopped just past me and I closed the gate with a satisfying click. I clambered back into the van and Adam drove slowly along the winding single lane.

'Wow!'

Adam chuckled softly beside me. 'I told you you'd like it.'

I nodded, speechless, unable to turn my gaze away from the view. Rolling green hills dropped into the ocean. A whitewashed lighthouse and long low buildings surrounded by a low grey stone wall stood sentry over all of it.

Adam pulled the van into the walled courtyard and stopped. 'I'll probably be a couple of hours,' he said as he pulled the handbrake on.

My heart swelled. There was a hint of apology in his tone, or perhaps regret.

'You can take a walk along the cliff path if you like and I'll text you when I'm done working in the holiday cottages. We can meet up and go for lunch at the café.'

I smiled. 'That sounds perfect.' I leaned towards him, gave him a quick kiss on his cheek and hurried out of the van, eager to start walking.

I heard Adam getting his tool bag out of the van, chuckling as I walked away. I didn't look back. I wouldn't.

I didn't want to know who might be in the cottages waiting for him. A client... A woman...

I shook my head and turned left out of the courtyard and headed down the stony path until I reached the edge of the clifftop. No, Adam was working. That's all this was, a job. He wouldn't have risked bringing me if it had been anything else.

I leaned forwards over the edge of the cliff and watched the waves crashing below. Adam was right. It was perfect here.

And he had brought me. No one else, just me.

* * *

I leaned back in the seat and felt my body relax. It had been a perfect day. Adam had joined me for lunch at the café at Durlston Park as promised. We'd talked. We'd laughed. And then we'd walked back to the van hand in hand. Just like we used to.

I'd made the right decision. Whatever that bottle of champagne had meant, it was in the past. Adam was with me now.

He'd chosen me.

It was as though we had reconnected. He'd been slipping away from me; changing. It wasn't just the receipt. It had started before that. Had his companion been the reason, or the result?

I shrugged. Some things were best left unknown.

'What are you thinking about?'

I turned and met Adam's gaze and smiled. 'Nothing important.'

He chuckled as he turned his attention back to the road ahead.

I read the road sign as we passed and tried to figure out how long it would take to get home. I couldn't wait to get back. Adam would put the TV on in his usual Saturday afternoon routine and we'd curl up on the sofa together. His arm wrapped around me as I nestled against his shoulder.

Adam flicked the indicator on and changed into the right lane. My head jolted forwards. 'Where are we going?'

'How long have you lived in Bournemouth?' Adam asked with a smile. 'I'd have thought you'd know your way around by now.'

I rolled my eyes. 'Well, obviously I know we are heading towards the town centre. But why?'

He shrugged. 'I have a couple of things to pick up.' Adam winked at me. 'It won't take long.'

'Okay.' I nodded, but felt my shoulders sag. Snuggling up on the sofa would have to wait a little longer.

Adam pulled into a space in the open air car park and we slid out. I met him the other side of the van and we walked hand in hand towards the shops. Maybe this wasn't so bad. It didn't really matter where we were as long as we were together.

'I'll meet you in the square,' Adam said as he slowed his pace and pulled his hand free from mine.

'What? Why?' I stopped and turned to face him.

'I just have a couple of things to get.'

I shrugged. 'I'll come with you.'

Adam shook his head. 'You'll be bored.'

'But—'

'You'll have more fun shoe shopping.'

'I don't need any new shoes.'

'Well, clothes, then,' Adam shrugged. 'Whatever you want.'

He leaned forward, kissed my lips lightly and then turned, cast a quick look up and down the road and dodged a bus as he raced across to the other side.

I stared at the back of his head as he merged into the crowd. I blinked. What just happened? It was our day together. Us.

A heavy weight descended in my stomach. What if it wasn't just us? What if he was meeting someone? Was that why he'd run off so fast? Was that why he was so adamant that I shouldn't join him?

I stepped forward off the kerb and a horn blasted beside me. I froze as a yellow taxi whizzed past me. My hand flew to my chest. I hadn't even looked. How stupid.

My gaze drifted to where I had last seen Adam. How desperate was I?

I bit my lower lip. I should trust him. We'd had a lovely day together. He was being thoughtful, not wanting to drag me along when he knew I'd be bored. I was just being suspicious. I should do as he said and go shopping by myself.

I swallowed and glanced up and down the road. I should, but I wouldn't.

The road was clear and I crossed quickly, my body still shaking from my near miss. I marched down the street, following Adam's path towards the square. I stopped in the square, my gaze searching the crowd for his familiar form. Which way had he gone?

I stepped forwards and collided with a man on his phone. He scowled at me as I mumbled apologies.

'What are you doing?' My question went unanswered amongst the Saturday shoppers as they veered around me.

This was crazy. I couldn't chase after Adam. What kind of relationship would we have if I couldn't trust him?

I'd made my decision last night, I had to stick to it and get over whatever doubts lingered at the back of my mind.

I nodded firmly.

I would do as Adam suggested. I would occupy myself for an hour and meet him as planned.

I meandered up the street, glancing in shop windows, but my heart wasn't really in it. Doubt gnawed at me. Would I have been so trusting if I had known which way Adam had gone? My gaze scanned the crowd around me. If I saw him now, what would I do?

I knew the answer without even needing to think about it. I would follow him in a heartbeat. Despite my best intentions, that trust I'd had in him had gone.

The question now was: what were we without trust?

* * *

I stirred the dregs of my now cold cup of hot chocolate as I sat outside Costa. It might be unusually mild for February, but it still wasn't really warm enough to be sitting outside. I snuggled deeper into my coat. I should have sat inside in the warm.

Except, inside I wouldn't have had such a good view of the street. I couldn't have watched the passers-by so easily. My eyes couldn't have searched for Adam in every face that passed.

I sighed. Perhaps that was exactly why I should have sat

inside. It certainly would have been better for my sanity.

It had been a pointless exercise anyway. I hadn't spotted Adam. Was that because he hadn't been this way, or because he'd seen me first?

I shook my head. I had to stop this.

I pushed my chair back and glanced at my watch. I took a sharp intake of breath. In my dismal failure to distract myself I hadn't paid attention to the time. I was late.

I grabbed my bag from the table and ran towards Bournemouth square. I cursed under my breath and dodged a woman with a pushchair. Adam would be waiting.

Adam.

He isn't Mum.

I slowed my pace, and pressed my hand against my side, trying to ease the stitch as my body objected to the unaccustomed exercise. Adam wouldn't judge me for being a few minutes late. He wouldn't mind that I'd got distracted. He'd just be happy to see me.

He always was.

Wasn't he? Doubt niggled at me with every step.

Things between us had changed recently. He still smiled at my arrival. He still kissed me. Still talked to me and told me he'd missed me. But his gaze no longer lingered on me, it dropped back to the phone in his hands. Something was taking his attention. Something or...

I froze. My gaze locked on Adam as he sat on the wall at the edge of the square. He smiled. His face lit up, his eyes crinkled. But it wasn't at me.

He wasn't alone.

A woman sat beside him. Her head bent towards him. She ran her hand through her long blonde hair, flicked it over her shoulder and laughed.

My feet found their momentum again. I moved towards them, unaware of anything else around me.

'Is that her?'

Their heads jolted up to look at me. They had the same expression. Surprise. Confusion. Guilt.

'What?' Adam asked.

'Is that her?' I repeated.

'What are you talking about, Jess? Her who?'

The woman stood up, fear and confusion etched across her creased brow. 'I should go.'

I nodded. 'Yes, you should.'

'Jess, you're making a fool of yourself.'

Adam's accusation was like a match being struck. It ignited a fire within me and indignance fuelled the flames.

'I'm not a fool.' My words were staccato, loud and sharp. I never snapped like that. Not at anyone. Except him. It was strange how he had that effect on me.

It wasn't that I was unaccustomed to insults or criticism. I was used to them. They were as natural to me as breathing. But with him it was different. I was different.

When we met I'd confessed to him that I was really quiet and shy. He'd raised his eyebrows. 'Really? You seem so confident.'

I'd laughed. He'd fallen for the act. I'd had a lifetime to perfect it.

'I just want the truth, Adam.'

'She's a client.'

My eyes narrowed. 'Like I was?'

Adam rubbed his hand across his forehead. 'No, Jess. Just a client. A big client. She's the manager for the hotel that's just taken me on.'

I glanced from Adam to the woman.

She looked nervous. Embarrassed.

'I'm so sorry about this.'

My anger softened at Adam's apologetic tone and I turned back. But he wasn't looking at me.

He was looking at her.

He was apologising to her.

For me.

Oh, my God. What had I done?

'Adam, I...'

'Leave it, Jess.'

I turned back to the woman. 'I thought...'

'She knows what you thought. Everyone knows what you thought.'

I glanced around. People were staring at me. People I didn't know.

I shrunk into my coat. I'd made a scene. I'd been so stupid. So wrong.

'I'll walk you to your car.'

I didn't even need to look this time. I knew Adam wasn't talking to me. He was trying to pacify his new customer. To make amends for my error. My humiliation.

'Don't you need to...?' I caught her sideways glance at me as she spoke.

'No, Jess and I have nothing to say to one another right now.'

I sank to the wall where they had been sitting and watched as they walked away side by side. I'd made a horrible mistake. I was so wrong.

It wasn't her.

Maybe it wasn't anyone.

I rubbed my head. What if the drinks had been innocent? A business deal. A celebration of a big new contract? Maybe I did have the right woman, but the wrong meaning.

35

NOW

It wasn't a conscious decision. I hadn't planned it. Or for that matter even thought about it at all. If I had I would have talked myself out of it. I wouldn't have even got in the car. Common sense would have prevailed.

This time.

My right foot lifted slightly from the accelerator. I could turn back. It wasn't too late. I could go home. Sanity could still take back control.

I tightened my grip on the steering wheel and pressed my foot back down. This wasn't about being sensible; it was about compulsion. Something inside me needed to do this. I needed to be there. To see.

I slowed as the turning came into view. An eerie chill crept though me, despite the car heater being turned up high.

I drove slowly around the one-way system of the car park. I edged forwards in my seat and peered out of the windscreen, my eyes darting back and forth. It felt wrong to be here. As though I was about to get caught doing something I shouldn't.

It was silly. Adam was already gone. All I was doing was...

I frowned as I pulled into a parking space. What was I doing?

Was it some morbid need to see this place again? To see for myself that it was real? Or maybe just to say goodbye?

I grabbed my woolly hat off the passenger seat and slid out of the car. I tugged the hat on, pulling it down over my ears, and shoved my hands in my pockets as I walked back through the car park.

I paused at the wooden gate intended to keep cars out.

Authorised Vehicles Only.

It hadn't kept Adam out.

I'm special.

Adam's laughter echoed in my memory. I missed that sound. He'd always seemed so young when he laughed. A big kid who hadn't grown up. Youthful. Fun. Carefree.

And yet, somehow he'd ended up here.

We'd ended up here.

I took a deep breath, shoved my hands deeper into my pockets and veered to the left through the pedestrian walkway beside the gate.

Rolling green hills swept downwards to the ocean. It was as breath-taking now as it had been the first time I'd seen it. Except now its beauty masked a shadowy secret.

I walked along the single lane road towards the lighthouse. It seemed much further by foot than when Adam had driven us here.

I paused beside the wall that surrounded the lighthouse and holiday cottages and stared at the cliff edge, before meandering forwards and peering down at the ocean below.

I don't know what I expected to find. Whatever it was, it wasn't there. Adam's van had gone.

Where was it now? In a scrapyard somewhere? Or had the

police taken it for further investigation? My mind raced with possibilities.

There wasn't any sign that anything significant had even occurred. The world carried on as though nothing had happened.

But then to them it hadn't. It hadn't made an impact on their day, their life.

In reality, the circle of people affected was small and distinct. Adam's family and friends would feel the void he left in their lives. His customers might be struck by momentary shock and pity. But it would be fleeting. They'd deal with the inconvenience of calling another plumber and go on with their day.

Perhaps Adam and I had more in common than I'd realised. We were both replaceable.

It's not like that, Jess. I love you. Just you.

I scrunched my eyes closed, blocking out the sound of Adam's voice.

Lies came so easily to him. Promises and assurances slipped from his tongue. But his words were like chocolate. Their silky sweetness hid the reality of how bad he was for me.

Dad had been the same.

He'd promised everything would be okay.

He'd lied.

Had Adam ever meant anything he'd said to me? Had it all been a lie? Or had there been a truth to it, even if it was only for a little while?

I shook my head. What was I doing? It was irrelevant if his feelings were real, when his availability wasn't. And yet it still mattered. It was relevant. I needed to know.

I needed to know that he'd loved me once. That he'd seen something in me that was worthwhile.

But what if all he had ever seen me as was weak? Pliable? Controllable?

The disturbing part was, he wouldn't have been entirely wrong. I was all of those things. But I was more than just that. I could be strong too. Adam just hadn't seen that side of me. I hadn't realised how strong I could be. He'd underestimated me and so had I.

I'd been so focused on keeping Adam happy that I hadn't questioned if I was actually happy. All that had mattered was that he stayed with me; that he loved me. Whereas all Adam wanted was... I took a deep breath. Someone else.

I shuffled closer to the edge. 'I guess neither of us will get what we want now, Adam.'

I peered at the waves as they crashed into the rocks below. I felt it then. The pain. The sorrow. The loss. The loneliness. Like a virus, it worked its way through my body, infecting every part of me.

I hadn't expected to feel it so strongly.

But beneath it all, there was something else too. I felt free.

36

THEN

Mum glanced around my open-plan kitchen and living room. She gripped her handbag tightly as it hung from her shoulder. 'I thought this dinner was supposed to be for the three of us to get better acquainted.'

My chest tightened. I knew what was coming.

'So, where is he, then?'

I resented the way Mum always referred to Adam as 'he'. It was her way of reminding me that she didn't approve of him, as though he wasn't even worthy of her uttering his name.

'*Adam* will be here soon.'

'I thought you said this was important to him?'

'It is. But Adam has a big job on over at the holiday cottages at Anvil Point.'

'Anvil Point,' Mum repeated slowly.

'Yes, it's past Swanage, at Durlston County Park.'

'I remember it.' She nodded, but her eyes were glazed over, as though her mind was somewhere beyond my apartment.

'You've been?'

Mum blinked. 'A long time ago, with my parents.' She smiled slightly. 'I haven't thought about that place for years.'

'It's beautiful. It's a shame we never went there when I was younger.'

She nodded, but I could tell from her vacant expression she was barely listening.

'Why don't you take a seat on the sofa and I'll join you in a minute? I've just got to put the vegetables on the hob.'

'Hmm?'

'Go and sit down, Mum.' I gave her a nudge towards the sofa, and she walked aimlessly towards it.

I frowned, as I poured the frozen mixed vegetables into a saucepan, filled it with water and set it on the hob to warm. This wasn't a good sign. I wanted tonight to go perfectly. I wanted Mum to like Adam, or at least give him a chance. But that was looking less and less likely if she was going to be in one of her weird moods. As good at small talk as Adam was, I doubted even he would be able to break through to Mum if she was off in her own world again.

I walked through to the living room. Maybe I could distract her and get her talking about something else. Something that would jolt her free from whatever was pulling her down.

Mum sat with her handbag resting on the sofa beside her, and a notebook open on her lap. She tapped her pen against the page, staring at the words that were written there.

I couldn't help myself. My gaze was drawn to the page.

Anvil Point???

'Planning a trip back there?'

Mum jumped. She slammed the notebook shut with such force the thud echoed through my sparsely decorated living room.

'Sorry, I didn't mean to startle you.'

'You didn't,' Mum snapped.

I stared at her. Why would she feel the need to deny it, when it was so clear that I had?

My gaze drifted to the notebook in her lap. My stomach tightened as I recognised the hard blue cover. It was *the* notebook. Mum's notebook. That notebook always gave me a sense of foreboding.

Mum jolted into action and hurriedly rammed the notebook into her handbag as though she couldn't bear to have it in her presence any longer.

I shook my head. I was being ridiculous. It was just a notebook.

Wasn't it?

My legs felt weak and I perched on the sofa beside Mum, my gaze fixed on her bag, where the corner of the notebook peeked out. Somehow that book seemed to have been present at every significant event in my life. The bad ones at least. Dad's departure, Matthew's, too. When Paul turned against me, and then Mike...

I closed my eyes as I tried to block out the memories that the notebook had triggered. Bad memories that were better left in the past, and yet somehow they were immortalised, their existence forever connected to that book.

But it was stupid. It was just a notebook. A way for Mum to cope, to process whatever she was dealing with at the time. Of course she wrote in it more during bad times, that would be when she needed it most of all. She didn't have Dad to turn to, to talk to, to share her thoughts and her fears with. She just had a pen and paper to confide in.

I leaned forwards and started to lift my arms, suddenly feeling an overwhelming need to wrap my arms around Mum's shoulders and hold her tight. But I stopped. It wasn't how she was. It wasn't how we were.

I let my hands fall to my lap. 'You know I'm always here for you, if you ever need to talk, don't you?'

Mum blinked and stared at me. 'Talk about what?'

'Anything.' My gaze dropped to her bag again. 'Dad...'

I saw her body tense out of the corner of my eye. 'We don't talk about him.'

'I know, but...' I turned back and my eyes met hers. 'Maybe it would help.'

'There's no point dwelling on the past, Jessica. It's gone, and so is your father.'

There was a familiar briskness to her voice. It was the same tone she'd had when she had told me he was never coming back. Cold, hard and unwavering, but this time perhaps there was something more there as well. A sadness that I'd never heard before, or perhaps I'd been too young, or too consumed by my own sorrow, to notice it.

I reached out and put my hand over Mum's. 'I know, and we are just fine without him. Just the two of us.'

I expected Mum to pull away, or brush me off with some curt reply, but she didn't. She sat for a moment, her expression unreadable. Not angry, but not sad, something in between, perhaps.

She nodded slowly. 'Yes, just the *two* of us.'

The way she emphasised that word sent a chill down my spine. I knew what she meant. Just us; no Dad and no Adam.

* * *

I peered at the leg of lamb through the mottled window in the oven door. We couldn't wait any longer for Adam, not unless I wanted to serve my mother a burnt roast dinner. I glanced back at her over my shoulder and shuddered. I really didn't want to do that.

I frowned as my attention was caught by the notebook in her lap. She was writing again.

I took a deep breath and walked into the living room. 'Well, it looks like Adam isn't going to make it in time for dinner.'

Mum's lips twitched upwards in a smirk. 'What a shame.'

'We should carry on without him,' I said, choosing to ignore her sarcastic tone. She was glad he wasn't there. Glad she didn't have to spend the evening pretending to be nice. But mostly she was happy that he'd screwed up. He'd let me down. He'd proved her theory right. He wasn't good enough. He was neglectful and rude. He hadn't even called to apologise.

She nodded and shoved the notebook back in her bag again. 'I'll just use your bathroom before we sit down to eat,' Mum said as she stood and walked out to the hallway.

I let out a deep sigh, grateful for the reprieve from her gloating. But it would only be temporary. We had a whole meal to get though together yet.

I started to turn back to the kitchen, but the sound of a key turning in the lock of the front door stopped me.

Relief washed over me as Adam stepped into the hall. 'Thank goodness you're here,' I whispered as I hurried towards him.

Adam frowned. 'Wh—' His words slipped away as his gaze fell upon Mum's bag on the sofa. He slapped his hand to his head. 'Your mother.'

'You forgot?'

'I was working.'

Guilt gnawed at me. It wasn't his fault he'd been distracted with his job. His work was important. I had the security of a regular salary, he depended on a fluctuating demand. He had to go when and where the work was. It was unfair of Mum and me to judge him for that.

'It's okay.' I smiled. 'You're here now, and just in time to join us for dinner.'

Adam winced. 'Where is she?'

She.

The word grated on me. It felt disrespectful. Dismissive.

They were as bad as one another.

'Mum's in the bathroom.'

We both glanced down the hallway to the closed bathroom door.

'Perfect, then she doesn't even need to know I'm here.'

My head jolted back and I stared at him, my eyes wide. 'Wait. What?'

'I'm knackered, Jess.'

A sinking feeling lodged itself in my stomach.

'I really can't deal with your mother right now.'

'But dinner...'

'I'll eat later.'

'But Mum...'

The sound of the toilet flushing caught our attention and we turned back towards the bathroom door.

'I've got to go.' Adam leaned towards me and his lips hurriedly brushed my cheek.

'Adam,' I hissed at his retreating back as he hurriedly crept down the hall and disappeared into our room. He didn't even turn back.

My body tensed with irritation. It was bad enough that he was late, but now he didn't even intend to join us at all. He was abandoning me to deal with the fallout from his absence alone.

The click of the bathroom door lock turning jolted me into action. I couldn't let Mum see me lurking by the front door. I couldn't let her know that Adam was avoiding her. Avoiding us. I scurried back to the kitchen. She mustn't know she was right, Adam wasn't quite the man I'd thought he was.

* * *

'That was delicious, Jessica.'

I beamed at Mum's praise as I cleared the plates from the table. 'I'm glad you enjoyed it.'

'Very much so,' Mum continued as she followed me into the kitchen area, carrying her empty wine glass. 'I miss your cooking. It's been a while since I had a proper Sunday roast, there's just no point when you're cooking for one...'

Her voice trailed off wistfully.

My hands shook as I placed the plates on the granite worktop beside the sink. 'I'm—' I clamped my mouth closed, biting back the apology that had almost slipped out.

I wasn't sorry, or at least I shouldn't be. I wasn't Mum's cook, I was her daughter. It wasn't my destiny to live with her forever so she could eat well.

'There's more wine in the fridge, if you'd like some?'

Mum blinked and her head drew back. 'Well, yes, actually, I could do with another glass.'

She turned her back to me as she set her glass down on the counter beside the fridge and opened the door.

I turned back to the sink and smiled as a movement in the living room caught my eye.

Adam.

He'd come to join us. Of course he had. He'd just been tired earlier. He'd needed a rest like he'd said. But he'd never intended to abandon me.

His eyes met mine and he froze. He looked awkward and pained. His right hand was tucked behind his back.

My hand flew to my chest. Was something wrong with his back? I started to open my mouth to ask, but something about the panicked expression in his eyes stopped me.

He lifted his left hand and pressed his finger to his lips as his gaze drifted over my shoulder. I turned automatically, though I already knew what, or rather who, had caught his attention. Behind me Mum poured a glass of wine with her back still to me. Somehow it was always about her.

I glanced back to the living room but Adam was gone.

I blinked.

Had I imagined him? Had I wanted him to join us so much that my mind had created an illusion?

It wouldn't have been the first time.

'Did you want another glass of wine, too?' Mum's voice pulled me back and I turned to face her.

I stared at the bottle of wine in her hand. 'No.' I shook my head firmly. 'Thanks, but I think I've had enough already.'

* * *

I turned the handle and pushed the bedroom door open.

Adam flinched as he leaned over his gym bag, which lay on the bed.

I shook my head. Since when had he become so jumpy? 'It's only me. Mum's gone.'

'I was just getting my stuff ready for tomorrow.'

I shrugged. 'I just thought you'd want to know.'

I pivoted on my heel and headed back out of the room.

'Jess?'

I turned back, hoping for an apology.

'There's something I need to talk to you about.'

I gripped the door handle tightly. Was this it? Was this the moment he confessed?

'I know you think I'm unfair on your mum.'

I swallowed. This wasn't the direction of the conversation I had anticipated.

'But you need to understand it comes from a place of love. I care about you. I see how she twists you around her little finger, how her words cut into your confidence, and it makes me mad. It hurts me to see you struggle. To see you suffer.'

'I'm not saying she's perfect, Adam. But she's still my mum.'

'But you don't know her.'

'And you do?'

'Better than you think.'

I sniffed. 'Look, Adam, I'm tired, I really don't want to get into this again right now.'

'Okay, okay, but I need to show you something.' Adam started to reach into his gym bag.

'Adam, if you're just going to tell me how bad my mum is for me, I don't want to hear it.'

Adam froze. 'Why do you always believe her? Even when she puts you down, you still think she's right? That she knows best?'

I leaned against the door frame. Why did I believe her? Mum's views were often negative and hurtful, but I still choose to listen. 'Maybe if you believe something for long enough then it becomes the truth.'

My gaze met Adam's and we stared at one another for a moment.

Adam sighed and zipped up his gym bag. 'Then I guess there's nothing more I can say.'

37

NOW

'You have reached your destination,' the SatNav informed me, as I cautiously weaved my car through the narrow one-way street lined with parked cars.

I pressed my foot on the brake gradually and glanced at the numbers on the building to my left.

116.

I edged forwards slowly.

118.

I pulled into an empty space by the kerb and studied the beige tower beside me. I felt small and insignificant in its shadow.

The engine was still running. My hands were still poised on the steering wheel.

I was here. But I wasn't sure if I wanted to be.

I wasn't sure if I should be.

You wouldn't like it there.

Adam was right. It wasn't the kind of area I was used to. Instead of a concierge, there were bars on the windows of the ground floor. His block of flats was very different to mine.

My gaze drifted up the building. Which floor was his flat on?

I felt a pang of guilt. That was a question I should know the answer to. I should know where my boyfriend lived. I should know what his life was like when he wasn't with me.

But I didn't.

I hadn't even known the address.

Helen had looked at me with such scorn when I had asked her for it. She thought I should have known too.

I reached for the car door handle, driven by a sudden urge to go inside the building and enter Adam's world.

But I stopped.

I didn't even have a key.

I was locked out.

I nibbled my lip. Was that Adam's intention? Had he always been keeping me at a distance?

Or had I never been interested enough to truly try to be part of his world?

38

THEN

I sat at the breakfast bar, my gaze locked on the clock on the wall. The second hand clicked loudly. Adam was late. Again.

It was the same every night. He'd come in and apologise for being late. He'd say a job had been trickier than expected or blame it on traffic. His excuses were all reasonable and perfectly acceptable. There was a time I would have believed them without hesitation. But not any more. Now there was a constant doubt that had lodged itself in my mind. It was persistent and unwavering. It ate into me; gnawing at everything I had believed. Everything I had hoped for.

I wound Adam's phone charger wire around my fingers as it lay on the counter. He was with *her.* I didn't know who she was. I didn't know what she looked like or what her voice sounded like. I didn't even know her name or her age. I didn't need to. I knew the most important thing about her. I knew she existed.

My blunder in the middle of Bournemouth town centre had been foolish. I'd let my jealousy and insecurity show. It had been weak. I swallowed. My accusation wasn't even right. All I'd achieved was to make things strained between us.

I nibbled my lip. But did that mean I was completely wrong? Or just wrong about that particular woman?

We never talked about what I'd thought. I never told him about the receipt. Adam said he wanted to put my accusation behind us and move on. But it was easier said than done.

His absences became more noticeable. His excuses more feeble. Had my outburst brought them closer together? Or had it just made him feel as though he didn't need to work so hard to hide it now? Perhaps to him my silence was my acceptance. But inside I screamed.

I knew the truth now. Adam wasn't what I'd wanted. He wasn't what I needed. He wasn't genuine. I ground my teeth together. The problem was, despite all that, he was still real. He was still mine, at least partially. But how much was mine? And how much was hers? He still lived in my apartment and slept in my bed each night, did that mean I was still his priority? Was she just a phase? Was I the real thing?

I rolled my shoulders trying to ease some of the tension that had built up. There was still a possibility that I was wrong. Or that he would realise his mistake. There was still a possibility that we could make it work. It didn't even matter how unlikely the possibilities were. All that counted was that there was still a chance for us; for me.

The sound of the front door opening jolted me from my thoughts. I cringed at the heavy thud of his tool bag being dumped on my pristine cream tiled floor. I knew that sound by heart.

Heavy footsteps grew closer behind me.

'Hey, Jess.' Adam's lips barely brushed my cheek, the scent of musty deodorant and sweat made my nose twitch. 'Sorry I'm late, traffic was a nightmare.'

The phone cable slipped from my fingers and unravelled across the breakfast bar.

'I'll take a shower before dinner,' Adam said as he started to walk back towards the hall.

I didn't acknowledge him.

Adam's footsteps stopped. 'Jess?'

I pivoted on the stool and our eyes met.

'I've been thinking.'

I waited for him continue.

'We'll never be happy here.'

'Wh-at?' My voice wobbled as my heart pounded. This was it. Adam was ending it. He'd made his choice and it wasn't me.

'It's this place.'

I blinked and my mind raced as I tried to catch up. 'This place?'

'There are too many things holding us back, making us crazy. It'll never really be just the two of us if we stay here. There will always be your mother and...'

He stopped abruptly and stared at the floor.

And who? The question burned on my lips but I refused to ask it. Did I even want to know what he called her?

He edged towards me. 'We should leave here. Just the two of us. We could start again.'

The two of us.

He wanted me. Just me.

My heart soared. It's what I'd wanted from the moment we met.

Except...

I glanced around my apartment. 'But this is my home.'

Adam rolled his eyes. 'It's just an apartment. You're the one who said it's never really felt like your home. It's your mother's taste, her influence. It's not you. It's not us.'

Us.

It was that word again. The one that made me feel part of something. But it wasn't enough. It wasn't real. It couldn't be.

Could it?

'We'd move far away. A new town. A new apartment. A new life.' Adam stepped towards me and reached for my hand. 'I can be a plumber anywhere and you can find a job you actually like.'

You should do something you love.

The words Adam's dad had said to me when I'd met him popped into my head. I'd dismissed his statement as flawed. Work was work. It wasn't meant to be fun. But maybe I'd been too hasty. Maybe there was another option.

Adam squeezed my hand. His warm touch felt calm and comforting. We were connected.

Maybe he was right. Maybe we needed a fresh start. If we moved away it would be just the two of us again. His indiscretion, his mistake, could be left here in the past.

I swallowed as I stared into Adam's eyes, trying to read his thoughts. I wanted to believe him. He was promising me everything I'd ever wanted. He painted a picture of our future that was so captivating that it almost felt real.

Almost.

I nibbled my lower lip as doubt began to creep into my thoughts. What if the past wasn't left behind? What if it couldn't be? His affair was part of him; part of his character; his nature. It had become part of us now too. We couldn't outrun it just by moving to a new place. It would follow us. We would carry it with us in the boxes we packed and memories we carried. It would always be there, the constant reminder of his betrayal. Proof that once again I hadn't been good enough to keep what I loved.

He might leave her behind, but there'd be women wherever

we ended up. There'd always be temptation. Would he succumb again? Would I believe him even if he didn't?

I'd made a life for myself here. It was a job I didn't like, and an apartment that would probably never feel like me, but they were mine.

Could I really walk away from all of that for someone who had cheated on me?

Adam's expression hardened. His hopeful pleading look morphed into a scowl. I might not be able to read his thoughts but he could read mine. 'You're such a coward, Jess.'

I bristled at his words. 'I'm not a coward. I'm just more grounded than you. I have ties here. Commitments.'

'You have tethers.'

I yanked my hand free from his. 'That's not fair.'

'You're so scared to break free, to take a chance, to do something different, go somewhere different.'

I slid down from the breakfast bar stool and stepped forwards. 'Where would we go, Adam? What would we do? What would I do?'

'Whatever you what, that's the point.'

'I...'

'Argh.' Adam let out a strangled groan. 'You're impossible. I have a plan, Jess, and you're screwing it up. You're so scared to leave your life here. It's as though you view it as some kind of safety net that's protecting you. But you don't realise it's not a safety net, Jess. It's a cage. You're trapped and I'm trapped right along with you.'

'You feel trapped? With me?'

'Where would you be without me, Jess? You'd have to start again with someone new. Do you really want that? Do you think you could find someone who could accept you the way I do?'

I shook my head. There was no one like him. Despite his flaws, despite his betrayal, I still wanted him. Still needed him.

'So make a decision, Jess. For once in your life, stop living by what your mother wants and what you're expected to do. Stop seeing every opportunity, every adventure, as a red flag.'

I squinted at him. There was something about his features that I'd never noticed before. The way his expression contorted as he mocked me. There was a harshness to it, just as there was in his words. It wasn't good-humoured teasing; it was spiteful and belittling, intended to hurt.

'What's that look for?'

I blinked. 'Wh-what look?'

'You look like a hurt animal.'

I drew back as though I'd been physically struck. 'I—'

Adam shrugged. 'I can't say anything to you without you getting all hurt and indignant.'

'You feel trapped with me. How am I not supposed to be hurt by that?'

'I told you.' Adam paced the living room. 'It's this place. It's everything. It's driving me crazy. I have to get away from it.'

My pulse raced. I was this place. I was part of it. It was part of me. Right now Adam wanted me to go with him, but what would happen when he realised he wanted to leave me behind too? I'd have given up everything for him. I'd have nothing. Was I willing to take that chance on us? On him?

Adam stopped pacing and glared at me. 'I don't know why I tried to talk to you about this. I knew you wouldn't listen. Not to me. You only listen to your crazy mother.'

'She's not crazy.' I spat the words at him. It was one thing to attack me, but how dare he insult my mother?

Adam snorted. 'You have no idea, Jess. You're clueless about everything. When are you going to wake up? You don't know her. Not the way you think you do.'

'What's that supposed to mean?'

'Your mum's right. You do have a selective memory. You choose to forget how she treats you. How she treats us. You'll always choose her over us, no matter what.'

He shook his head and marched out of the living room. The front door slammed behind him. I stared at the empty doorway. He'd left. We were in the middle of a row and he'd just left.

When things got tough, he left. Just like the others. Just like Dad.

My shoulders slumped as my strength evaporated. So that was it. It was over. I'd known it days ago, but I hadn't wanted to admit it. I was still hoping it would change. That Adam would return, and everything would be okay, my Adam, the one I'd fallen in love with, not the imposter he had become. But, of course, it wasn't going to be that simple.

It was stupid, really. I, of all people, knew better than to hope. Or at least I should have done. But hope was a crafty little thing. It had sneaked up on me without me even noticing, until it was too late. And then there was no escape. It had lodged itself in my routine and nothing I could do could shake it free. Even when everything was clearly set against me, it remained, causing me to constantly cling on to the impossible. I never learned.

I guess as much as I'd known the truth, I still couldn't let go of the fantasy. He saw me. For the first time someone saw through my invisibility and liked me for who I was. I was good enough. I was better than good enough, to him I was beautiful and wanted. At least in the beginning.

Everything was hinged on the belief that the version he saw of me was real. But the only way I could keep believing was if he kept saying those wonderful things. It felt like our relationship was crumbling and with it so was the illusion of that version of me.

Where did that leave me?

Even now, even after he'd walked away, he'd abandoned me, I was still waiting, still hoping that somehow we could figure it out. We'd find a way.

It was foolish.

I was foolish.

I was pinning my hopes on someone else again. Waiting for them to make me feel valid. To feel worth something.

My gaze fell upon Adam's tool bag, dumped in the middle of the hallway. He never put it away. He left it there obstructing the pathway. I never complained. I just walked around it. I didn't want to make a fuss.

I felt something shift inside me, like a sudden change of the tide.

I should be stronger.

I picked up his bag, opened the front door and slung it out into the corridor. It landed with a satisfying thud.

'You can't keep doing this to me, Adam. I won't let you!' I yelled. I heard his footsteps pause, before continuing down the stairs and out of the building.

I nodded and slammed the door.

I was stronger.

Anger burned inside me. How dare he yell at me and insult me and then just walk away as though I didn't matter? How dare he think he could dictate my life and not listen to my concerns?

If he didn't feel I was good enough for him then so be it. Maybe he wasn't good enough for me.

I marched to the bedroom and flung the wardrobe door open.

I'd been so wrong about Adam. It would never have been what I imagined in my head; in my heart. It was always going to fail.

I grabbed his clothes; there weren't many, he never left much here, just a couple of shirts and a spare pair of jeans. I threw them in a heap on the floor.

I stopped. I could throw him out but then what? What if he ended up with her? I'd have cleared the path. I'd have given him to her.

I clenched my fists.

She'd have won.

My nails dug into my palms, but I didn't care. It felt good to feel something; pain, anger, hatred. It was invigorating. Like a charge of electricity running though my body.

I kicked the pile of clothes, sending them sprawling across the bedroom floor. There had to be another way. A better way. I wasn't going to lose. Not this time.

I knew I was spiralling and desperate. It felt like Adam had been key to help me find myself and learn how to have fun, to live, not just to survive. I didn't want to go back to my life without him. But the black and white reality was crashing in on me. It was terrifying. What would I do to keep someone who I didn't even like?

39

NOW

It felt strange. Wrong.

This was our place. Adam's and mine. I glared at the crowd that was gathering on the clifftop as I stood a little further down the path. They were encroaching on our space.

'I'm so glad you're here, Jess,' Helen said as she appeared beside me.

I blinked. I hadn't even noticed her approaching.

Her gaze drifted to the growing crowd. 'Adam would love this.'

A pang of guilt struck against me. She was right. He would.

Today wasn't about me. It wasn't even about Adam and me, what we'd had, or what we had lost. It was about him. Just him.

And Adam had always loved being the centre of attention.

'I wasn't sure what to expect. I wasn't even sure if a vigil was the right thing to do.'

I tried to muster a smile. I still wasn't convinced it was.

'But under the circumstances, we needed to do something, right?'

I nodded. 'Of course. It was a lovely idea, Helen. Everyone can unite in their...' I paused. It felt wrong to say grief. Adam was still missing. There was still a chance.

Helen cleared her throat. 'It's a good turn out.'

'Adam was very popular.' I cringed at the 'was' that had slipped out unguarded.

Helen smiled. She hadn't noticed. She was too preoccupied. She thought my observation had been a compliment, that I was praising her son for his social skills. I wasn't. I hated that side of him.

Not at first.

In the beginning I had envied him his ability to talk to anyone, to laugh and joke and fit into any situation with ease. I wanted to learn from him, to replicate that skill. I had managed it, to an extent. Adam had helped with that. Just his presence had been enough to make me feel like I belonged, or at least, to feel less of an outsider.

But it was also his friendliness that had been our undoing. He was too friendly. At least with someone.

Someone who wasn't me.

'Where is your candle?'

Helen's question jolted me from my thoughts and I glanced down at my empty hands. 'I, er...'

'Here.' Helen rammed a plastic candle into my palm. 'Take mine, I'll get another.'

I stared at it.

'The minister is going to say a few words, then I'll read a poem, and then we will switch the candles on for the prayer.'

I glanced at the sun, still high in the sky.

Helen must have followed my gaze. 'I know the candles would have been more effective at night, but the park closes early. The cliff path would be too dangerous in the dark.' Helen clamped her mouth shut, and pressed her hand to her chest. She blinked and I saw tears sparkle in her eyes. 'It's too dangerous at any time.'

I nodded again. It seemed to be the only thing I could do. It wasn't as though there were words for this kind of occasion.

I watched as Helen hurried away. The vigil was a distraction for her. A way to feel useful. A way to break up the monotony of waiting for news. I couldn't blame her for needing that.

Unfortunately, I needed the opposite. I needed the silence. The solitude. I needed to be anywhere but here.

My attention drifted back to the crowd again. My gaze flitted from face to face. I recognised them all. They all knew me, too. Adam made sure of it. He made a point of including me in his social life. He held my hand and led me around, introducing me to everyone he knew. He was proud of me. It was as though my presence somehow made him feel a little more important. Part of me cherished feeling worthy of being included. Wanted. But another part. A tiny, nagging part, wondered if it was really about me at all.

I tilted my head as a figure in the background caught my attention. She lingered a few steps removed from everyone else. The fact I didn't recognise her was strange enough, but her manner raised the hairs on the back of my neck.

She was trying too hard to be undetected, as though she thought she could somehow make herself invisible. I glanced around; no one else seemed to have noticed her. Maybe it was only obvious to me. Maybe I recognised that desperate need to hide, because I'd spent a lifetime feeling that way. Until I met Adam.

I closed my eyes as fresh tears seeped from the corners of my eyes. Every day I was struck by another memory, another way he had changed my life, another thing I missed about him. And yet it never overrode one thing; he'd lied.

I opened my eyes and my gaze met hers. Her face flushed, despite the cool afternoon air and she turned away quickly. But it was too late. That split second had been enough. I knew who she was. Not her name. Not her identity. But I knew who Adam was to her. I could see it in her red rimmed glossy eyes that had looked so guilty. She was the reason Adam would never truly have been mine.

My feet were striding towards her before I even realised what I was doing. She seemed to sense my approach and turned back to face me, her eyes wide with fear. She stepped back and glanced around her, as though searching for an escape. But all that surrounded us was a clifftop and crashing waves below. There was nowhere to hide here, not for the living.

She swallowed as she turned back towards me. Her shoulders tensed and her jaw clenched, as though bracing herself for an impact. She was scared. Of me.

That realisation struck me as ironic. The woman who'd been in control of my destiny was afraid of me. No one was ever afraid of me. I was nothing to them. Insignificant. Irrelevant. Or at least I used to be.

I stopped just in front of her. Now that I was finally face to face with her, I didn't know what to say. A battle raged in my head, torn between the desire to physically remove her from trespassing on my farewell to the man I loved, and pity because the truth was, looking at her I could see she probably loved him more.

'Why?' My voice was flat but clear.

Confusion passed over her pale face. 'I don't...' She shook her head.

I couldn't blame her. There were a thousand 'whys' I could have meant. Why was she here? Why did they do it? Why cheat? Why didn't he leave me for her? Or her for me? Why did she accept being the other woman? Why didn't she want more? Why didn't he?

'Why did he stay with me?'

She blinked. My question had surprised her. It wasn't what she'd expected. But then, it wasn't what I'd intended to ask either.

'You loved him, didn't you?'

She hesitated. I could see her debating how to answer. Her instincts were probably telling her to deny it, to lie, but there was something else as well. A need to say how she felt perhaps.

'Yes.'

'And he loved you?'

Another pause.

'Yes,' she repeated more tentatively.

I nodded. I was glad she at least had the decency to be honest.

'Then why didn't he leave me for you?'

She glanced down and I followed her gaze to her left hand. Her thumb stroked a gold band on her ring finger.

'Ah.' I nodded again. 'You're married.'

It wasn't a question, but she answered anyway. 'Yes.'

'You could have divorced him—'

She winced.

'But you didn't want to.'

She shook her head. 'I know what you must think of me. I know how bad it sounds. How bad it is. I love my husband, but Adam...'

'Was different,' I finished for her.

'Exactly.'

Our eyes met and I felt a strange fleeting moment of connection. Adam was different. He had an ability to see inside me and know how I felt, and how to reach me.

A heaviness pressed against my chest. I'd thought that it had been a sign that we belonged together. As corny as it sounded, I believed we fitted like soulmates. But now I realised it was just who he was. Intuitive. Observant. Attentive.

There was nothing unique about us or our relationship. We weren't special. I wasn't special.

She licked her lips. 'I should go.'

She didn't move. Perhaps on some level she was hoping I'd stop her, that I'd tell her it was okay for her to be here and allow her to pray for his safety like Helen, or perhaps, like me, to say her final goodbyes. But I didn't.

It wasn't okay.

She turned and took a step towards the path that led to the car park.

'How long?'

My question stopped her and she looked back at me over her shoulder. 'Four years.'

I flinched as her admission struck me like a punch in my heart. 'But we only met in May.' My head spun. He'd been seeing her before we'd even met. Bile rose at the back of my throat. She wasn't the other woman. I was.

I watched her expression. It wasn't surprise. Or even disappointment. 'You knew?'

She nodded. 'He ended things with me when he met you. He said he'd found someone special, someone he wanted to be with completely.'

He'd ended it for me. He wanted us to make it work. He did care. He did love me. Except... 'No, that doesn't make sense. He can't have ended it. You were still together. Those late-night call-outs. The cancelled dates.'

'We missed each other too much for it to ever really end.'

'When did...' The words stuck in my throat. When did he decide that I wasn't enough?

'August.'

And there it was. The truth. I stepped back, fighting the urge to scream, to cry, to throw up, to do something, anything that would free me from the pain that was tearing through every part of me.

'I'm sorry.'

I glared at her. 'But not sorry enough not to cheat on your husband. Not sorry enough to have let me have the one good thing I had in my life. Not sorry enough to stay away today.'

'I...' She looked stunned at my sudden outburst.

The calm numbness that had kept me moving through each moment had worn off, washed away by the truth. I finally knew it now. Before I had only suspected. Now I knew.

Adam hadn't loved me. Not enough. He'd given up on us, on me, after barely three months.

She'd been there in the background the whole time. I was always being compared to her. And I always failed to measure up.

I should walk away. She was nothing to me now. But my feet wouldn't move. There was still something I needed to know. Something I needed to ask.

'What's your name?'

She blinked. 'My name?'

'You were there the whole time, a shadow over our relationship, it seems only fair that I should at least know what to call you.'

She nibbled her lower lip. 'Natalie.'

I nodded. Whatever I had hoped to gain from knowing her name was disappointingly elusive. Nothing had changed.

She swept her brown shoulder-length hair back and tucked it behind her ear. Her watery brown eyes stared at me.

I frowned. There was something so familiar about her. Her hairstyle, her eyes, her clothes, even the shade of her eyeshadow.

A cold chill washed over me. It was almost like looking in a mirror.

I fought to find my voice. 'Did Adam suggest what you should wear? Did he help you shop?'

A frown creased her brow. 'No, why?'

I shook my head. 'It doesn't matter.'

But it did matter. It all made sense now. What was it about me that had attracted him? Was it ever about me, or was it just about the similarity I bore to her?

He'd been trying to make me in her mould. To replicate the woman he loved but couldn't have completely. But I was never good enough. I was only ever going to be a mere copy. The original would always be better. She possessed something that was out of my league. Authenticity.

40

'Come on in.' I ushered Karen inside my flat.

'I brought wine, as promised,' she said and handed me a bottle of Zinfandel.

'You didn't need to.'

She rolled her eyes as she slipped off her coat. 'I wanted to.'

I smiled and gave her a hug.

I guided her through to the living room.

'Your flat is beautiful.'

'Thank you,' I said.

I fetched a couple of wine glasses as I watched Karen gaze around the room approvingly and I felt a pang of guilt that this was the first time I'd ever invited her round. We'd grown closer over the last few months, and yet I still kept her at a distance.

'I'm sorry, I should have invited you sooner,' I said as I set the glasses down on the coffee table and opened the wine.

'You've had a lot going on. You needed some space. It's natural.'

'No, I don't just mean now. I should have invited you months ago.'

'Oh,' Karen shrugged. 'That's okay. You didn't have to—'

'I don't know why I didn't.'

'Really, it's fi—'

'No,' I winced. 'Actually, that's not true. I do know.' It was time I stopped hiding from the truth. 'I was afraid.'

Karen's eyes widened. 'Afraid? Of me?'

'No.' I shook my head. This was coming out all wrong. 'I shouldn't have said anything.'

'You can't leave it there. Not now you've made me worried.' Karen edged towards me. 'Was it something I said?'

'No, of course not.'

'I know I can be a little pushy sometimes.'

'Kar—'

'Okay, very pushy. But it's only because I care.'

I smiled. 'I know.' It seemed strange to think that Karen's pushiness had been something I had found intimidating to begin with, but now I realised it was what made her so special.

'But—'

'It wasn't because of you. It was me.'

'I don't understand.'

I poured a glass of wine and took a large gulp. 'I keep people at a distance. Not just you. Adam, too.'

'Why?'

'Because I'm scared I'll screw everything up again.'

'Again?'

'If I keep the people I care about far enough away, then maybe they won't get tired of me. Maybe they won't leave.'

Karen and I stared at one another.

What had I done? I'd blurted out too much information. Things I had barely even begun to admit to myself and now I had voiced them aloud.

I took another large gulp of wine before topping up my glass and pouring one for Karen. She looked like she could use it too.

'Why would I get tired of you?'

I nibbled my lip. I'd already said too much. I should stop there. Tell her I was being stupid. It had been an emotional few days. She'd understand.

But some part of me didn't want to just let it drop. I needed to say what was on my mind. I needed a friend to confide in.

'I'm too negative. Too afraid. Adam had started to realise it. He'd started to pull away from me—'

'No, Jess. Adam loves you.'

Loves.

The word tore into me. Loves, not loved. It was full of hope. It implied a future. Maybe Karen still thought there was a chance Adam was okay after all. A chance he would come back to me.

But I knew better.

'He used to love me.'

Karen's eyes widened. 'You split up?'

'No, we were still together. He still lived here, sort of. But it wasn't the same. He wasn't the same.'

'Oh, Jess. I'm so sorry.'

'I think I was also afraid that if you spent time here with us, without the distractions and noise of crowed bars, then you'd see the cracks.'

'Would that have been so bad? I wouldn't have judged you. I would just have been there for you if you'd wanted to talk.'

'But that's just it. I couldn't talk about it. I couldn't even admit it to myself. But if you'd realised...'

'Then you wouldn't have been able to stay in denial any longer.'

'Crazy, right?' I lifted my glass to my lips.

Karen shook her head. 'Not crazy. Just lonely.'

I paused, my wine glass still pressed against my bottom lip. Karen was right. It was lonely. I was lonely. I always had been.

Even with Adam.

'That's what friends are for, you know. Someone to help us through the difficult times. Someone to talk through the things we can't face alone.'

Friends.

I set my glass down on the coffee table, and sank onto the sofa. 'It's been a long time since I've had a friend.'

'You have one now.'

'Really?' I cringed at the surprise and desperation in my voice. Over the last few days I'd started to view Karen as a friend. But somehow I never thought of it working the other way too.

'You don't believe me?'

'It's not that I don't believe you.' I screwed my nose up as I searched for the right words. 'I just don't really understand why.'

I lowered my head and stared at my lap. Those were bad words. They sounded needy and clingy. But it wasn't that I was seeking praise or attention. I simply didn't understand why anyone would want me as a friend.

I was different. An outsider. Adam had helped me to fit in, or at least look more like I did. But what was I without him? He and Mum were all I'd had, and I couldn't help wondering now if either had really been good for me.

Karen sat on the sofa beside me and placed her hand on my shoulder. 'You really don't see it, do you?'

I heard the awe in Karen's voice.

'Jess, you are a beautiful, brilliant, caring and funny woman.'

I shook my head. 'That's not me. That's just the illusion Adam created. He made me look better. He made me...' I shrugged. 'More than I was.'

I took a long shaky breath. 'Sometimes I wonder if I ever really progressed at all.'

'What do you mean?'

I lifted my head and gazed around the room. 'I thought things would be different when I moved in here. It was meant to be a fresh start. But all I did was change my address. Everything else stayed the same. I stayed the same. Even with Adam. He changed my appearance. But I was still the same underneath.' I still felt the same. Still acted the same. I was still just as alone.

What if that was never going to change? Maybe I was too weak to change; too broken.

Mum was right. What I wanted really didn't matter. It wasn't realistic. It wasn't achievable. And the saddest part was, all I'd ever really wanted was for someone to want me.

'What's wrong with who you are?'

I stared at her, my eyes wide, stunned that she even needed to ask that question. 'Everything.' My voice cracked. It was the first time I'd ever said it aloud. The first time I'd acknowledged my failings to someone. Partly because I knew how it would make me sound; weak and pathetic, but mostly because as much as I knew the truth already, saying it aloud somehow made it more real.

As long as things weren't talked about they could be ignored. It was like an ugly piece of furniture in the corner of a room. Everyone knew it was there, it was unmissable, detestable. The key was not to focus on it, because the moment you looked directly at it, the moment you acknowledged its existence, it became all you could see. And whatever attractive qualities the rest of the room may hold, they instantly became irrelevant and invisible.

Just like me.

'I'm not good enough.'

'Whose voice is that?'

I blinked and peered at Karen through watery eyes. 'What?'

Karen edged forwards on the sofa. 'You have such a negative view of yourself, Jess. And the thing is I don't even think it comes from you.'

I shuffled. 'Where else would it come from?' I dreaded the answer. And yet at the same time, I needed to hear it.

'Stacey was wrong when she said you made up an excuse about visiting your mum, just to get out of hanging out with us, wasn't she?'

I shrugged. 'What's that got to do with anything?' I was being cagey. Deflecting her questions. I could sense what she was building up to, but I couldn't help her get there.

'Before Adam, she was the only person you talked about. The only person in your life.'

'There were other people. Sometimes.'

'But she's the only one whose opinion matters, isn't she? She's the one you channel when you say something negative about yourself?'

I scoffed. 'That's ridiculous.' But my protest was just out of loyalty. Something inside me screamed at me that it wasn't ridiculous at all. Weren't Karen's accusations the very same thing that I had been wondering myself? Wasn't it the same thing that Adam had tried to tell me over and over again?

Were the voices in my head my own self-doubt and overthinking, or were they echoes of Mum's criticisms?

'I see how stressed you get on the evenings you're going to see your mum after work. I heard the digs Adam made occasionally about you doing too much for her; about how controlling she is.'

'N—'

'Jess, it's okay. You don't need to tell me. Just think about what I've said. Ask yourself if it's really your voice in your head, or someone else's. If it's yours, then forget what I've said. Just chalk it up to an ignorant friend with good intentions jumping to the wrong conclusions.'

'And if you're right?'

Karen and I stared at one another, equally surprised by my question.

'Then we'll have to figure out how to turn up the volume on your own voice.'

'We?'

Karen smiled. 'That's what friends are for.'

41

I paced Mum's living room, feeling restless. What was I even doing here? Ever since I'd talked to Karen my mind had been filled with endless questions. Adam had voiced the same questions before, but I'd always ignored him. I was loyal to Mum. But now the questions wouldn't subside.

Neither would the guilt.

I was wrong to think badly of her. She was my mum. Her actions had always been driven by her love. She had always done what she believed was best for me.

Her intentions were pure. Who was I to criticise her for any mistakes she might have made? I was hardly perfect. And yet I had talked about her behind her back. I'd led Karen to believe my negative beliefs were Mum's fault.

I took a deep breath as another wave of nausea washed over me. I felt so guilty. I was a bad daughter to even think such things. And yet, I still couldn't help but wonder if Karen was right.

'So, what brings you here?' Mum asked as she carried a tray of tea into the living room.

'I just needed to see you.'

Mum smiled. 'I knew you'd be back eventually. You're not strong enough to stay in that apartment alone.'

You're not strong enough.

I swallowed. Wasn't that practically what I had said to Karen, that I wasn't good enough? Was Karen right? Had 'you're not' become 'I'm not'? Had Mum's opinions become mine?

And if so, when had it happened?

Why hadn't I seen it?

Why hadn't I stopped it?

My grandparents' photo on the sideboard caught my attention. I picked it up and studied the faces. I tried to remember what things had been like before they'd died; before we moved here.

'What were they like?' I asked Mum, without shifting my gaze.

'Don't you remember?' She sounded hurt. They were her parents and I had forgotten them.

'Not properly. I was only little when we lost them. I remember I loved them a lot and I used to love our visits here.'

'They were...' Mum paused. 'Passionate about what they believed in.'

I tilted my head to the right. 'That doesn't necessarily sound like a good quality.' At least not the way Mum said it.

'They were good people. Just a little hard to please. They had high expectations.'

I perched on the arm of the sofa. How had I not known that before? Mum had always spoken of her parents with such admiration. She idolised them.

Didn't she?

'You always seemed so close.'

'I wanted to be. I'd have done anything for them.'

'Even moving into their house to fulfil their dream.'

Mum nodded and leaned forward to pour the tea. 'It's their legacy. It's all I have left of them.'

'But does it make you happy?'

Mum's head jolted up and she stared at me. 'Your dad asked me that same question a long time ago.'

I stared at her. She'd mentioned Dad. She never spoke of him. And yet for the second time this week she had brought him into the conversation.

I swallowed. 'And what was your reply?'

Mum frowned. 'I don't think I gave him an answer.'

'Why not?'

'The question was irrelevant.'

'No, it's not. Your happiness should never be irrelevant. It matters. It should matter to you, too.'

I took a shaky breath. My words had been full of conviction and passion. But it wasn't just Mum who needed to listen to them; I did too. Hadn't I been doing exactly what she had done? I'd put her happiness above my own. I thought that made me a good daughter. A good person. But was I really responsible for her happiness?

Mum was still living her life in a way that made her parents happy, even though they'd been gone for twenty-four years. Where did it end? When was enough?

I'd done the same. I'd spent my life trying to make Mum happy; to be the daughter she needed; the company; the support; the help. But it was never enough. It had never been what she needed. It didn't matter what I did, I would never be able to make her happy. Only she could do that.

Adam had tried to tell me.

'No matter how much you do, Jess, it'll never be enough.'

'That's not fair. You make Mum sound greedy, as though she'll always want more.'

'It's not her fault. Not entirely. It's just that she's set you an impossible task, but neither of you even realise it.'

'What I do has an impact on Mum. We're connected. My words and actions affect her. I can make her happy or I can make her sad. I'm responsible for that.'

'No, you're not. You're only responsible for your own happiness, Jess. No one else's.'

'But my actions have repercussions.'

'I'm not saying you should intentionally hurt her. You can still act compassionately, but ultimately what you do should be based on what you want. Only she is responsible for how she chooses to feel about things. Yes, you might disappoint her if you don't visit her occasionally. But it's her decision whether to dwell on that or move on. It's her decision whether she sits at home alone engulfed in self-pity, or picks up her bag and goes out to the cinema, or takes up a cooking class.'

I studied him silently. Logically what he was saying made sense, but it wasn't that simple. Mum and I were different. Our relationship was different.

'You don't decide her reactions. You only decide your own.'

I'd ignored Adam's words. I hadn't listened. Not properly. I hadn't wanted to hear. But I understood it now.

I wanted Mum to be happy, but maybe her needs shouldn't outweigh my own. Wanting her to be happy shouldn't mean my own happiness was sacrificed.

My hand shook as I stood up and placed the photo back on the sideboard.

My beliefs and feelings about myself were defined by Mum. Dating Adam was the first time I'd gone against her. I'd finally taken a small step to putting what I wanted first. He made me feel better about myself. I craved his encouragement. His approval. I was dependent on it. It wasn't just Mum's voice in my head now, it was Adam's too.

And I would never live up to either of them.

Adam was right, I had been trying to achieve something that

was impossible. I'd measured my self-worth by how happy I made someone else. I'd made myself feel guilty and inadequate because, no matter what I did, I always failed. But Mum's happiness had never been in my control. Success was always going to be out of reach.

Just as it was for Mum.

'What would you do if you didn't feel compelled to live here? If you ignored what your parents wanted for a moment and just thought about what you want?'

'I won't discard what they wanted for me. They worked hard to give me everything they could.' Mum sniffed. 'Everything they had.'

'But was their house really what you wanted from them? Wasn't their unconditional love more important, regardless of whether you did as they dictated?'

'They loved me.' Mum's eyes glazed over as she stared at the photo. 'In their own way.'

'But isn't it time to think about what you want?'

Mum stared at me for a moment before reaching out her hand towards me. I stepped forwards and took her hand in mine.

'I have what I want. You are my world.'

A cold chill ran through my body. She would never be free of her parents' hold over her.

And neither would I.

42

PC Davidson stepped back off the doorstep and waited for me to join him. I hesitated in the doorway. His steely expression wasn't exactly encouraging me to comply, but then it wasn't as though I had any alternative. My presence at the police station wasn't just requested; this time I was being escorted.

'Jessica, don't tell them anything,' Mum said beside me as she handed me my coat.

I froze. Mum believed there was something to tell. Something that would betray my guilt.

I glanced at PC Davidson. He was studying me intently.

'I have nothing to hide,' I told him.

He nodded, but I could see his scepticism. I couldn't really blame him. If my own mother didn't believe it, then why would he?

We drove to the police station in silence. I felt compelled to say something to break the tension in the car, but what? Would my aimless chatter demonstrate my openness and innocence, or would it make me look nervous and more suspicious?

'We talked before about your jealousy affecting your past relationships,' PC Davidson said once we were seated in the now overly familiar interview room and he had started the recording, and reminded me of my rights.

'I explained that already. It wasn't what it seemed.'

'And what about with Adam?'

I blinked. 'With Adam?'

'You were jealous, weren't you?'

'I...' My voice trailed off. How could I answer that without looking guilty?

'You suspected him of having an affair?' PC Davidson asked softly.

The room closed in around me. How could he know that? I'd never told anyone.

'You were angry, weren't you? Furious, even?'

'No.'

'We have a witness.'

The word dug into me. A witness to what? What had they seen?

You know your memory isn't reliable.

What had I done?

Could Mum be right?

'We spoke to his recent clients. We know you confronted him in the street, accused him of cheating.'

Realisation dawned on me in a wave of relief. 'The woman in the square.'

PC Davidson's eyes narrowed. 'You thought I was talking about something else?'

'No.'

I tried not to cringe. I'd answered too quickly, I could tell from the way PC Davidson sat a little straighter. I'd given too much away. He knew I was lying. Perhaps I wasn't as good at it as I'd thought.

'I made a mistake. She was a client.'

'Adam was having an affair, though, wasn't he?'

My face flushed. 'He, erm…'

'What gave him away?'

I swallowed. I could deny it. The receipt had gone. There was no evidence that it had ever existed. No evidence that I'd known. 'A receipt.'

A flicker of surprise passed over PC Davidson's face and I realised he hadn't expected me to admit it. But then I hadn't expected to say it either.

'It was for a bar we'd planned to go to for our six-month anniversary, but…'

'He took someone else instead.'

I shrugged. 'It might have been nothing.'

'You don't really believe that. You think he was having an affair.'

'I didn't know. Not for sure.' I phrased my reply carefully. It wasn't a lie. I didn't know. Not then.

'That must have been an awful betrayal.' PC Davidson ignored my caveats. To him it didn't matter if I'd had proof or not. I'd believed it was possible, that was enough.

He was right, of course. The uncertainty didn't make it hurt any less.

I shrugged.

'Hope is a dangerous thing. It's powerful. It makes you powerful too. You can achieve amazing things if you have hope. It keeps you fighting against adversity. It keeps you going when everything else tells you to give up. It lets you imagine a future that's better than the present. A future that could be yours.'

I slouched back in the chair. 'The problem is, when you have hope you have something to lose.' I arched an eyebrow as I studied PC Davidson. 'What happens when that future you'd been clinging to and dreaming of shatters and dies?'

He tipped his head to the right but didn't respond.

'You die, too.'

His forehead twitched slightly. Perhaps he thought I was being melodramatic. He couldn't know how it felt. No one could. Not unless they'd been through it. Not unless they'd lost everything.

'Not fully. Never fully. But something inside; the part of you that kept you going, that kept you strong, withers a little. It leaves you weaker, more pessimistic, and more sceptical.'

'And that's what happened with Adam? When you learned of his affair, of his betrayal, something in you "died"?'

I nodded slowly. 'I'd been there before. I'd vowed never to go through it again. But then I met Adam...' I took a long breath. 'He gave me hope. But it was false hope.'

I wasn't in love with him. I never had been. I knew that now. I was in love with the idea of him. The life that could have been mine with him by my side. My version of him anyway. The version where I knew him; where I knew his character; his likes and dislikes; his hopes and dreams. Instead, all I had was a reality where I hadn't really known him at all.

'Everything had been different to what I'd thought. He'd been different.'

Even if he was still here, still with me, it wouldn't have worked out between us. I knew that now. There were too many differences between truth and fantasy for that to have been possible.

'I keep trying to figure out what I did wrong. What I always do wrong. They always betray me. They always leave.'

'What makes you so sure that it's you?'

My head jolted up and I stared at him. 'Who else would it be?'

PC Davidson paused as he studied me. 'Them.'

I blinked. It was such a simple word, but one that was so

powerful. It absolved me of guilt, of blame. I shook my head. It was wrong. I didn't hide from my flaws or my responsibilities. I wouldn't shirk the blame here.

I straightened my back. 'I'm the common denominator.'

He shrugged. 'That doesn't prove anything other than you've had bad luck.'

'Luck?' I scoffed. 'I thought you wouldn't believe in luck in your line of work.'

PC Davidson chuckled. 'Let's just say this case has got me questioning a lot of things I used to be sure of.'

I frowned. What things? The question burned on my lips, desperate to be asked, but I shook my head. It didn't matter. It didn't change anything. 'Pinning my failures on bad luck is the easy way out. It's pretending that there is something bigger at play. But the truth is we control our own fate. We either work hard or we don't. We either make good decisions or bad ones.'

'Is that what Adam was? A bad decision?'

I took a deep breath and let it out slowly. 'Yes.'

My admission hung in the air. PC Davidson looked startled. Was it the word that had surprised him or the fact that I had admitted it?

I shrugged. It didn't matter. It seemed futile to pretend any longer. Adam was a mistake. I knew that now. I'd known it for a while.

'He wasn't at the start, though,' I added, for some reason feeling the need to defend what Adam and I had once had. 'When we met, Adam was...'

'What?'

'Everything I needed.'

'But in the end...?'

He was prompting me to elaborate, no doubt hoping my

sudden willingness to share information would lead to a confession. My confession.

But it wouldn't. It couldn't. I wanted to know what had happened to Adam just as much as the police did, more even. The problem was I didn't hold the key to that mystery. Just like all of the strange things that had happened in my life, the truth was just a little out of my reach.

'In the end...' I took another deep breath. 'In the end Adam wasn't who I thought he was.'

'Because he cheated?'

I smiled ruefully. 'No.' I watched PC Davidson and DC Fisher exchange a look. They didn't believe me. 'Adam's affair was a betrayal. It made him a cheat, but...' I paused, searching for the words that could explain.

'You loved him anyway.'

I started to nod but hesitated. 'I think, more accurately, I loved the idea of him.'

'Cheating and all?'

I snorted. 'I didn't love that part. But I could have overlooked it, accepted it, even.'

PC Davidson ran his hand through his short brown hair. I could see the confusion etched into his eyebrows. I had destroyed his theory. I wasn't the jealous girlfriend who'd killed in a fit of rage at Adam's betrayal. I was...

I bit my lip. What was I?

'So, what changed?'

'Adam died.'

DC Fisher frowned. 'You're saying Adam wasn't who you thought he was because he died?'

I laughed. It felt strange to laugh. It had been so long since I had done so, not since long before Adam's disappearance.

'No, Adam's death is what made me realise he wasn't who I'd thought.'

PC Davidson shuffled forwards in his chair. 'In what way?'

'Natalie.'

A frown passed across his face.

'You've met her, right?'

He nodded. 'Have you?'

'Yes, at the vigil.'

'Okay, but you already knew about her, so what did meeting her change?'

'Everything. Didn't you see it?' I smiled at his confusion. 'The similarities between us? The same hairstyle? The same fashion?'

PC Davidson shrugged. 'So, Adam had a type.'

'No.' I shook my head. 'Adam had Natalie. I was just an imitation. Someone he tried to reshape in her design.'

His eyes widened as understanding dawned. 'The gifts…'

'Yes, all of Adam's gifts, the clothes, the make-up, everything was to make me a little bit more like her.'

'Then that gives you more motive to kill him,' DC Fisher said, with a smug smile on his lips. 'If it wasn't bad enough that he was cheating on you, it must have been humiliating to realise he wanted you to be more like her.'

PC Davidson shook his head. 'But if you didn't meet Natalie until the vigil…'

'I would have stayed with him.' I wrung my hands on the table in front of me. 'Things weren't good between us, but he was all I had. I couldn't lose him, because I didn't know how to live without him.'

'So, you didn't kill Adam?'

'No.' I shook my head and leaned back in the chair. I felt a strange calmness wash over me. I'd told them the truth. No matter how mad at Adam I had been that night, I would never have hurt him. I couldn't. I needed him too much.

'Or maybe you just don't remember...'

PC Davidson's words struck to my core. My hands trembled and I shoved them under the table out of sight.

He knew.

43

'You've had issues with your memory before.'

I stared at PC Davidson. It sounded like a statement rather than a question, but he paused as though waiting for me to respond.

What could I say? If I denied it I would look like a liar, but from my perspective my memory worked fine. It was other people who thought it was faulty.

They talked about things that hadn't happened. Things I'd done. Things I'd said. But it wasn't real. It couldn't be.

'I see from your file that you received counselling for it.'

Another statement.

I shuffled.

'How is your memory now, Jess?'

'It's fine,' I replied through clenched teeth.

What if...?

Mum's question hung in the air. What if I'd done it? What if I'd killed him?

I could tell PC Davidson everything. I could explain our troubled relationship, reveal my past mistakes. I could tell him the truth, the whole truth, and let him investigate. He'd find the answer. He'd resolve it for me. I'd finally know one way or the other.

'Miss Harper?'

I blinked and felt my face flush.

'You looked like you wanted to say something.'

'I just...' I took a deep breath. 'I just wanted to say thank you for what you're doing for Adam.'

Disappointment weighed heavily in my stomach. I was a coward.

'We'll find out what happened to him soon, I promise.' There was a steeliness to his eyes as they locked with mine. Were his words meant to reassure or unnerve me?

I nodded slowly. 'I hope so.'

Another lie.

I didn't want him to find the truth. Not really. I wasn't sure I could handle it. Some things were better left unknown.

I should be stopped. If I'd killed Adam, then what would be next? *Who* would be next?

Yet there was a little voice in my head that screamed at me that it wasn't me. I couldn't have been me. It was the same voice that had been with me for years, constantly protesting my innocence no matter what happened. Even against overwhelming evidence to the contrary, that voice held strong. It never quit. It never wavered.

That voice had been wrong before.

He arched an eyebrow. 'What was your mother's relationship with Adam like?'

I blinked at the sudden change in topic.

'She didn't like Adam, did she?'

I snorted. 'She detested him.'

'That must have been hard.'

I tried to shrug his comment off, but I couldn't. 'I wanted her to see him the way I did.'

'But she couldn't.' He paused and tapped his pen against his notepad. 'Or wouldn't.'

'No. She never gave him a chance. She never gave *us* a chance.'

'So, when you discovered Adam was cheating on you...' PC Davidson drew in a deep breath and shook his head. 'You realised that she'd been right about him all along.'

I gritted my teeth. 'Yes.' It grated on me to admit it. It was almost worse than Adam's betrayal, the fact that Mum had been right about him. About me.

'You must have hated that.'

I squirmed. His insight was too accurate. It was unnerving.

'You're close to your mother, aren't you?'

'Of course. She's my mother.'

'It's been just the two of you for a long time.'

I nodded. 'Dad left when I was seven.'

'I'm sorry.'

I squinted at him. There seemed to be genuine sympathy in his voice. I hadn't expected that. Not from him.

'The details about your dad came up in our background check on you.'

I nodded. I wondered what else his file said. Abandoned as a child. Emotionally scarred. Unwanted. Unloved.

'I can't imagine how difficult it must have been for you to cope with a loss like that.'

'I missed him so much.' I sniffed. 'I'd always been Daddy's little girl. It was hard to accept that he could just leave me like that.' I blinked and wiped away my tears with the back of my hand. The truth was it was still hard to accept it. Even now.

'Grief is difficult for anyone, especially a child.'

'Grief?' I frowned. I'd never thought of it in that way before, but... 'Yes, I suppose that's what it was.' I nibbled my lip. 'But I think the hardest thing was knowing it was his choice.'

'I'm sorry?'

'He chose to leave us. To leave me. He chose not to come back.'

I leaned against the window, my nose pressed against the cold glass.

'What are you doing?'

I kept my back to her. I didn't want to answer. I knew Mummy would disapprove. I was being naughty. No, not naughty. Silly. That was worse.

'Jessica?'

'Waiting,' I mumbled quietly, hoping she wouldn't hear.

'For what?'

I heard her heavy footsteps cross the living room and stop behind me. I twisted round to look at her through bleary tearful eyes. 'Daddy.'

Her lips pursed and deep creases dug into her forehead.

I shuffled closer to the window.

'What did I tell you about Daddy?'

I dropped my head and stared at my fluffy pink slippers. 'That he's never coming back.'

'Exactly. So stop moping around looking for him. He's not coming.'

A tear left a cold damp path down my cheek. 'But...' I paused, searching for courage. 'It's my birthday.' I looked up at Mum and her gaze met mine. 'He'll come back for my birthday.'

Mum's eyes narrowed as she glared at me. I'd made her mad. I tried to step back but bumped into the window behind me.

She grabbed my arm and pulled me towards her as she leaned down over me. 'Never means never, Jessica. He's not coming back for your birthday, for Christmas, for anything. He's gone, do you hear me?'

Tears streamed down my face. I nodded frantically.

Mum's grip tightened as she shook my arm. 'Stop snivelling.'

I tried to stem my tears, but it just made them flow more.

'Is it any wonder why he left? Why would he want to be here with a cry baby like you?'

A sob escaped my lips.

'I said that's enough.'

I nodded and balled my fists together, fighting to regain control. My fingernails dug into my palms. I winced in pain, but it felt good. Calming.

Mum nodded slightly and took a deep breath.

'You have me, Jess. I'm still here.' Her voice had softened, but there was still an edge to it. 'Or aren't I good enough?'

Guilt and fear engulfed me, surging through my sorrow. I shook my head. 'No, Mummy. Don't say that.' I swung my arms around her waist and clung to her. She couldn't leave me too. 'You're good enough. I promise, you are.'

'Miss Harper, what exactly do you think happened to your dad?'

I stared at him. It was a strange question. 'I thought you said you had it in your records?'

'We do, but...' The two men exchanged a look. There was something about it. The way their brows furrowed. It was almost as though they were confused. Bewildered, even.

'He left.'

'Left, as in...?' PC Davidson arched his eyebrow as he leaned forward on the table.

'Left as in left.' I shrugged. How much more simply could I put it? 'He went to work one morning and just never came home. He left.'

The same look passed between them again.

'What's going on? Why all the questions about my dad?'

'Your dad didn't just leave, Miss Harper.' PC Davidson cleared his throat. 'I'm sorry, but he died.'

44

Died.

The word repeated over in my head.

'W-hat?' I struggled to speak. I hadn't seen my dad in over twenty-three years. I never expected to see him again, but there was still some part of me that had hoped... I was like a child who was too old to believe in Father Christmas, but still went to bed on time, lay still and didn't dare peek, just in case he was actually real. I knew Dad wasn't coming back, but there was still the possibility that he could.

'When? How?' It was irrelevant now, but I needed to know. How long had I been holding on to an empty hope?

PC Davidson swallowed.

'Why didn't anyone contact us to tell us?' So many questions formed in my brain.

He stared at me. The colour seemed to drain from his face. 'Your mother knew, Miss Harper.'

I shook my head. 'No, you're mistaken. If Mum had known she would have told me.'

Wouldn't she?

I swung my legs as I sat on the big comfy chair in the corridor outside the headmaster's office. I studied the certificates on the wall. They looked important. Like Mr Travis.

My stomach twisted in knots. I shuffled and sat on my hands. I hadn't been sent to his office before. Only the naughty kids had to face him. I rarely even saw him, other than in morning assembly. That was enough. He was big and tall, and spoke with a booming voice that could be heard from every corner of the school hall. I shuddered. I didn't want to go into his office.

'She doesn't need to talk to anyone.'

I smiled slightly at the sound of Mummy's voice. At least I wouldn't have to face him alone. Mummy was already in his office.

I screwed my nose up, trying to work out what I'd done wrong. It must have been something very bad for Mummy to have been called to see the headmaster too.

'Mrs Harper, I can't imagine how difficult this is for you, but you have to think about your daughter.'

I leaned back in the chair and strained my ears waiting for Mummy's reply.

'I am thinking about her. I always think about her.'

'Her teacher is concerned about Jessica, and so am I.'

'She's fine.'

'She's in denial.'

'It's her way of coping.'

'It's not healthy, Mrs Harper. At some point it will catch up to her. Eventually Jessica will have to face what really happened.'

I frowned. What would I have to face? I slid off the chair and edged closer to the door.

'No.' Mummy's voice was icy cold. 'She never needs to be confronted by that.'

Mr Travis took a sharp breath. 'Mrs Harper, Jessica does know what happened to her father, doesn't she?'

'Of course she does. But she's just a child. How can a child understand something like that? How can any of us?'

The door swung open and I jumped back.

Mummy stared at me.

'What can't I understand?'

For a second she looked afraid, but then she shook her head and her expression cleared. 'Pick up your bag, Jess. We're going home.'

'But I have PE.'

'Now, Jess.'

I turned and picked up my bag. 'Did I do something wrong again?'

'Again?' Mr Travis peered at me over Mummy's shoulder.

'No, Jess. You didn't do anything wrong. You're a good girl.'

I beamed at her. I was good. I liked being good.

'That's why you get to go home early today. It's a treat.'

My eyes widened as I grinned. 'Really? Does Susan get to go home early as well? She's a good girl too.'

Mummy shook her head. 'No, just you, Jess.' Mummy put her hand on my shoulder and guided me down the corridor.

'Miss Harper, your Mum was the one who found your father.'

I blinked. 'Mum found him?' I shook my head. 'How could that be? Mum hasn't seen him since he left when I was seven.'

'It was a little over twenty-three years ago.'

'Yes.'

'No, Jess.' PC Davidson shook his head. 'He died twenty-three years ago.'

My breath caught in my throat. 'That's why he never came back.' Everything made sense now. Or at least more than it had. He hadn't kept in touch because he couldn't, not because he hadn't wanted to.

'That's why he "left".'

My forehead creased as I frowned. 'I don't understand.'

'Your dad didn't walk out on you, Jess. That's the day he died.'

'But...' I blinked.

'The file said he fell down the stairs. Your mum heard and, well...' His words trailed away.

'But that would mean Mum knew?' I shook my head. 'No, that's not right. Your file is wrong.'

'According to your mum's statement, your dad had returned home after dropping you off at school. Apparently he'd forgotten something. It made him late and he was hurrying.'

You forgot your briefcase.

I put my hand to my mouth. 'He'd left his briefcase behind. It would have been in the spare room upstairs, the one he used as a study.'

PC Davidson nodded. 'I see.'

'I should have gone back for it.'

'You?'

'I knew he'd left it. I told him. But he wanted to get me to school on time.'

'Jess—'

'I should have gone back.' My words tumbled out. 'If I'd gone back, then...'

'You weren't to know.'

'No.' I stared at him. 'I didn't know. I didn't know any of it.' I brushed my tears away with the back of my hand. 'I should have known, though, shouldn't I?'

He gazed at me helplessly.

'How could I not know?'

'Maybe your memory... the trauma...'

Somethings are best forgotten.

I started at him. 'My memory.' Was it possible? Was my memory really faulty after all? Had it been faulty then, too? Or was that the cause?

'I think we should end the interview there for today.'

45

I stared out of the window, watching the traffic go past as PC Davidson drove me home. There was a time when I would have been embarrassed to arrive at my apartment block in the back of a police car, but right now it didn't seem to matter. Nothing did.

'Are you sure you don't want to go back to your mother's house?'

'I don't want to see her.'

He nodded. 'Okay.'

The past was running through my mind on a loop. Had I remembered it wrong? Had I missed something? Had Mum told me? Had I been in denial?

I'd been so little. Perhaps I couldn't understand Dad's death. Perhaps I couldn't accept it. Had I pretended Dad left us? Had it been easier for me that way? It had still hurt, but at least I'd been able to imagine him out there somewhere, still living, still happy.

The car stopped and PC Davidson stepped out and opened the door for me. I hesitated for a moment. I didn't want to go home. I didn't want to do anything. I didn't know what was real any more. Not Adam, not my life, not even me. Everything was twisted and distorted.

PC Davidson would arrest me if he could, I had no doubt about that. And yet, in a weird way he was my only ally. He was neutral and independent.

'Everyone has their own past, their own way of seeing things and they are rarely the same,' PC Davidson said, as I stepped out of the car. 'Maybe you should hear your mum out.'

I nodded. 'Maybe.' But I knew I wouldn't, not yet. It was too soon.

I started to walk towards the building but stopped as my gaze fell upon my car in the car park. Maybe there was somewhere I could go. Someone who could help me. Someone who would understand.

46

'You're back!' Susan stared at me through her open front door. 'I didn't expect to see you again after the way you left.'

'Why didn't you tell me?' Anger bubbled inside me, punctuating each syllable.

She flinched at my tone. 'Tell you what?'

'You knew, didn't you? Ever since we were kids, you knew.'

Susan sighed. 'Jess, what are you talking about?' There was an impatience to her tone, but I didn't care. She'd blamed me for failing her but it was the other way round. Her betrayal had been far worse than any she had ever accused me of.

'My dad—' My voice cracked. 'My dad's dead.' Tears welled in my eyes and I blinked furiously. 'Isn't he?'

I don't know why I asked. The police wouldn't have made a mistake, not about this. But some part of me still refused to believe it. Inside I was still that same little girl who had watched for him to walk through the door each night.

'Oh, Jess.' Susan pressed her hand to her chest. 'You knew that.'

I glared at her. 'You helped me make him a card for every

Father's Day, every birthday, every Christmas that he was gone, you think I would have done that if I'd known?'

Susan frowned and her eyes darted back and forth in confusion. 'But your mum said...'

'She said what?' My gaze narrowed, waiting for her excuses. It wouldn't be enough. There was no explanation she could offer that would make me forgive her betrayal. She'd played along, letting me believe he was coming back, when all the time she had known that he wouldn't. He couldn't.

'That it was your way of coping. That it was a game you were playing, like make believe. You knew your dad was gone, but it helped you to pretend that he would come home someday. She told me if I was your friend that I would be there for you. I would play along. I wouldn't shatter that fantasy.'

The ground shifted beneath my feet and I reached for the doorframe for support.

'Oh, my God.' Susan slumped as her body crumpled. 'You really didn't know.'

I shook my head. 'He left.'

'Oh, Jess.' Susan flung her arms around me and I clung to her as I sobbed into her shoulder. My dad was gone. Completely gone.

The fading hope that I had hung on to for twenty-three years had finally been extinguished. He wouldn't be coming back for me. He never had been.

'Come and sit down,' Susan instructed as she tugged me inside. She guided me helplessly to the living room and I lowered myself down onto the sofa. There was nothing else I could do but comply. I didn't have the strength or inclination to resist.

Dad was gone.

Susan sat beside me, her hand clasped over mine. I stared at our hands. It was the same thing Mum had done when I heard about Adam's accident. Yet, this felt different. This time I could feel the warmth and compassion emanating from Susan's hands as she grasped mine as though she was afraid to let go. She was offering me a lifeline. After everything that we had been through, and all the years that had separated us, she was still the one person who understood right now. She was still the person I could count on.

'How is it possible that you didn't know?' Susan's voice was quiet and hesitant. She shook her head slowly. 'It's just incredible that you could have been in such denial.'

Denial.

The word circled in my brain. Denial implied I'd known but had chosen not to. I frowned as I searched back through my memories... Had it been a choice? Even an unconscious one? Or... I swallowed.

He's never coming back.

I screwed my eyes closed and allowed the past to engulf me. I could see it so clearly. I felt the tears, smelt the egg and toast. It was so vivid. So real.

I opened my eyes slowly. 'I don't think it was denial.'

'What do you mean?'

'I don't think I ever knew.' Even as I said it, it felt crazy. Wrong. How could I not have known?

'You must have done. Your mum would have told you.' Our eyes met and we stared at one another in silence. 'Wouldn't she?'

The question hung between us. The loyal daughter in me wanted to object and instinctively jump to Mum's defence. Of course she must have told me. She wouldn't keep something so momentous from me. She wouldn't have let me think he had left me by choice.

But I couldn't. There was an uncertainty to Susan's voice. It wasn't a foregone conclusion that Mum would have told me what happened. There was doubt. It wasn't just my doubt, I could see from her pale face and anxious expression that Susan felt it too.

A cold wave washed over me, draining me of all energy.

'Mum didn't just not tell me, she lied to me.'

'But she's your mum...'

I shook my head slowly. There was an expectation that her being my mother meant she wouldn't hurt me; that she wouldn't deceive me. 'Mum said he'd left.'

'No, you must be mistaken, Jess. She wouldn't have kept something like this from you. She wouldn't lie to you about it.'

'But she did. I'm sure she did.' Mum hadn't just not told me that Dad had died, she'd lied to me about his absence.

I felt numb. Everything I had believed had come unravelled in the last few hours.

Mum and I had always had a strange relationship. We'd been so different. Dad had been the glue that bound us together. In a weird way, his departure had strengthened that connection. We were united in our sadness, our loneliness. We were all each other had left.

And yet she had deceived me.

'Why would she do that?'

Susan's question echoed the one that had been repeating in my mind. Why? Why would Mum lie? Why would she hide Dad's death?

'Unless she thought she was protecting you somehow...'

Images from the past whirled through my head.

They will ask what you did wrong.

My hand flew to my mouth as I gasped. 'It was my fault.'

'What?'

'That's why Mum didn't tell me, she was shielding me from the truth.' It made sense. It was the only explanation that did. It was how it was meant to be; a parent protecting their child. A mother protecting her daughter from bearing the guilt of knowing she was responsible for the death of the father she adored. Mum had protected me then, just as she had my whole life. Our relationship was complex but it was ours.

'No.' I heard the shock in Susan's voice; the disbelief. 'You were just a child, you couldn't have been responsible.'

I stood up, suddenly feeling restless. I couldn't sit beside Susan, with her hand over mine. I didn't deserve her sympathy. Something I'd done had caused Dad's death.

But what?

I knew he'd left his case. I should have gone back for it. I could have prevented him falling. But why would Mum lie about that? It was an accident, tragic and pointless, but it wasn't enough of a reason to keep his death from me. She could have omitted the details. I didn't need to know that I could have saved him.

My stomach heaved. How did Mum even know to protect me from that detail? She wasn't there when I realised Dad had forgotten his case. She couldn't have heard me. So how would she know to hide it from me?

I paced the living room as I tried to catch hold of the memories that eluded me. Somewhere in my past the answers lay. There had to be a reason. 'Mum said it was something I'd done.'

But his accident happened when I was at school. I wasn't there.

Was I?

'She said that to you?' She shook her head. 'No, that can't be right. What kind of mother would say that to their child?'

I paused in my pacing and gazed desperately at Susan. 'He left because of me, I've always known that. His leaving was just...' I closed my eyes as fresh tears fell. 'More final than I'd thought.'

'You were his world, Jess.' Susan's voice grew closer as she spoke. I opened my eyes and saw her walking towards me.

I shook my head. 'I couldn't have been, or he wouldn't have left me.'

'Jess—'

'I drove him away, Susan. What if I did something...? It—' My voice cracked and I swallowed again. 'It must have been so unforgivable that—'

'What could you have done? You were seven years old.'

I raised an eyebrow. 'You, of all people, are asking me that?'

Confusion flickered across her brow.

'You know what I am capable of.'

Susan took a step backwards. 'You said it wasn't you. You said—'

'You said I didn't remember doing it, Susan. Like so many things that have happened in my life, so many bad things... You, Paul, Adam...' Another tear left a cold wet trail down my cheek.

Adam.

His name repeated over and over in my head.

I'd loved him. I couldn't have hurt him. It was unthinkable. And yet...

'But what if...?' I swallowed, unable to finish the question.

What if?

Those words were torture. They opened up so many possibilities, so many doubts. I could deny it to the police, to Mum, but could I really keep denying it to myself?

Susan stared at me. I willed her to speak, to say something, anything. I needed to hear her tell me I was being crazy. It wasn't possible. None of it could have been me. Not really. Not ever.

She didn't move. She didn't speak. She just stared. Not even Susan could defend me now.

They'll ask what you did wrong.

It always came back to that. I tried to claim innocence through ignorance, but was I innocent?

Mum had taught me not to lie. It was the foundation of my being. At least I thought it was. But maybe I was just a more accomplished liar than I could have imagined. So good that I had even fooled myself.

I turned and ran out of the living room.

'Jess...?' Susan's voice was hesitant and quiet. Afraid.

I ran through her hallway and down the drive to my car. What now? I couldn't confess to something I couldn't remember, could I? And if I did, then what? They would lock me away.

For life.

But the alternative was to do nothing. To wait for PC Davidson to find the proof he needed to arrest me by himself. It would only be a matter of time. I might not recall my crimes, but the past had proved I was no criminal mastermind. I always slipped up. I made a mistake. I got caught.

Mum had made the problems disappear in the past. She had looked out for me just as she had with Dad, but what had happened with Adam was too big even for her.

This was murder.

I shuddered as I clambered into my car and slammed the door. It seemed incredible to think I could have killed someone when even the mere thought of it made me feel nauseous. But the truth was inescapable. And it wasn't just someone. It was Adam.

My Adam.

If I could kill him... I closed my eyes. If I could kill Adam then no one was safe from me. I was a danger to anyone who crossed me. Any betrayal, whether real or just perceived, was punishable by me. Who would be next?

I rammed the key into the ignition and started the engine. Adam had been my way out, my escape from the trap I had made for myself, but even he couldn't save me. No one could.

47

Tears streamed down my face as I drove. There were so many lies, now. So many things I didn't say. Half-truths. Omitted facts. I thought it was new, a behaviour I'd learnt since Adam's disappearance, but the reality was the lies had started long before that.

I'd been lying to everyone for years; mostly to myself. Pretending I was fine; happy, even. Pretending I fitted in and belonged. Pretending I was just like everyone else; normal.

The things I couldn't talk about mounted up inside me.

They'll ask what you did wrong.

Mum had been protecting me from myself. She'd kept me close, where she could fix the things that I destroyed. She covered up my mistakes and kept me safe. She deserved better than me. Better than a daughter who was a burden. And the worst part was I had doubted her. I had questioned her motives. I'd let Adam poison me against her.

She'd been right all along about Adam; about me. It was time I finally accepted that my memory was faulty. But did I choose to forget? Or was it something within me, something so broken, so wrong, that the only way I could live with myself was to block my deeds from my memory?

But there were no glaring gaps. No missing time. Mum's theory meant I hadn't just forgotten parts of my life; I'd rewritten it.

Somehow it still didn't feel real, it didn't feel possible. And yet...

How could I ever really have known Adam, when the reality was I didn't even know myself?

The route had become familiar to me now. It was strange how a place that I hadn't even heard of until a few weeks ago had now become the centre of my world. Everything revolved around it.

It had a pull over me now. It drew me to it, whether I wanted to go or not. It was a place that had brought me such happiness, and also such sorrow. It had brought finality. It seemed a fitting place to go now. The only place to go.

I couldn't keep doing this, not alone. And I couldn't be trusted to be around anyone else. It was too dangerous. I was too dangerous.

Who knew what I would do tomorrow? Who knew who else I might hurt?

I pulled into the car park, and drew to a halt.

What if tomorrow didn't come? It didn't always. Not for everyone. Not for Adam. It didn't have to for me, either.

A sob escaped my lips and a torrent of fresh tears fell. I sat in the deserted car park, rocking gently in my seat as my mistakes weighed heavily on me. It no longer mattered that I couldn't remember my part in them. The truth was inescapable. My memory was unreliable. Ignorance was no defence. I was guilty of everything, more than I had ever imagined.

I sniffed and reached across to the glovebox. I opened the flap and reached in and pulled a tissue from the packet I kept in there.

My hand brushed something unfamiliar and I frowned as I peered in the glovebox through bleary, tear-filled eyes.

It was a book. A notebook. The seatbelt pulled against me as I leaned further forwards and picked the notebook up. I rested it on my lap and ran my fingers along the cover. It looked like Mum's book. The colour. The worn corners.

She'd been looking everywhere for it. What was it doing here?

I shrugged. She must have left it last time she was in the car. I leaned back in my seat as my brain whirled. When had that been? I hadn't driven Mum anywhere in weeks; months, even. Had I?

I must have done. Mum had only lost her notebook recently.

My shoulders sagged. Something else that I couldn't remember.

I should call her and let her know I'd found it, she'd been so distraught at its disappearance.

I started to reach for the phone in my bag but stopped. It seemed so mundane, so trivial. My gaze drifted to the path that led to the lighthouse. What did an old notebook matter when I'd come here to...

I closed my eyes. If I called Mum, I'd lose my nerve. Her voice would make me feel guilty. I was planning on abandoning her, like Dad had.

My breath caught in my chest. No, it was worse. Dad's departure hadn't been his choice. It had been something he'd had no control over. Something I could have prevented.

Mum knew my part in it. She must have done. She had hidden his death from me. She'd tried to protect me from my failure.

It was time for that to stop. I wouldn't be a burden to her any longer. She'd shielded me for long enough. There was so much I didn't know, so much I couldn't remember. Only Mum knew the truth about me; who I was; what I was capable of.

I lowered my gaze to the notebook resting in my lap. Mum

would never tell me what I'd done. She would always protect me from myself. But maybe there was someone; something she had confided in.

Memories of Mum scribbling frantically flashed through my mind. The book had been present at every big event in my life. Dad's departure, a new boyfriend, a failed relationship, even when Susan had shunned me. Mum would never tell me my secrets, but perhaps her notebook would.

I ran my fingers along the edge of the pages. It felt wrong to open it. It wasn't mine. I nibbled my lip. Mum had always been so protective of it. So secretive. It could be a diary, filled with Mum's personal thoughts and feelings.

I frowned. But how could she have the same notebook after all these years? I tilted my head to the right as I studied the notebook. Maybe it wasn't the same. Maybe it was just identical. But then how would she have found twenty-three years' worth of notebooks that looked the same?

There was only one way to know for sure what was inside, one way to know the secrets that Mum would never tell me herself. I wanted answers. I needed them.

What you want doesn't matter.

I shook my head. Maybe this time it did matter. Maybe it always should have mattered.

I opened the book at a random page. My gaze fell upon the name at the top.

Susan.

I frowned. I only knew one Susan.

She's gone. Finally.

My eyes widened as I carried on reading. My heart pounded a little faster. It couldn't be.

With hindsight I should have ended the friendship years ago. It had seemed harmless enough. She was the one person I hadn't anticipated would try and take Jessica away from me.

I could have let their friendship be, if only she hadn't put those crazy ideas of universities in London in Jessica's head.

The plans will die now, though. Susan will never forgive Jessica for her betrayal and Jessica will be too lost without her best friend to even contemplate going alone.

She will stay here now. With me.

I read the passage again.

With hindsight I should have ended the friendship years ago.

I couldn't take my eyes off those words. Mum had ended it. I hadn't kissed Tim. My memory of that time wasn't distorted or faulty. Mum had lied to Susan. She hadn't been apologising for me; she'd been sabotaging me.

I turned to the next page.

Paul.

It's working. She thinks he is cheating on her now. It's just a matter of time until she confronts him.

I jumped ahead as my head span.

I bought paint today; gold. It seemed a little classier and more unusual. It will be harder for Jessica to explain when Paul finds it. Too much of a coincidence.

Cold dread washed over me. Mum had vandalised Paul's car. I'd been arrested and questioned. Paul blamed me for the damage and the police had believed him. I had the evidence in my car. I only escaped being charged because Mum paid for the repairs. She persuaded Paul to drop the charges. She saved me from the trap she had set for me.

How could she do this? How could she alienate the people I'd loved? She'd poisoned them against me. She'd chased them away. And she'd blamed me for it.

My hand flew to my mouth. If she'd done that to Susan and to Paul, then what about...

Frantically, I flicked through the pages as years whizzed by, until...

Adam.

My gaze skimmed the lines until...

Anvil Point???

Jessica says Adam is working there. It would be the ideal spot. It's quiet in the winter.

My heart pounded as bile rose in my throat. I knew I should stop reading, but I couldn't. Disbelief battled with horror. I had to know now. I couldn't put the book down.

He would need to be unconscious. A mix of alcohol and sleeping pills should do it. I could invite him to the house. Tell him I wanted to make peace. We could toast our truce with a glass of good whisky...

I could drive his van out to Anvil Point. The cliff is steep. It would look like suicide. Or an accident. Just like before.

My hands shook as I lowered the book to my lap.

Adam.

My Adam.

48

I stared at the words scrawled on the pages. 'I don't understand.' My voice sounded strange and hollow. It was Mum's notebook. It was her writing. And yet, it couldn't be. Because if it was, then...

A cold drop of water splashed onto my hand as I held the notebook. Everything I'd known. Everything I believed had been thrown into chaos.

That book had changed everything.

The past. The present.

Adam had tried to warn me. We'd had so many arguments about Mum. He was certain that she was bad for me. I'd never listened. I hadn't wanted to hear it. Hadn't wanted to believe it.

But now I knew.

I'd read it with my own eyes.

I'd read it in her own words.

I gagged and I flung the car door open. The notebook slipped from my fingers as I ran to the bushes to throw up.

'Miss Harper?'

I closed my eyes. My head spun. It couldn't be real.

None of it could be real.

'Jess?'

I blinked and turned my head at the sound of a familiar voice. PC Davidson ran towards me and I groaned.

I wiped my mouth with the tissue I still held in my hands and tried to summon the strength to stand up straight.

I stared at him. 'You're here?'

'I followed you.'

'You...' I shook my head. It didn't matter.

'Are you all right?'

I gazed at him blankly.

All right.

The concept felt so unfamiliar. Nothing in my life had been all right for a long time. More so than I'd realised.

'Jess, what are you doing here?'

'Adam... I...' I glanced towards the path that lead to the clifftop.

'What happened to Adam, Jess?'

My gaze met his as my body swayed. PC Davidson reached out his hand and held my arm, gently steadying me.

'I should get you a doctor.'

I shook my head. 'I don't need a doctor. I need...' I ran out of words. What did I need?

I thought I'd wanted answers. Now I had them. But they weren't the answers I'd expected. They weren't even the ones I wanted.

'It wasn't me.'

My voice was quiet and hesitant. As much as I'd fought against it, part of me had always feared that I had been responsible. Not just for Adam, but for everything. There had always been a doubt that niggled at the back of my mind. A question that I refused to consider for too long, just in case.

'I didn't kill Adam.' My voice was firmer this time. Clearer. More certain.

My body shook with an overwhelming sense of relief, my palms felt sweaty and my hands trembled. I had actually believed that I was capable of killing the man I had once loved.

That fear had driven me here. If I hadn't found that notebook… I glanced back at the path. I'd almost met the same fate as Adam, and this time it would have been at my own hand.

'I think we should talk about this back at the station.'

I shook my head. 'It wasn't me.'

'Jess—'

'It wasn't.' I grasped his arm with my other hand. 'I know that now.'

PC Davidson's eyes narrowed. 'You really didn't remember, did you?'

'I…' I frowned, as I tried to make sense of the tangled mess of facts in my head. 'I was afraid I didn't.'

He tilted his head to the left.

'But there was never anything for me to remember. I hadn't forgotten. I had never been there. I didn't do it. I didn't do any of it.'

'Then who did?'

I turned back to my car, and my gaze fell upon the notebook sprawled open in the dirt. There was only one person it could have been. And yet that was the one person that it couldn't possibly be. The one person who would never hurt me. The one who always stood by me. The one who loved me, no matter what.

'What is that?' PC Davidson pulled free from my grasp and my hands fell to my sides as I watched him walk over to my car. He crouched beside it and studied the open pages.

He glanced back at me. 'You wrote this?'

I shook my head, my feet welded to the spot.

He pulled a pair of gloves from his pocket, slipped them on and picked up the notebook. I peered over his shoulder as he flicked through the pages. 'There's a lot of detail here about Paul, the damage to his car...'

'Everything is in there. Everyone I've ever loved. Everything that happened to them.'

He arched an eyebrow. 'And yet you're telling me it's not yours?'

I shook my head again.

'So whose is it, then?'

'Mum's.' The word felt like a betrayal. I was accusing her of the impossible. It was unthinkable. I was wrong. I was evil to even think such a thing; to doubt her.

PC Davidson glanced at the notebook and then back at me.

'Mum had hated them. She'd hated all of them.' Every person in my life who had meant anything to me was recorded in that book. Their faults were scrawled across the pages. Their arrival was detested and their departure plotted and savoured.

'Your mum wrote this?'

I nodded.

'But then that would mean...'

I stared at him, willing him to explain; to tell me the thought that repeated in my head was wrong; to tell me Mum hadn't done this.

His eyes met mine and I could almost see the pieces of the puzzle falling into place in his mind. In that instant I knew the truth. It was her. It had always been her.

49

'Have you heard what they are accusing me of? It's ridiculous.' Mum gripped my hand, her anguished face pale in the stark hospital lighting. 'They actually think I killed him.'

'Hush, Mum.' I glanced at the police officer by the door, praying he wouldn't call a nurse to sedate Mum again. I needed answers. I needed explanations. Neither of which I would get if Mum became hysterical again.

She sat up in the bed, rocking back and forth.

'I didn't do it.'

Something contracted in my chest. I wanted to believe her.

But I couldn't. Not now. Not ever again.

Her face contorted. 'I couldn't have done.'

Her grip tightened on my hand, and I winced. 'They're sending me for a psychological evaluation. Can you believe it?'

I shook my head. I couldn't. None of this seemed possible and yet somehow here we were. 'They're going to help you, Mum. You'll get the treatment you need—'

'I don't need treatment. There's nothing wrong with me.'

The sight of her in the hospital bed contradicted her words.

She seemed so erratic, her eyes wide and darting, despite the sedatives.

It tore at my heart to see her like this. It wasn't her. None of this was her. There had to be a way to reach her. To save her. She was my mum. She'd made mistakes. Horrendous mistakes. But it wasn't her. Not the real her. I just needed to find her again. To remind her who she was. Remind her how to be good.

'That police officer turned up on my doorstep, muttering on about placing me under arrest, but for what?'

I stared at her. Had she forgotten already? 'For Adam.'

Mum scoffed. 'He's not worth this.'

'You ki…' I couldn't finish the word. I couldn't voice that accusation. 'You resisted arrest.'

'Of course I did.' She glared at me. 'I wasn't going to let them drag me from my home like that.'

'They said you became hysterical.'

'Because I didn't do it. I couldn't have done. I would remember.'

'You don't remember?' I stared at her. It seemed incredulous. I'd protested my innocence for years, I'd never been able to remember doing any of the things I had been accused of, and now Mum was claiming the same thing. Except the difference was that I couldn't remember because it was never me that had done it. It was her.

'I wanted to. I planned to. I had it all worked out.'

'I know. I read your notebook.'

'You have my book?' Mum glared at me as her nails dug into my flesh. 'Give it back. It's not yours. It's mine.'

I gritted my teeth to prevent myself from crying out. I couldn't risk the policeman hearing. He would interrupt and then Mum would never tell me what I needed to know.

I tried to prise her fingers back with my other hand. 'I don't have it any more. The police took it.'

The strength withered from Mum's grip. 'They have my notebook?'

I nodded.

'How did they get it? I've been looking for it for days.'

I frowned. 'When was the last time you were in my car, Mum?'

'Your car?' She looked at me blankly. 'Why would I have been in your car?'

It was a valid question. Mum usually drove if we went anywhere together. But if she hadn't been in my car, then how did her notebook get in the glovebox?

'You wrote about Adam in your notebook, Mum.' I edged closer to the bed. 'You wrote about all of them.'

'That's private.' She resumed her rocking.

'You bribed Matthew. You bought him a car so he would stop dating me. And the graffiti on Paul's car, that was you too, wasn't it?'

'It was for your own good.'

I stared at her. She couldn't actually believe that, could she?

'They weren't right for you. It wouldn't have worked with any of them.'

'You don't know that.' I glared at her, full of indignance. 'You never gave us a chance. You never gave *me* a chance.'

'I was protecting you. I'm your mother. It's my job.'

Her words tugged at my heart, chipping away at my anger. She'd been looking out for me. Maybe I should feel grateful to her for that at least. Her methods were flawed, but her intentions had been good. She loved me. She wanted what was best for me.

It didn't make it right, but it was something. Beneath all the craziness and the manipulation, beneath the lies and the hatred, there was still a tiny sliver of the woman I thought I'd known.

Despite what she'd done, she was still a mother protecting her child. She was still my mother.

Maybe she was right. Perhaps none of the guys I'd dated had been good enough. They'd all fled. They'd all fallen for her manipulation and lies. None of them had thought enough of me to question it. None of them had fought to stay with me.

But then not every relationship is destined to last. She curtailed them before their time. She deprived me of the excitement of being part of a couple. Of dating. Of being happy and enjoying life. She'd isolated me, to keep me safe, but she'd hurt me more than anyone else could have done.

I put my hand over hers. 'You can't protect me from life, Mum. All you did was stop me from living it.'

Maybe if I could reach her, I could help her understand that what she'd done was wrong. Maybe I could save her.

'Jess...' She leaned forwards, her eyes glossy as her gaze met mine. 'I...' She licked her lips as she struggled to speak.

A lump lodged in my throat. She was going to apologise. I squeezed her hand, urging her to continue and say the words I wanted to hear; I needed to hear.

It wouldn't change anything. It wouldn't undo the past. But if she was able to admit her mistakes then maybe, just maybe, in time we would find a way to move past it. Together.

'I need you to promise me you won't date any more.'

I pulled my hand away from hers as though her touch had burned me. 'What?' My mind raced. How could she ask me to do that? To give up on love? To give up on life?

'You're better off alone. They'll never love you. None of them.'

Her words were like shards of ice piercing my skin.

'It's not your fault, Jess. You can't help the way you are. You were born that way.'

I frowned at her. 'Born what way?' I cursed the words as I said them. I knew I shouldn't ask. I should ignore her and walk away. But I couldn't.

'Unlovable.'

My breath caught in my throat. 'You think I'm unlovable?'

She shook her head. 'Not to me, Jess. I love you despite it. I'm your mother. It's my job to love you unconditionally. I always have. I always will.'

It wasn't that she thought the guys I'd dated weren't right for me, instead she thought I wasn't good enough for them. They'd never be able to love me.

'That's why Daddy left.' She shook her head slowly. 'He just couldn't love you.'

It wasn't the apology I'd expected. She wasn't sorry. She never would be.

Had any of it really been about keeping me safe, or just about keeping me alone? Like her?

'But Dad didn't leave, did he?'

'Of course he did. He abandoned us.'

'You were arguing a lot. You were so mad at him.'

'He wanted to go back to the old house. My parents left us everything and he wanted to throw it all away.'

Just like before.

The words from the notebook repeated on a loop in my head.

'What happened to Dad, was it really an accident?'

Mum stared at me. 'Daddy left.'

'And what about Adam?'

'He...'

'He what, Mum?'

She clamped her mouth closed.

'You wrote about Anvil Point, Mum. You wrote it exactly the way it happened.'

'That doesn't mean...' She shook her head. 'I wrote it, but I hadn't got round to actually doing it. Not yet.' She frowned. 'I don't think.'

'You don't think?'

Mum leaned closer to me. 'There's a gap.' She whispered. 'In my head. Time is missing. He was alive and in the way, and then suddenly he was gone.'

'You don't remember pushing him off the cliff?'

'I don't remember going to Anvil Point at all. I couldn't have done, could I? I would remember, wouldn't I?'

I gasped. It was like I was looking in a mirror. All the anguish and questions that had tormented me for years were now reflected in her face. She didn't remember.

Perhaps Adam had been one step too far for her to come back from. In the past she had paid people to leave, or scared them away from me, but with Adam her actions had been more severe. More final. How did you come back from something like that? From taking a life?

I drew back in the chair away from her. I wasn't sure why I had come here. Perhaps I had hoped for an explanation, one that would change what I had read in that notebook. One that would disprove the conclusions I had drawn from it. One that would prove Mum's innocence.

All I'd found was a certainty of her guilt.

But was Mum right about me? Was I unlovable? Had I needed her protection? Not in the way she had actioned it, but had my choices been so bad for me that my mother had needed to intervene?

An unfamiliar queasiness stirred in the pit of my stomach. I wasn't accustomed to doubting anything. Everything in my life had been so certain. So planned. I always did what was right. Expected. I didn't make decisions. I didn't question things. I simply obeyed.

Even with Adam. I'd replaced following Mum's path with following his. It had felt freeing for a while. It felt like I'd escaped. It was different. More exciting. Rebellious.

But I wasn't really rebelling, I was still obeying the rules. Only the person issuing them had changed.

But now something felt different. I felt different. I had a choice. I could accept Mum's words and correct my course. I could revert back to who she thought I was, or at least who she thought I should be. She had always been my lighthouse. A beacon to keep me on course and avoid crashing on the rocks. She'd been helping me. Protecting me.

Hadn't she?

It's what I'd always believed. If I struggled with her path, it was my fault. It was because I wasn't good enough. I needed to try harder. I needed to be better. But what if the problem wasn't me? What if it was the path? Her path? Had it ever really been mine?

A chill crept through my body. Before Adam, I'd been afraid that all I was ever going to have was Mum's love; no one else's.

But now I realised I didn't even have that. Not the way I'd thought. The way I'd needed. It was manipulative and poisonous. It was suffocating me. Reminding me of my weaknesses. Never letting me grow and be myself.

I stood up. 'Mum, I need to go now.'

She didn't answer. She just stared at the wall ahead of her.

I picked up my bag and walked out of her room. I didn't look back. I wouldn't. My boots clunked down the ward, the only intrusion to the silence of our goodbye.

It felt wrong to hate her. She'd destroyed so much of my life, my happiness, but she was still my mother. Deep down, I knew she loved me. Her actions had been driven by her own hardships and her own failed choices. She'd simply been doing what she thought was best to protect me from the same fate.

She hadn't asked me to come back and I'd made no promises to return. I wasn't sure it would do either of us any good. We both needed to learn to live our own lives.

I felt more alone now. I hadn't just lost Adam, I'd lost everything. Mum was still here; except she wasn't. Not the way I'd thought. Not the version of her I'd known. She hadn't changed but my perspective of her had.

It was like one of those perspective tests, where you could look at a picture for years and see two faces, until one day someone tells you it's a candle. You squint at it until finally you see it too and then suddenly that's all you can see. The original picture disappears and no matter how hard you try you can't see it that way again.

Mum was that picture. I couldn't see her the same way now. That version of her had gone. Maybe she'd never existed. Or maybe the truth lay somewhere between the two versions. She wasn't one or the other, she was both.

50

I hung up my mobile and slipped it back into my pocket as I stood outside the hospital.

'Jess?'

I glanced up at the familiar voice.

I swallowed. 'PC Davidson.' I nodded cautiously as he walked away from the entrance towards me. 'Are you here to see me?'

He shook his head. 'No, I was here on another case.'

I let out the breath I had been holding.

'Were you visiting your mother?'

I nodded. 'I'm just waiting for my friend to give me a lift, so I can go and get my car from Anvil Point.'

'Are you sure there isn't someone else who could collect your car for you?'

I smiled. 'Probably, but I feel like it's something I needed to do myself.'

'Do you think it's a good idea for you to go back there again?'

I nodded. 'I think I need to see it one last time.'

'One last time? You're not...' His voice trailed away. 'Last time you went there you were so distressed, I wondered if you were...'

'Going to join Adam?'

His nod was so slight it was barely visible.

'It had crossed my mind.' I cringed. It had more than crossed my mind. 'I thought I'd...'

'You thought you'd killed Adam.'

'There were so many things I couldn't remember. Bad things.'

'Because you were never responsible.'

I nodded. 'I know that now, but right then I was so scared. Scared of what I could already have done. Scared of what else I might do. I didn't want to be like that. I didn't want to risk hurting anyone else.'

'But it wasn't you.'

'You thought it was.'

His cheeks flushed. 'It was a possibility.'

I raised an eyebrow.

'Okay, a strong possibility,' he admitted grudgingly. 'But I wasn't convinced.'

'Why not?'

He shook his head. 'Call it gut instinct, I guess. Something just never quite added up to me.'

I frowned. 'Is that why you followed me?'

He cleared his throat. 'After I dropped you off at your apartment, I saw you head straight to your car.' He shrugged. 'It seemed strange. You were so distraught. I was curious about where you would go in that state.'

I chuckled. 'So much for believing my innocence.'

He shrugged again. 'I needed to be sure, one way or the other.'

'So did I.'

'Do you want some company while you wait for your friend?'

I glanced at him and could see the hesitation in his eyes. Was he afraid that I might still try and join Adam? I might know the truth now, I wasn't responsible for his death, but my world had crumbled. I'd lost everything now. Everyone.

'I'd like that.' My answer surprised me. Surely the police officer who had been digging into my life for the past few days was the last person I should voluntarily want to spend more time with.

He gestured to a bench and we fell into step as we walked towards it. 'Thanks for your help with everything, PC Davidson.'

'It's Simon.' I glanced at him and he smiled. 'You're not a suspect any more.'

I nodded. It felt freeing to hear those words. It was over.

Almost.

'I need to see the notebook again.'

He shook his head. 'It's evidence, Jess.'

'I need to check…' We reached the bench and I sat down slowly. 'Mum started writing in that book after Dad left.'

Died.

I closed my eyes as the correction reverberated through me. I knew the truth now. He hadn't just left. He'd died. But had there been something about that moment that triggered a change in Mum?

'I opened the book part way through. I never read the beginning.'

'I'm sorry, Jess.'

'But you've read it?' If he wouldn't let me see it, maybe he would at least tell me what it said.

'I have.'

'And?'

'I told you, it's evidence.'

'It's my life.'

'Jess.' There was a warning tone to his voice.

I shoved my hands into my pockets as a cold wind whipped up around us. I glanced up at the dull sky. There was a storm coming.

'I need to understand. She's my mum. She framed me.' I took a breath. 'My own mother framed me.' I stared into his eyes, pleading with him to understand; to help me. 'If Mum chased people out of my life to protect me, to keep me close to her, then why would she frame me? Why would she want me to believe I was capable of those things?'

'Maybe she hoped that by destroying your trust in yourself, you would become dependent on her. You wouldn't make new friends, you wouldn't want to date, because you would always be afraid of what might happen to anyone you let into your life.'

'You mean she wanted me to be afraid of what I might do to them.'

'I wish I could say something that would make this less painful for you.'

I took a deep breath of the cold February air. 'And my dad? Why would Mum lie about what happened to him?'

Simon shook his head. 'Maybe she was traumatised. Maybe she couldn't process his death and needed to believe he was still alive, that there was a possibility that he could come home. Or maybe to protect you from the pain of knowing the truth.'

I nibbled my lower lip. I wanted to accept it. His theories were plausible. And yet doubts had lodged themselves firmly in my head.

'Mum wasn't protecting me, though. She didn't create a fairy-tale where Dad was alive and going to return. She was adamant that he was never coming back and that it was all my fault. She wanted me to believe he had a choice. She wanted me to believe I was the reason he abandoned us. She wanted to punish me.'

'Grief can do strange things to people.'

'Or maybe she blamed me.'

Simon frowned. 'For what?'

'Dad's death. He'd been in a hurry to get me to school on time. If he hadn't been rushing...'

'You don't know that, Jess. You don't know if he fell because he was in a hurry, or if he tripped at the top of the stairs, or if—' He stopped abruptly.

'Or if...?'

He kept his gaze fixed on the hospital building.

Just like before.

'Or if it wasn't an accident?'

It was the question that had burned in my mind since I'd read Mum's notebook. If she could kill Adam, then who was safe?

Simon inhaled deeply. 'There is no evidence to suggest that it was anything other than an accident.'

'But Mum's notebook?'

'She never actually admits to any wrongdoing.'

'But you think she did it? You think she was capable?'

'Hard to say for sure. The evidence against her for Adam's disappearance is mostly circumstantial, but...'

I studied him closely. 'You think she could have done it, though?'

Simon lowered his gaze to the ground, avoiding meeting my eyes.

'Will Mum be charged for Dad's death, too?'

'It's doubtful.'

I stopped. 'But you will investigate?'

'Of course, Jess. But it was a long time ago. His death was ruled an accident. His body was cremated. Unless your mum confesses...'

'There's no proof.'

He shook his head.

'She'll get away with it.'

'Maybe. We have enough to charge her for Adam's disappearance. We've found sleeping pills at her house along with a receipt for a bottle of whisky. And when we recover Adam's body that should give us more evidence.'

I nodded but somehow it didn't seem enough.

'What will you do now?' Simon asked.

I gazed at him blankly. 'I don't know.'

'You have to find a way to let go, Jess.'

'Why should I?' I cringed, aware that I sounded like an insolent child. 'I have the right to be indignant, don't I? The people I loved most lied to me and betrayed me. They were the two people who were meant to care about me, to love me, and yet...'

'Yes, you have the right to be hurt and angry and every other emotion that you are feeling right now, but at some point you have to let go.'

I opened my mouth, ready to object again, but Simon put his hand on my shoulder. 'Because they have stolen enough of your life, of your time, your heart. Do you really want to let them take any more?'

I clamped my mouth shut. It was a valid question. Of course I didn't.

'How can you ever move on, Jess, if you can't let go?'

He was right. I had to find a way to move forward. I couldn't go back to how things had been; to how I had been. I knew that. Too much had changed. I'd changed. But what else was there? What if I'd left it too late to start again? What if I repeated the same mistakes? What if I wasn't able to be different?

'I'm afraid that...' I paused. How could I explain? How could anyone ever understand? To anyone else it would sound weird and stupid. On the surface it seemed so simple, so easy to avoid the same pattern. Just do what you want. Be what you want. Live.

'I don't know how to live.' The confession slipped from my lips.

I could feel his gaze on me. He was studying me. No doubt assessing my sanity. Only a short time ago that would have made me want to disappear and hide. But strangely, today it didn't bother me. He'd uncovered all there was to know about me. He'd seen the worst parts of my life. He'd thought I could have murdered a man. It was doubtful that I could fall lower in his expectation than I already had. And yet he was still here, patiently waiting for me to continue.

'I don't know how to. Not really. I never did. I'd slipped from the world without anyone noticing. Not even me. Not at first.'

Had I been kept away, or had I chosen it? Perhaps it didn't even matter now. The only thing knowing achieved would be to know where to lay the blame.

I knew where Adam thought the blame lay. But maybe it wasn't that clear cut.

'Maybe none of us really know,' Simon said quietly. 'I think most of us are just making it up as we go along. I know I am.'

Now it was my turn to stare at him.

'You?' I frowned. 'But you seem so confident. So self-assured.'

He chuckled. 'I have faith in my abilities as a police officer. I work hard. I do a good job. But that doesn't mean I know everything. I'm always learning. And beyond work...' He shrugged. 'Well, that's just a case of testing things out. Going new places. Meeting new people. Seeing what fits.'

'I'm still scared.'

He nodded. 'Yeah, it'll be daunting at first. I've been finding my way my whole life and it still catches me off guard sometimes. For you it will all be new. But that doesn't mean it won't be worth it.'

'I don't think I even know where to start.'

'Make a list of things you want to do. Start at the top and work your way down.'

I ground my toe against the pavement. 'I don't even know what I want to do.'

He nudged my arm with his elbow. 'In that case you'll just have to try everything until you figure it out. It could be kind of fun.'

'I'm...' My voice cracked. 'I'm not sure I'm brave enough. Not without Adam. Not alone.'

'One thing I am certain of is that you are stronger than you realise.' He smiled. A wobbly, tentative smile that made him look nervous. 'But maybe you don't have to do it alone. Not because you can't, but because you choose not to.'

51

I saw Karen's car pull up in front of the hospital. 'My friend's here,' I announced, feeling slightly disappointed that she had arrived so quickly.

Simon nodded.

We both stood up and started walking back towards the hospital entrance.

'Thank you,' I said, as we reached the car.

'For investigating you?'

'For perceiving. For seeking the truth, not just an arrest.'

'It's my job.'

I nodded. 'I know, but even so…'

I opened the car door and slid into the passenger seat.

'He's cute.' Karen's gaze was fixed on Simon as he raised his hand in a half wave before heading off towards his own car.

I raised my eyebrows and stared at Karen. 'He's the guy that's been investigating me for Adam's murder.'

Karen smirked. 'But he never actually arrested you, did he?'

'No, but—'

'So, he obviously never really thought you did it.'

'Or possibly the lack of evidence might have had something to do with it.'

'A mere technicality.' Karen shrugged.

I rolled my eyes.

'He likes you, though,' she said as she started the engine and flicked the windscreen wipers on, as the first drops of rain fell.

'What? Don't be ridiculous,' I scolded her, but I couldn't help sneaking a glance back over my shoulder as we drove out of the car park.

'I saw that.'

'I didn't do anything. He's not even there.'

Karen laughed. 'You were looking for him, though.'

I swatted her arm gently. 'I'm admitting nothing.'

'But seriously, Jess,' Karen said as she stopped at the junction and turned to look at me. 'I think someone like him would be good for you.'

'Someone who wants to arrest me?'

'Someone who accepts you for who you are.'

My cheeks flushed. 'Thanks, but I think right now I need to spend some time alone. I think I need to learn to accept myself first.'

'That makes sense.'

I smiled, grateful for her understanding.

'Besides, I'd be worried if he made a move too soon. I mean, you were a suspect after all.'

I laughed. It felt good to laugh again. It felt different now; lighter; more genuine.

'Well, it's not like anything would ever happen with us anyway. I'm probably never even going to see him again. I am aiming to lead a much quieter life from now on, with no more trips to police interview rooms.'

'You know there'll be a trial, right?' Karen asked tentatively.

I cringed. 'I hadn't even thought about that.' Mum's life would be publicly debated, and mine along with it.

'But at least you'll get to see the cute police officer again.' Karen winked at me. 'And once the trial is out of the way...'

I rolled my eyes again, but the corner of my mouth twitched upwards.

52

I huddled by the door as I fumbled in my pocket for the key. The rain pounded against my back and the wind whipped around me. I slipped the key in the lock and pushed the door open. I stepped inside and hurriedly shut it behind me.

I should have just driven straight to my apartment after collecting my car from Anvil Point. But I couldn't. I needed to come here. I needed to see the past again, but this time with fresh eyes.

I lingered by the door. I'd entered this house countless times over the years. I knew every inch of it and yet today it seemed different. It looked the same, it even smelt the same, but it felt different now.

The life I'd lived here, the memories I had, were all tarnished and warped. Nothing had been as it had seemed. I turned to face the staircase and my gaze fell upon the wood flooring at the base of the bottom step.

I could imagine Dad lying there. His body twisted and lifeless. He hadn't abandoned me. At least not by choice.

I'd given up on him too easily. I'd believed he was capable of leaving. I'd believed Mum. I should have known him better than that. He was my dad, my hero, my strength. The one person who believed I could do anything and encouraged me to chase my dreams. The one person who had never given up on me.

I walked towards the stairs. My trainers squelched with each step. I glanced back at the trail of muddy footprints I had left, and the drops of water that dripped from my winter coat. Mum would scold me if she could see the mess I had made. I shrugged. It didn't matter. Not now.

I leaned against the staircase. The prospect of Dad leaving me had jarred with everything I'd believed, everything I'd known, but I'd still accepted it as the truth. I'd trusted Mum when she said he'd left. I believed her when she said it was my fault.

Perhaps she was right. Perhaps if I'd gone back for his briefcase he would still be with me. He wouldn't have raced home that day. He wouldn't have hurried up the stairs to his office. He wouldn't have fallen as he wouldn't have been there.

At least, not then. Not that day. Not that moment.

But what about the next?

Maybe I could have prevented an accident, but what if there was more to it than that?

It was a question I would probably never know the answer to. Not for sure.

Mummy and I need to sort some things out first.

I froze as Dad's words from that morning played in my head. He had stopped me running back for his case. He hadn't hurried back for it after dropping me at school. He'd planned to return home. He wanted to talk to Mum.

'Oh, Dad.' I sank to the floor and sobbed. I cried for him, for the way he had died. I cried for us and the years together that we had been deprived of. And I cried for me and the life I might have had if he had still been part of it.

His death had changed everything. It changed me. It changed how I saw people, how I kept my distance, how I built walls to protect me.

His death changed my life.

Slowly my sobs quietened. I had no more tears left to cry. They wouldn't bring him back. They wouldn't change the past.

I clambered to my feet. This wasn't the way I wanted to remember my dad.

I turned and walked through the kitchen. I unlocked the patio door and swung it open. The wind howled through the doorway, and I staggered backwards. I hunched my shoulders and ploughed forwards. I needed to return to the place where we had been happiest. I needed to reconnect with the memories I treasured most. Dad and I and our view of the ocean. I needed to see it one last time. I needed to remember him as he had been; happy and caring.

The icy air stung my face, but I didn't care. I rammed my hands in my pockets and fought against the wind as the rain obscured my vision. Not even that would keep me from saying goodbye. Nothing would. Not this time.

I stopped near the edge of the clifftop. It was our spot. The place we sat together watching the waves lapping against the shore. But today the waves looked angry. They rolled up, engulfing the entire beach. I edged forwards; even the promenade was submerged as huge waves crashed against the cliff side.

I drew back. I'd never seen it like that before.

It wasn't just my life that had turned upside down, the world had too. It was angry and crazed. The rhythm and pattern had been disrupted and lost. Everything was out of sync. All that was left was chaos.

'Jess?'

I shuddered. I was losing it. I could almost hear Adam's voice calling to me on the wind.

'Jess?'

I turned.

My hand flew to my mouth as my eyes grew wide. I stepped backwards instinctively.

'No, Jess. The cliff.'

I swung back as a hand grabbed me and pulled me away from the cliff edge.

'Adam?' My voice was a breathless whisper.

'Hey, Jess.' He smiled at me. That adorable lopsided smile that had always made my heart melt.

I shook my head and pulled free of his grasp. I was as crazy as my mother. Perhaps it ran in the genes. Adam wasn't here. He wasn't real. He was dead.

I blinked, furiously trying to clear my vision. I expected his image to disappear. It was just grief distorting reality.

But he remained.

Adam stared at me silently, his hair plastered to his head from the heavy rain, as though he had just stepped out of the shower.

My heart lurched at the memory. I missed those simple things. His presence. His voice. His touch.

I pressed my hand against my arm where he had grabbed me. I could still feel the dull throb in my muscles from his powerful grip. But how? He wasn't real, so neither was the pain.

It was this place. The memories. It was making me crazy.

Just like Mum.

I veered around him. I had to get back to the house. I had to get out of here. Out of this house. This town.

'Jess, it's me.'

Adam stepped in front of me.

'No, you're dead. Argh.' I groaned in frustration. I was talking to my illusion now. Did that make me more or less insane?

He grabbed my arms. 'I'm not dead.' He reached for my hand and pressed it against his chest. I felt his heart pounding against my palm. 'I'm alive, Jess.'

53

I stared at my hand against his chest. My lips parted and closed as I fought for air. The wind howled around me, but I couldn't feel it. I was numb.

'You can't...' My words were nothing more than a whisper that evaporated in the wind.

My hand shook as I pulled it away from him, unable to bear the feel of the impossible any longer.

No matter how real his touch felt, it wasn't possible. It had to be a hallucination. He was dead. Mum had killed him. 'The cliff. Your van.' I screwed my eyes closed, forcing away the memories. 'The police said you couldn't have survived that fall.'

'I wasn't in the van, Jess.'

'What?' My eyes flew open and I gazed at his familiar face.

'I never went over the cliff.'

'But Mum...'

'I staged the whole thing.'

Staged.

'No, it was Mum. She wrote—'

'I set her up, Jess.'

'You? But...' My head span. 'How? Why?'

Nothing made sense. It was crazy to think that Mum had killed him, but now he was here, claiming none of it was real. He couldn't have faked his death. He wouldn't do that. Not to me.

I swallowed. But then, I hadn't believed he could cheat on me either.

My knees buckled and I sank to the soggy grass.

'We should go inside.'

I shook my head. I couldn't move. I didn't want to. I didn't care that the rain was pounding down on me. Adam was alive.

He knelt in front of me. 'I had to do it. It was the only way.'

The shock that had kept me paralysed ebbed away. I was no longer numb. Pain seeped into my body, like the rain that soaked through my clothes. He'd made me believe he was dead. I'd lost him. I'd even thought I could have been responsible. And yet, the whole time he'd been alive.

'I read your mum's notebook.'

'You've seen that?'

'I stole it. She was always carrying it around with her; she was always scribbling in it and then hiding it when she saw me. I wanted to know what she wrote about me. About us.'

'How did you get it?' The question seemed almost irrelevant, but some part of me needed the details. I needed to piece it all together. To understand. To make it plausible; real. To make *him* real.

'The day she came for dinner.'

I squinted as I remembered that day. 'You came home late and then wouldn't join us for dinner.'

'I was too tired to deal with her. But then I realised her guard would be down. She didn't know I was there. Her bag would be unattended. She trusted you. She knew you'd never go in her bag and read her notebook. But me...'

'That's why you crept into the living room while I was clearing away.'

Adam nodded.

'You faked the entry. Set it up to look like she was plotting against you—'

'No,' Adam interrupted. 'The notebook was all real. All her. I only read it. At first it was horrifying realising how much she wanted me dead. She wanted to kill me, Jess. I was so freaked out that I almost ran.'

'You were going to leave me?'

'But I didn't.'

I glared at him. 'No, you faked your death instead.' My tone was full of anger. He hadn't just abandoned me. He'd destroyed me.

'You've seen her notebook, Jess. You know what she is capable of now. You know what she's done. Your mother is insane. The stuff she had written...' He shuddered. 'The things she had already done.'

'You could have told me.' He'd chosen to run from Mum, instead of staying with me. He hadn't even tried to fight for us.

'You would never have believed me.'

'You could have showed me the notebook.' He was right, I wouldn't have believed him. Who could believe that of their own mother? But the notebook changed everything. It was her confession. Even I couldn't argue her innocence against that.

'I thought about it. But something you said stuck in my head. You told me if you believe something for long enough then it becomes the truth.'

My eyes narrowed. 'So you decided to make us believe that you were dead.'

Adam smiled. 'Not just dead; murdered.'

My stomach heaved and I pressed my hands against the ground to steady me.

'I still had her notebook. I went through it again, this time more carefully. I needed something I could work with, something where there didn't need to be a body. She made it so easy. All I had to do was follow her plan, with just enough careless mistakes to show it wasn't an accident.'

'You wanted to hurt her. Torment her.'

'Yes.'

'But it wasn't just her. It was me too. You let me believe you were dead. I mourned for you. I went to your vigil.'

'I had to. It was the only way I could help you. I had to rescue you from your mother, from that life.'

I stared at him. I'd pushed him to this. My refusal to take a chance; to be brave; to break away from my mother, had led him here. He'd done it all for me. To save me. To be with me. My own handsome hero who'd battled demons and even faced death, all to save the girl he loved.

It was the fairy-tale I'd always wanted, but it was all messed up. It didn't mean anything and, like all fairy-tales, it wasn't entirely true. He'd rescued me from Mum's control, not to save me, but to remove the competition. He'd freed up my time and attention so it could be redirected towards him. He hadn't done it out of love for me, but out of jealousy.

'We can be together now. You and me. Forever.'

Together.

He still wanted to be with me. He'd come back for me. He hadn't abandoned me. He still loved me. It was a sick and twisted kind of love. But it was love none the less.

'But you're dead.' I closed my eyes and shook my head. 'I mean, everyone thinks you're dead. How can you live? How can you work, or—'

'Jess.' Adam laughed. 'I don't need to work.' He swung his arms wide open. 'We have this.'

I frowned.

'Your mum gave you power of attorney. With her incapacitated—'

'H-how did you know that?'

'I found the papers in your filing cabinet.'

'You went through my personal papers?' It wasn't just Mum he'd been spying on, it was me too.

'We're in control of all of it now. This will be ours.'

Ours.

We'd become an *us* again. A couple. He wanted me now. He needed me.

I glanced back at the house that had once been a home. Was I so desperate to have the fairy-tale that I'd settle for the illusion?

'No,' I said quietly.

'What?'

I turned back to him. 'No.' My voice was firmer this time. More certain. More determined. 'This was never about me. This was about what you could get from me.' I shook my head. 'Well, you'll get *nothing*.' I spat the word at him. I deserved better than him. Better than his lies and betrayals.

The colour drained from his face. 'Look, Jess—'

'I hate you.' I glared at him. The fear and heartache that I had been desperately keeping in check inside me for months suddenly erupted into anger. 'You put me through hell. Your death. The police. The questions. They thought I'd killed you. Did you know that? They kept questioning me. I was terrified they were going to arrest me. That I would spend the rest of my life in prison—'

'I wouldn't have let that happen. I didn't let that happen. I left the notebook where you would find it. I made sure I left enough evidence to lead them to your mother.'

I nodded slowly, regaining my composure. 'Yes, my mother. The woman who has been hospitalised because of you. They've charged her with your murder and you're not even dead.'

'She deserves what she got.'

'She was innocent,' I yelled above the storm.

'Was she?' Adam stared at me. His eyes wide with disbelief. 'She wanted me gone, Jess. She'd have gone to great lengths to get rid of me.'

'But not to kill you.'

'We don't know that.' He shuffled closer towards me. 'She was planning it.'

I shook my head. 'She'd thought about it.' I cringed. 'That's bad, but it's not the same. She wouldn't actually have done it.'

'Are you sure? Until today you believed she had. You believed she was capable of it.'

'Because you *made* me believe it. You made me think...' I closed my eyes. 'You made me think my mother was a murderer.' I opened my eyes and searched his face for any signs of remorse. There weren't any. 'You made her believe it, too. It crushed her. It pushed her over the edge. It destroyed her, her life, her sanity.'

Adam reached out and held my hand in his. 'She planned to kill me, Jess. That's what drove her crazy. Not me. Not what I did. The fact is, she can't live with herself, knowing what she wanted to do.'

I snorted. 'No, it's probably the fact that she thinks you're actually dead that did it. She kept talking about missing time. She thinks she lost time because she can't remember killing you. But she didn't lose anything. You used her against herself. You used her hatred for you. You used her need for control.'

Adam laughed. 'She took it further than I'd expected. I knew her need to control things overrode everything else, but I didn't realise how she'd react when I took that control away. She destroyed herself when she realised she wasn't in control of anything, not even her own actions.'

I clambered to my feet, and pulled my phone from my pocket. 'Hopefully, when she learns that you are alive it will help her recover.'

'What are you doing? You can't be serious?'

Adam charged at me and knocked the phone from my hands.

I glared at him. 'Did you really think I'd go along with this? That I'd accept all you've done and let my mother stay locked up in that place?'

'She's better off there. You're better off with her there. She's crazy, Jess. Even before this. She wasn't right. The way she treated you, the way she made you feel.' He reached out and his fingers stroked my cheek. 'It wasn't right.'

I pushed him away from me. 'And you think the way you treat me is?'

Adam flinched. 'I'm going to change.'

I shook my head. 'No, you won't. You'll still cheat. You'll still lie. You'll still control me. Just like you're trying to do now.' I turned back to the house.

'Where are you going?'

I didn't answer, I just marched forwards.

'You can't just leave.' There was a desperation to his voice that I had never heard before. 'I gave up everything for this.'

I paused and glanced back as the silence stretched between us.

'For you.'

His correction was too slow. It wasn't for me, it never had been.

'My family, my friends, they all think I'm dead.'

I frowned. How would they feel when they discovered Adam was alive? How did I feel? Happy? Relieved? I should be, shouldn't I? I probed the emotions inside me, searching for some tiny sliver of light. But all I felt was disappointed and trapped.

'You need me.'

I stared at him. His statement was filled with so much uncertainty it almost sounded like a question.

Did I need him? A little while ago I would have said yes. But now... things were different. I was different. Over the last few days, I'd proved to myself how capable I could be, how capable I was. I always had been. I understood that now. It had been other people who had made me feel weak and incapable. And I had let them. I'd chosen to accept their view of me, instead of deciding for myself. I'd taken on board their criticisms. I'd complied with their demands. I'd accepted their control.

But not any more.

'I heard someone say that we all have two lives.' Adam spoke slowly, as though determined to get the quote perfect. 'One to learn and one to live.'

I tipped my head to the right. 'I like that.' There was a comfort in that idea. It made it seem like the years that had slipped through my fingers hadn't been wasted. I'd been learning. And now...

I took a deep breath. Now I wanted to live. I still wasn't sure I knew all the answers yet. Despite all the years of 'learning', there was still so much I didn't know, mostly about myself. But I'd made a start; a wobbly, tentative first step.

Simon's face popped into my head and the corners of my lips turned upwards. Maybe nothing would happen with him. It didn't matter. It wasn't really about him. It was the possibility he represented. The possibility that there could be someone in my future. Not yet, but when I was ready, I could start again.

I would start again.

A movement caught my eye and I blinked as I realised Adam was walking slowly towards me.

You'd have to start again with someone new. You'd be back at the beginning. Alone.

Adam's words repeated in my head. He'd been desperate for me not to leave him. So desperate that he had made me afraid to lose him. Not because we were good together. Not because I was the only woman he wanted. But because he wanted me to believe no one else could put up with me. Without him, I would be unloved and alone.

Adam was right. Without him, I would be back at the beginning. But maybe that wasn't such a bad thing. It was a chance for a fresh start, not just for a new relationship, but a fresh start for me, too. A chance to put my past mistakes behind me, mistakes I had learned from and didn't intend to repeat again.

I was no longer afraid to be alone. I didn't need someone else to define me. I was me. For all my flaws and insecurities, I was okay on my own; without my mother; without Adam.

I started to walk towards the house again.

'No!' Adam charged past me and blocked my path.

I froze. My stomach tightened. The shock of seeing him and my indignation at what he'd done had given me clarity about so much of our relationship, but it had blinded me to one thing; he couldn't let me turn him in.

He'd faked his death and framed my mother for murder. I didn't know what his punishment would be for that, but surely it wouldn't be good?

'You're my future, Jess. This house. This lifestyle.' He laughed. 'Your mother thought it was all I was ever interested in.'

'She was right.' There was a coldness to my voice. I wasn't sure which bothered me more; was it that he'd disappointed me, or that Mum had been right about him all along?

'Not at first.' Adam shook his head. 'In the beginning I was interested in you. Your smile. Your laugh. Your...' His gaze trailed across my body. 'Everything.'

'In the beginning...?'

He shrugged. 'I liked you. You liked me. We had a connection. I felt something for you. Something strong. I could see you were struggling with so much. I wanted to help you.'

'You felt pity for me? That was it? That was our connection?'

'No!' Adam shook his head. 'Not pity. Admiration.'

I raised my eyebrows. 'Seriously?'

Adam took a small step forward. 'You still can't see it, can you?' He shook his head slowly. 'You don't realise how strong you are. I loved that about you. That inner strength that kept you going no matter how bad things were. You always had that beautiful smile, even when everything was weighing you down inside.'

'So, what changed?' I cursed myself for asking the question. But I was driven by some morbid desire to pick over the bones of our relationship and discover where it had gone wrong. Where I had gone wrong.

'I discovered it's not possible to love two people. Not equally.'

My stomach contracted. I'd wanted the truth. Now I had it. It was what I had thought. I never quite measured up to *her*. I was always second best.

'Your mother was so worried that I was using you as a means to an end.'

'She was right, you were.'

'No!' There was a hurt tone to his voice. He gazed at me with wide glossy eyes, like a hurt little boy. Except his indignance was misplaced.

'Everything you've done proves it. You were after her money. You were after this house.' I waved my hand at the building in front of me.

'No, you have it all wrong. It's not about the money. I wanted freedom. For you. For me. My death, this house, it can give us that freedom.'

I frowned at him. Our views would never be aligned. He saw himself as a hero. All I saw now was a liar.

'I freed us from our lives. From the traps we had made for ourselves. You with your mother, me with...' He swallowed, as though forcing his guilt back down. 'Natalie.'

I blinked as my mind raced, trying to make sense of his reasoning.

'Your mother was never going to let you be your own person. She was always going to sabotage your life.'

'She was protecting me.' I cringed as I said the words. 'In her own way.'

'Her way was poisonous.'

I didn't reply. I couldn't really disagree. Not now. Not after learning all the things she had done, and all the people I had lost because of her.

But I haven't lost Adam.

That thought struck me without warning. I'd wanted him back. I'd cried for him. For us. For the future that we couldn't have. And now, here he was...

But it hadn't been his death that I had mourned him for, but his betrayal. He'd cheated. He loved someone else.

'And I'm free from Natalie now too. What we had is over. Finished. She thinks I'm dead.'

'For now.'

'You think I'd go back to her? You think I'd tell her that I'm alive?'

'Why not? You've told me.'

'Because I want a life with you.'

'You want a life with my mother's money.'

Adam sighed. 'Do you really think so little of me?'

I snorted. 'You don't exactly have a good track record, do you?'

'Okay, fair point. But I've changed. This is it. A fresh start. We can sell up here and move away. Anywhere you want. Somewhere no one knows us. Somewhere we can be ourselves. Just us. No distractions. No more secrets and lies.'

I studied him. There was an earnestness to his plea. He really seemed to want this. To be with me. Just us.

But then I'd thought that before.

'It wasn't me who was keeping secrets or telling lies.'

'Weren't you?'

I squirmed.

'You never told me about your past. You never mentioned what happened with your previous boyfriends. You never mentioned your arrest.'

'Because it wasn't true. It wasn't me that had done any of it.'

'But you thought it was. Your mother made you think that. She made you doubt yourself and your sanity. And that's why you couldn't tell me. Because to say it out loud would—'

'Make it real,' I finished for him, as I finally acknowledged the reason I had never talked about my past.

A chill washed over me. He knew me too well. He could read me better than I could read myself.

'You had secrets, Jess. Your smile hid them well, but they were still there.'

Adam slipped his hand into mine. It felt familiar and warm. Could I really let him go again?

'You don't need to hide any more, Jess. Not from me. Not even from yourself. We can be together. Just you and me. All of this can be ours.'

'But it wouldn't be just you and me, would it? There will always be Natalie.'

'I want to be with you. Just you.'

'For how long? Three months?'

His eyebrows drew together.

'Like last time?'

Understanding straightened the creases in his brow.

'You know.'

'I'm much wiser than I used to be.' I took a deep breath. 'About so many things.' The truth hadn't been kind to me, but Mum had been right, it was still better than a lie.

'It's different now, Jess. I choose you. I want you. Only you.'

My chest tightened. They were the words I had wanted him to say for so long. I'd wanted him to cast Natalie aside for me. I'd wanted to be his choice, his priority. Now, finally, I was.

I expected to feel some surge of emotion. I was wanted. Accepted.

But all I felt was empty.

I'd waited my whole life to be accepted, by someone, anyone. And now, when I finally was, it was worthless. His wasn't the opinion that mattered. It never had been. I just hadn't realised it until now.

My opinion was all that should ever have counted.

It hadn't before.

But it did now.

I shrugged. 'But I don't want you.'

Adam let my hand fall. 'I don't need you, you know?'

I froze. My eyes locked with his.

'I know everything about you. Your accounts. Your passwords. Even your signature.'

'What are you saying?' I asked the question even though my gut already knew the answer.

I was expendable.

54

'No one would be surprised if you disappeared for a while.' Adam shrugged and shook his head slowly. 'Your mum killed your boyfriend, everyone would understand if you needed to be alone to deal with that.'

'Adam...' My legs trembled beneath me as I edged backwards away from him. This was the man I had once loved. The man who had been my life. Surely he wouldn't hurt me. Not physically.

But then I was starting to realise that people were capable of anything. Even people that supposedly loved me.

'You'd send them a postcard or two, just so they don't worry about you.'

I couldn't stand here and be helpless. I'd spent my life doing that. Look where it had got me.

Fear and frustration coursed through my veins and I sprinted to the left, but Adam lunged forward. He grabbed my arm and tugged me towards the house.

'What are you doing? Where are you taking me?' I fought against him, twisting and turning, desperate to break free from his grasp.

'Somewhere where you can't tell anyone what you know.'

'Somewhere you can lock me away?' I'd be a prisoner, more than I already had been. I'd spent a lifetime trapped in the shadows, fearful of what I might do, of who I might be. But I was never the villain.

'I know this is a lot to take in. You just need a little time to come around to the idea.'

'You're kidnapping me.'

'I'm helping you. It's for your own good.'

Adam had never seen me as a villain. Only a victim. He'd wanted to change me; to help me. To make me stronger; to make me his.

I was done being the victim of my own naivety. I was done trusting other people more than I trusted myself.

I didn't need him to save me. In truth, I never really had. All I'd needed was to realise that there was another way; that I had a choice. I'd been so blinkered by the past, by Mum's blame, that I had lost sight of who I was and how strong I could be.

I'd never fought for myself, because I didn't think I was worth it. I'd been taught that I was worthless, that what I wanted didn't matter.

But it did.

It was the one thing that mattered most.

And I wanted more than this. More than him.

I kicked his shins, but his grip tightened. 'I don't want to hurt you, Jess.'

I shoved my hand in my pocket, my fingers wrapped around the house key. It wasn't much. But it was all I had.

I pulled my hand free from the pocket and lunged at him with the key. He yelled as I scraped it against his cheek. He pushed me away, loosening his grip and I staggered backwards.

An angry line of red blood surged from his skin as he glared at me. 'What do you think you are doing, Jess? Where do you think you can go? Look around you, the only escape is past me.'

My eyes darted left and right, searching for a way out. But Adam was right. The house was behind him. He would never let me get to it. I cast a nervous glance behind me.

Can you get down to the beach from here?

Adam's question sprang into my brain from the first day I had brought him here to meet Mum.

I staggered closer to the cliff edge. It wasn't a smart idea. The cliff was steep and unstable, and in the midst of a storm... I shuddered. What choice did I have?

Adam edged towards me. 'Your Mum was right, you know, you should watch your footing up here.' His voice sounded nervous.

I glared at him. 'You expect me to believe you care?'

'I do care, Jess. It's not too late. You can still join me.' He held his hand out.

It was tempting. I could take his hand. We could walk together away from the cliff. Away from this madness. I could play along. I could bide my time. I could wait for an opportunity to escape.

But what if no opportunity arose? What if this was it?

I gritted my teeth. I was tired of doing what I was supposed to. Of being meek and obedient. I was tired of playing it safe and being afraid to take a chance.

This was my chance.

I pivoted and rushed to the edge.

'Jess, no!'

I took a tentative step on the slope.

Adam rushed towards me. He grabbed my arm and pulled me back up to the top. 'I can't let you do this. You'll fall.'

I fought against him.

'What do you care? You're going to kill me, anyway.'

'No, I don't want to hurt you. I just need to keep you quiet.'

'I loved you.' My voice was barely a whisper against the wind.

Adam shrugged and I felt his grip relax. 'Sometimes that isn't enough.'

I shook my head. 'It should be. It should be everything.'

'Not this time, Jess.'

I took a deep breath. 'Every time,' I said as I jerked to the right and dove to the ground, pulling free from Adam's grip again.

He lunged at me, but I kicked him. He staggered backwards. Fear flashed in his eyes as his footing slipped. 'Jess!'

'Adam!' I scrambled to the edge, as his arms flailed.

He disappeared from view. I peered over the edge. I half expected him to be clinging to the side, ready to reach out and pull me over. But he was gone. The only sign of him were the ripples in the waves where he had splashed into the water.

I covered my mouth and watched as they dissipated. Until it was as though he'd never been there at all.

I backed away, before turning back to the garden. My eyes scanned the grass, searching for my phone. I saw it and ran towards it. I dropped to my knees and keyed in my passcode. I hit the phone icon and the keypad appeared: 9... 9... I stared at it. Calling the police was the right thing to do. It was self-defence. I hadn't done anything wrong. Surely they would see that. But what if they didn't believe me? What if they didn't believe it had been an accident?

I pressed the delete key and watched the numbers disappear.

A stranger might not believe me, but there was one person who would.

Call me if you think of anything.

Simon had given me his number at the beginning. He'd called me from it when he'd asked me to go into the station. I'd saved it in my contacts list. I scrolled through the numbers until his name appeared.

I hit the dial button and pressed the phone to my ear.

It rang once…

What would happen once he knew? Everything would change. Mum would be innocent. Would she be released? Would she be free to return to her life? To my life?

She hadn't killed Adam, but she'd thought about it. She'd planned it. If Adam hadn't beaten her to it, would she have gone through with it?

Twice…

I shuddered. The frightening thing was, I knew it was possible. Given all the things I had learnt about her, I no longer had the luxury of trusting my mother. She'd poisoned people against me, damaged their property, all for simply dating me. She'd made me think the reason I was alone was because I wasn't good enough. She'd messed with my life, but also with my head. My innocence was no longer in question now, but that didn't eradicate my memories.

She'd let the police arrest me for what she had done. She'd sent me to psychologists to help me control my behaviour. But it was never me that had really needed the help.

Three times…

And what about Dad?

Just like before.

Would Adam have been her first victim? Or had Dad been?

I glanced back over my shoulder at the waves in the distance. My freedom wasn't at risk. At least not from the police. But my mother…

What would happen to me if she was released? Somehow she'd find her way back into my life. Interfering. Controlling. I'd never be free of her. And next time maybe she really would kill someone. Adam was right, I believed she was capable of it now.

Four times…

I'd spent a lifetime in the shadows, first Mum's, then Adam's. Was it possible to change? To take everything I'd known, everything I was and become something different? Someone different?

Not if Mum was with me.

If Mum was free then I never would be. It wouldn't matter where I went, or who I was with, I'd always be looking over my shoulder, waiting for her to find me. Waiting for her to destroy me. Again.

But without her…

What if it was too late? What if I'd missed my opportunity? What if I'd missed my chance of having my own life? A good life?

'Hi, Jess. Is everything all right?'

All I had to do was tell him. I could save Mum like she'd always tried to save me. I'd be free of the guilt. Free of the burden. The truth would finally be out there.

Except Mum hadn't saved me. Not really.

She never had.

'Jess?'

I could hear concern in his voice.

Maybe it wasn't too late. Maybe I could still have the life I'd always wanted.

There was only one way to find out.

'Is something wrong?'

This was it, my chance to tell the truth.

I lied.

ACKNOWLEDGMENTS

Thank you to Mum and Dad for your love and support and for always being there. You taught me to never give up.

Special thanks to my amazing friend, Ellie Henshaw, for the brainstorming, editing, motivational chats and endless hot chocolates. My book wouldn't have made it this far without you.

Thank you to friend and writing tutor, Alison May, for all your encouragement and wisdom. And to my mentor, Jonathan Eyers, for your time and insight.

Thank you to Katie Fforde for believing in me. Your bursary gave me hope that one day I might make it.

Huge thanks to all my friends in the RNA, who taught me that a writer is never truly alone. And to my dear friends Abhi, Vicky, Katie, Linda, Kath McGurl, Josie Bonham and Diane Saxon for sticking with my endless conversations about fictional people.

And to Ahl, the best bubble mate a girl could have.

Thank you to Lucy for the beach walks that kept me sane through lockdowns and beyond. And to all my wonderful colleagues for being such an amazing cheering squad.

And finally, thank you to my wonderful editor, Emily Ruston, for having faith in my writing and being so enthusiastic and supportive of this novel. And to all the team at Boldwood Books for making my seemingly impossible dream become a reality.

ABOUT THE AUTHOR

Alex Stone, originally an accountant from the West Midlands, is now a psychological suspense writer based in Dorset. This beautiful and dramatic coastline is the inspiration and setting for her novels. She was awarded the Katie Fforde Bursary in 2019.

Sign up to Alex Stone's mailing list here for news, competitions and updates on future books.

Follow Alex on social media:

x.com/AlexStoneAuthor
instagram.com/AlexStoneAuthor
facebook.com/AlexStoneWriter

ALSO BY ALEX STONE

The Perfect Daughter

The Other Girlfriend

The Good Patient